The Christmas Market Murder

ALSO BY PETER BOLAND

THE CHARITY SHOP DETECTIVE
AGENCY MYSTERIES
Book 1: The Charity Shop Detective Agency
Book 2: The Beach Hut Murders
Book 3: Death at the Dog Show
Book 4: The Vanilla Killer
Book 5: Death of a Wild Swimmer
Book 6: The Christmas Market Murder

The Christmas Market Murder

PETER BOLAND

JOFFE BOOKS

Joffe Books, London
www.joffebooks.com

First published in Great Britain in 2025

© Peter Boland

This book is a work of fiction. Names, characters, businesses, organisations, places and events are either the product of the author's imagination or are used fictitiously. Any resemblance to actual persons, living or dead, events or locales is entirely coincidental. The spelling used is British English except where fidelity to the author's rendering of accent or dialect supersedes this. The right of Peter Boland to be identified as author of this work has been asserted in accordance with the Copyright, Designs and Patents Act 1988.

No part of this book may be used or reproduced in any manner for the purpose of training artificial intelligence technologies or systems. In accordance with Article 4(3) of the Digital Single Market Directive 2019/790, Joffe Books expressly reserves this work from the text and data mining exception.

Cover art by Cherie Chapman

ISBN: 978-1-80573-284-6

PROLOGUE

I like the fear. Other people's, I mean. Stalking them late at night, I follow behind them, matching them step for step, feeding off their growing dread. It's an addictive sensation, being the piper who calls the tune to their march of terror.

The victim I'm currently following quickens their pace and I receive a delicious hit of pleasure. I imagine their amygdala lit up like the Christmas lights around us — that's the part of the brain that processes fear. I looked it up online. I'm always reading about this stuff. The amygdala is the most important part of the brain, if you ask me. If it wasn't for these two little almond shapes buried deep in the temporal lobe then we'd have died out long ago. You see, the amygdala is responsible for ensuring natural selection doesn't unselect us and turn us into another dead branch on the evolutionary tree. Triggering the fight-or-flight response, it's kept us alive for millions of years. And up ahead, the trigger has just been pulled.

My intended victim chooses flight, scurrying across to the other side of the road. A move I know well. All my previous victims have embarked on this futile manoeuvre. I've witnessed it enough times that I'm getting pretty good at predicting when it will happen. This one went a bit early. I thought they'd hang on a bit longer, maintaining a straight course along the pavement as if nothing was wrong. But no. Over the road without checking for traffic. Not that there's any need to look for cars. The streets are deserted. Damp and eerie at this time of night, but even more so under the surreal blinking fairy lights and inflatable Santas bulging in front gardens.

My frightened little mouse is hoping the pursuit has ended. But it's really just begun. I follow them, increasing speed, my footfalls landing a touch heavier than they really need to, broadcasting in no uncertain terms that, yep, I'm stalking you.

They should make a run for it. But they're in denial. Convinced that this will all go away if they just ignore me. Not going to happen, I'm afraid. I'm addicted to this now. Hooked on the rush.

I've even made a name for myself — the Southbourne Stalker, they call me. I don't kill anyone. I just give them a light tap on the back of the head with my little wooden mallet. A slapstick pop, more in the realms of Laurel and Hardy than the Yorkshire Ripper. Just enough to knock them unconscious or at least make them drowsy so I can steal their valuables. No permanent damage. To be honest, I'm not bothered about what I take. It's just a fringe benefit. For me, this is all about the fame. Or the infamy. I'm the notorious Southbourne Stalker — people speak my name and tremble. Pity I can't reveal who I really am and get all the glory. But then they'd put me away.

There's no way that's going to happen. I'm too good at this. Too slick and stealthy. And I'm hooked on the power and the fear I wield, knowing that the whole of Southbourne is terrified of me.

People do stupid things when they're scared, just like this one's gone and done. Which makes my task a whole lot easier. I watch with immense delight as my little mouse pivots under the glow of a street light and disappears into a convenient alleyway. There's nowhere better for the Southbourne Stalker to strike.

As I follow them in, joyfully I sing a modified Christmas carol to myself: 'Tis the season to be wary, fa-la-la-la-la, la-la, la-la.

CHAPTER 1

When it came to walking, Fiona was an as-the-crow-flies type of person. She wasn't prone to following her nose and certainly not idly meandering for the sake of it. For her, perambulating had to have purpose. Whether it was taking Simon Le Bon, her scruffy terrier cross, for his daily wants or popping to the shops, bag for life under one arm, she rarely strayed from the beaten path, especially when it came to the morning walk to work. As far as she was concerned, there was only one way to get to Dogs Need Nice Homes, the charity shop she managed, and that was the quickest.

However, since last week, that strict attitude had slipped and her route had become distinctly circuitous, favouring a long detour through Southbourne's one and only park. Well, there were other parks, but Fiona considered them to be more recreation grounds, designed for running around and getting sweaty on, rather than looking pretty and lifting the spirits.

Fisherman's Walk was definitely the latter. Of modest proportions, it was a majestic if somewhat narrow slice of nature slotted among the urban sprawl. It could be walked end to end in about three minutes, linking the clifftop above the beach to the shops of Southbourne Grove. But what it lacked in dimension, it certainly made up for in substance. There was a handsome 1920s bandstand at one end and a lozenge-shaped ornamental pool at the other. Between these two were mature woodlands that dappled the light over secluded glades of lush grass peppered with rustic benches, just begging for someone to park themselves with a book.

The place had history, too, of the ancient kind. Fisherman's Walk, as its name suggested, was the last surviving leg of a route used by early inland settlers, who would trek to the sea to hook a fish or two for their supper. It would have been lost for ever had it not been for a plucky individual in the 1900s, who had probably smoked a pipe and spoke with a plummy accent, and had the foresight to declare that it might be a jolly good idea to preserve it. After all, future generations might need somewhere to sit and eat their meal deals.

Fiona often did at lunchtime — however, she'd never frequent Fisherman's Walk on her way to work. Though it would be a pleasant start to the day, it was much too big a detour, adding another seven minutes to her journey (she needed every one of those precious minutes to make it in on time).

But that all changed last week, because something marvellous had happened there. This already enchanting sliver of nature had been transformed into a winter wonderland, becoming the most perfect venue for a Christmas market. Two lines of festive stalls nestled together along its gently meandering central path to form a seasonal avenue of wonder and curiosity. Okay, the stalls were glorified garden sheds with double doors at the front, and the market wasn't as large and impressive as the ones in the big towns. There was no ice rink, nor Ferris wheel, but what Fisherman's Walk had that they did not were living Scots and Monterey pines towering overhead. These giants had been commandeered for the festive period, their mighty limbs draped in all manner of decorations of the brightest red, gold and purple. Fairy lights were strewn from tree to tree, criss-crossing the high branches. There was no consistent design behind any of it and the overall effect was a bit DIY, but that's what made it so charming.

Fiona was a firm believer that Christmas should start in December, but she'd made an exception on this occasion. Since the market opened in mid-November, she had modified her daily route to work to catch a festive morning fix. Most people would argue that evening would be the best time to experience a Christmas market, the warm glow emanating from each stall, the dazzling lights and damp night air laced with cinnamon, candy and roast chestnuts, overwhelming one's senses. But Fiona thought the morning was a far more magical prospect.

As her breath clouded in front of her, she got a thrill watching the market come to life. Wooden doors were thrown open, revealing an eclectic and sometimes baffling mix of goods to fill up Christmas stockings. There were drinking horns (for that hard-to-please Viking in the family) and leather-bound parchment journals (for aspiring sorcerers), giant lollipops and candy canes, and mythical ceramic dragons. These were interspersed with various food stalls, cooking up bubbling pots of sweet gooeyness, while hotplates sizzled and spat with meaty treats. As they prepared for the day ahead, stall-holders cheerfully nattered to their neighbours, clutching steaming cups of coffee in mittened hands. If she squinted hard enough, Fiona almost felt as if she was in a medieval scene on a Christmas card. She couldn't get enough of the place, and neither could Simon Le Bon, judging by the way he strained on his lead at all the delectable smells.

It had all been the brainchild of Malorie Granger, ex-counsellor and current manager of the local community centre. Fiona didn't often see eye to eye with her. She was a brash, blunt object of a woman, who'd earned the name the Bulldozer in Barbour. However, sometimes you needed a bulldozer or a blunt object to get things done, and despite all the protests and disapprovals, Malorie had definitely got things done. Securing funding by pulling in a ton of favours from here, there and everywhere, she had pushed the idea like a prop forward in a rugby scrum until the Christmas market had become a reality. Hats off to her. Malorie had done an amazing job, not so ably assisted by Sophie Haverford, the scheming socialite who managed the Cats' Alliance, a rival charity shop across the road.

Sophie had kept her distance from the project, smartly biding her time to see which way it would go. But when she had an inkling of possible success, not wanting to be left out of any ensuing glory, she stepped in at the eleventh hour to offer her services. Malorie didn't really need them, but as they were friends, she had given her the one and only job of hiring the market stalls, which Sophie had carried out very badly, ordering one too many. Space was minimal among the tightly huddled stalls and there was nowhere for the spare one to go. Luckily, a side road adjacent to the park provided a more modest position — a wide patch of pavement in front of a garage, a shoe repairer and one of those pottery places where you handed over money to paint things. The spare stall was plonked there and offered at discounted rental. It was snapped up by someone who sold not particularly nice hot chocolate, according to reports. The Wicker Man, who owned the shop next to Fiona's, had likened the taste to a discarded old boot that had been steeped in puddle water.

Through the narrow gaps between the stalls in the park, Fiona caught fleeting glimpses of the lonely, superfluous hot chocolate stall, standing all alone. Normally it wouldn't have caught her attention but this morning a small group of people had gathered outside. They appeared agitated, their raised voices carrying tones of fear and desperation. Increasing her pace, she feared that the Southbourne Stalker had struck again.

CHAPTER 2

Since the infamous mugger had begun roaming the streets, the locals had been terrified to go out, worried they'd receive a crack on the back of the head and wake up with all their valuables gone. Genteel Southbourne simply wasn't a place where muggings happened. One would have been bad enough, but to have had a spate of them, all following the same pattern, had altered Southbourne's happy vibe. The place had lost its allure and the mood in the usually cheerful community was distinctly gloomy. Police had warned everyone to be on their guard. Visitors were down and footfall on the streets had dwindled. Fiona, along with Daisy and Partial Sue, her fellow charity shop detectives, had tried to get to the bottom of it. But they'd had no luck finding the culprit.

In a bid to shame them for not catching the mugger, and a bit of self-glorification, Sophie Haverford had started a campaign entitled Make Southbourne Safe Again, complete with red baseball caps, which she sold from her charity shop. They hadn't caught on. But Fiona hoped the appearance of the Christmas market would bring some much-needed joy back to the town, which it certainly had, as far as she was concerned.

Reaching the bandstand, there was a break in the line of market stalls, offering a clearer view of what was occurring. She recognised one man, Scott Preston. Everyone knew Scott. He and his wife ran the local post office. A dedicated and trusted pillar of the community, she wondered what the sub-postmaster was doing outside the appendage of the Christmas market at this time of the morning when he should have been opening up for the day.

She realised something was definitely wrong when he began shouldering the two front doors of the market stall, shoving his full body weight against it. A tallish fellow in his early thirties with not much girth, Scott bounced off the stall with the energy of a flicked chopstick. As Fiona made her way over there, others attempted to ram the doors, several of them all at once, but they remained firmly closed.

"What's wrong?" Fiona asked.

A flustered Scott spun around, his eyes wide with terror. "My dad's in there. It's locked from the inside and he's not answering his phone. I'm worried something terrible's happened to him."

Fiona's detective brain immediately kicked in. "How do you know he's in there?"

Scott pulled out his phone and dialled a number. From within the stall, she could hear a muffled ringtone — a cheesy repeating blues piano riff, completely at odds with the gravity of the situation. "That's his phone, no doubt about it."

"Maybe he left it there yesterday. I presume this is his stall?"

Scott bit his lip and nodded.

Two overalled men appeared from out of the garage. Judging by the resemblance they were father and son, sharing the same thick black hair, although the father's was streaked with white at the temples. The son uncoiled an extension lead, while his father kept telling him to hurry up.

"Don't worry," the older mechanic reassured Scott. "We'll have your dad out of there in a jiffy." He was carrying a hefty electric saw with a brutal-looking blade attached to one end. "This'll cut through the bolt in no time."

He plugged the saw into the extension cable, then barked at his son to get back inside. The lad jumped and did as he was told while his father knelt down and poked the blade between the two wooden doors. With a high-pitched squeal, the blade began cutting, jabbing back and forth faster than the eye could follow.

Fiona moved back as Simon Le Bon cowered at the din. The air immediately filled with the hot tang of lacerated metal and friction-burned wood. It didn't take long. The tone of the saw suddenly changed abruptly as the blade made it all the way through the bolt. The mechanic retracted the tool and threw open the doors.

The gathered crowd gasped in horror at the harrowing sight. A man hung lifelessly by his neck.

Fiona flicked a glance at Scott, who stood frozen, mesmerised by the ghastly vision. A second later, he came back to life, cried out then rushed inside. "Dad!"

CHAPTER 3

The Christmas market and side road were sealed off for the rest of Saturday. Cold, authoritarian blue police tape stretched everywhere, not mixing well with the warm festive colours of the surroundings. Blending in a little better, a white forensics tent was set up around the fateful stall. The casual observer might have thought it was all part of the Christmas market, where you got to meet Santa, with the white coveralled forensics team darting in and out as his sort of low-budget little helpers. But that illusion was all destroyed by the large, uniformed police presence. As was the case with many a crime scene, the officers appeared to be hanging around with not much to do, apart from keeping the public out.

Police procedure had to be followed, of course, despite the fact that it was so obviously a suicide, as Fiona explained to DI Fincher and DS Thomas. The DI was her usual businesslike self, dressed up to the nines in a long, double-breasted burgundy frock coat and black riding boots. DS Thomas, on the other hand, had made no effort. In grubby sportswear, he was a man who'd not so much given up on fashion but had never started in the first place.

They listened patiently as Fiona presented them with the simple but hard facts as she and everyone else had observed them. The door had been firmly locked from the inside until the mechanic had poked his electric saw through the tiny gap and cut through the sliding bolt. Clive Preston had hung himself from one of the rafters. It looked as if he'd used his own belt. A large wholesale tin of hot chocolate was on its side near his feet, presumably where he'd stood on it before kicking it away. There were no signs of a struggle, nothing broken, not even a dent in the shiny metal water boiler perched at the side of the counter or the large fridge at the back. It was all very tidy. Everything put away.

The two detectives appeared satisfied with everyone's corroborating statements, which would no doubt be backed up by a swift, straightforward post-mortem. A nice open-and-shut case. Next day, the whole macabre police carnival had left, and the market resumed business as usual. Although it was far from usual. Sunday was the market's busiest day but a subdued, melancholic cloud hung over the whole place.

Christmas was meant to be a celebration, but celebrating was the last thing anyone wanted to do. A few market stalls stayed shut, their doors locked up tight — this time bolted and padlocked from the outside, either out of respect or perhaps because the stall-holders just didn't have the stomach to be jolly after what had happened.

Attendance was down and it didn't help that the infamous "suicide stall", as it had become known, remained *in situ*, locked up and lassoed with more police tape. A ghoulish reminder of what had happened within. It would have stayed that way had Malorie Granger not stepped in, almost certainly after much provocation from the remaining stall-holders, who, though sympathetic, were becoming increasingly disgruntled that customers were avoiding the place. Malorie immediately contacted DI Fincher and asked if the offending stall could be removed. To her credit, the young detective agreed, on the proviso that it would remain secure and untouched, and stored somewhere safe. The next day, the supplier's massive truck arrived with its hefty hydraulic built-in crane. Two thick harnesses were slung under the base of the stall and it was hoisted, creaking and swaying, onto the back, lashed down securely and taken away.

Gradually, the market returned to something resembling normal, although still not what you would class as heaving or rammed. But behind the brave faces and festive smiles, the dark and gloomy feelings still lurked. These turned into unpleasant thoughts, grew into nasty theories, and eventually festered into rumours and gossip that ran the length of Southbourne. They were fuelled by one simple fact: not forty-eight hours after his father's suicide, Scott had returned to work, first thing on Monday morning. Many thought this was very odd behaviour, verging on downright cold. His father had just died in the worst way possible, yet he was back selling stamps and helping pensioners pay their gas bills.

Fiona didn't agree. People dealt with grief in different ways. Some wanted to shut themselves away from the world and cry until they had no tears left, while others, like Scott, preferred to keep their sorrow at bay, distracting themselves from the pain with everyday regularity and routine. But also, knowing Scott — as everyone did — he'd have felt he had a duty to the local community. As a sub-postmaster, he wouldn't have wanted to let anyone down, especially at this time of year, when the post office was at its busiest.

But no matter how much she told herself this, Fiona couldn't help a niggling feeling jabbing at her mind like a tiny boxer. Did he have something to do with his father's death? Fiona had no justification or evidence for this, other than Scott's reaction when the stall doors were opened. Everyone had gasped in horror, except him. He'd just stood there, unresponsive. Of course, this could also have been a completely normal reaction on Scott's part to the chilling sight of his father in the most horrific of circumstances imaginable. Perhaps Fiona might have reacted the same way. She decided to put her suspicion on the back burner for now, only shifting it forward if she uncovered something that pointed to Scott's involvement.

CHAPTER 4

Fiona watched Daisy from the safe distance of the counter at Dogs Need Nice Homes, not wanting to get involved. Her gentle friend had become obsessed with the Christmas window display, fiddling with it every few minutes in a bid to attract more customers. It wasn't just the market that had suffered. With the stalker and now the suicide, all the shops along Southbourne Grove were experiencing a loss of feet through the door. Though she admired Daisy's resolve, she didn't think window dressing would make any difference. Besides, Fiona couldn't face attacking the Christmas decorations again. Not until they were ready to come down in the New Year.

Putting them up had been quite the festive marathon, though admittedly a very joyous one. Yesterday had been their annual Deck the Halls Day, as it was called, and took place on the first Sunday every December. The ladies would forgo their day off, cranking up the carols while they decorated the shop merrily on high. It was their favourite day of the year. Fuelled by endless mince pies, tea and Christmas spirit, they'd start early in the morning, not stopping until every one of the many storage boxes had been emptied of decorations, and every corner of the shop glittered and shone. By about 5 p.m., the ladies would put their feet up and chink their cups for one last round of tea in celebration, sitting back to enjoy their handiwork.

Once was enough, and she didn't think there was anything that could be added to a shop whose decor most people would describe as festive maximalist overkill. But today, Daisy thought otherwise and had been tweaking the window every spare moment, of which, due to a distinct lack of customers, there had been plenty.

By lunchtime she decided that it needed a complete overhaul. There'd been some breezy weather recently, so she went out foraging for windfallen pinecones. Deciding they would make a nice feature, she'd gathered them up and deposited them in the window. But Daisy hadn't stopped there. The pinecone base had provided the perfect medium in which to plant candy canes, creating a miniature forest of swirly red sugar sticks. Artificial Christmas trees of all shapes and sizes, tangled with lights and tinsel, formed a backdrop, throwing off the scale of the forest. She would have finished there but after lunch, someone had donated a train set and Daisy had pounced on it for her display. Currently, she was squeezed between the Christmas trees, her little fingers delicately laying out the track on the uneven pinecones, so the toy train and its carriages could weave in and out of the candy canes.

"Shouldn't that train set be on the shelves?" Partial Sue commented without looking up from her phone. "Make a nice present for someone's grandkids."

"I'll put a note by it," Daisy replied. "Announcing it's for sale."

"You might be going to a lot of trouble only to pull it all out again when someone wants to buy it," Partial Sue warned. "I'm just saying."

Daisy extracted herself from the window and faced Partial Sue. "Yes, but before that happens it'll look wonderful. Just like the Polar Express. Attract lots of customers. What are you doing, by the way? You've been staring at your phone all day."

"Come and see."

"Don't! You won't be able to tear your eyes away," Fiona warned, as if it was the head of Medusa.

Unable to resist the temptation, Daisy headed over to the table and gazed into the screen. "Knitting?"

"Yes," Partial Sue grinned. "It's a couple who livestream themselves every day. They're called Purl and Dean. I am partial to watching a bit of knitting. I find it very relaxing."

"Look away, Daisy. It's not too late," Fiona advised.

Daisy ignored her. "Is that a Christmas jumper they're making?"

"Certainly is."

Catnip to Daisy, she slotted herself into a chair beside Partial Sue, ensnared by the hypnotic, repetitive motion of clacking needles and interlacing strands of wool.

Fiona rolled her eyes. How long her colleagues would remain in this state of stupefaction was anyone's guess.

Thankfully, it didn't last long. A distraction appeared in the form of a customer — a fairly rare occurrence these days. A woman came in, weighed down with so many bags she had to edge through the door sideways. "I like your window display," she said enthusiastically.

"Thank you," Daisy replied, then shot Partial Sue an *I told you* so smirk.

"Tell me, that train set you're building. Is it for sale?" the woman asked.

Partial Sue sent Daisy an equally smug grin.

Before Daisy could answer, the woman shook her head. "Sorry, I'm getting distracted by your lovely shop. That's not why I'm here at all." She dropped her bags and went round them one by one, vigorously shaking her hands like an overenthusiastic Joyce Grenfell character. "I'm Daph, by the way. Daph Richardson." Her hair was unkempt and hadn't been troubled by a brush since Brexit. Eccentrically dressed, her clothes clashed as if she'd selected them from the shop's rails while blindfolded. A heavily patterned pashmina was wrapped around a chunky-knit cardigan, not too dissimilar to the ones

Fiona wore, except this one almost reached down to her knees. A pop of green leggings led to a pair of heavy-duty walking boots that hadn't been cleaned in a while.

Daph gathered up her bags, which, Fiona noticed, did not contain shopping but a ton of paperwork. Without being asked, she pulled up a chair and plonked herself down at the table, sighing contentedly. "Right, then. I hear you're rather good at investigating things."

"We have been known to solve a case or two." Fiona came out from behind the counter, accompanied by Simon Le Bon, who cautiously sniffed the visitor, before giving in to friendly wags of his tail.

"No need to be modest." Daph leaned down and gave the terrier cross a tickle behind the ear. Satisfied, he returned to his bed. Daph straightened up. "And from what I've heard, you're good at investigating things that aren't all they seem. To put it another way, changing the verdict on open-and-shut cases."

Partial Sue got straight to the point. "What is it you'd like us to do?"

Daph leaned back in her chair. "Plain speaking, I'm here about Clive Preston, the chap found dead in his market stall. I'm a freelance claims investigator. I was hired by Tyndale Life — strictly off the books, mind. His son has made a claim on his life assurance policy. It's a hefty sum."

The three ladies stared at her, nonplussed.

Daph misread the confusion in their eyes. "I know, I don't look like a claims investigator. Perks of being freelance. Work from home and cut corners in the presentation department." She giggled and gestured to her outfit and the bags by her feet.

Fiona was of the mind that anyone could dress how they pleased. "It's not that. You do know that Clive Preston took his own life?"

"Oh, yes," Daph replied casually.

"But doesn't suicide invalidate his policy?"

Daph rummaged around in one of her bags and pulled out a printed sheet of conditions and shoved it across the table. "Nope. The policy covers that too. Most of them do these days. Mental health conditions are legitimate illnesses, no different from physical ones, as long as the claim is made two years after the policy is taken out, which it was."

"Well, I never," Partial Sue exclaimed.

Daph snatched back the sheet of paper and stuffed it into the carrier bag. "I've seen the coroner's report. Cause of death was asphyxia due to an external compression of the neck by means of an encircling ligature. Toxicology showed alcohol in his system. Taking into account various factors when the body was found, et cetera, his blood-alcohol levels were back counted. In simple terms, he'd had the equivalent of about four pints of beer at the time of death. It's only an approximation, but he definitely wasn't sober, but not paralytic either. Maybe enough for a bit of Dutch courage."

"Doesn't the alcohol break the rules of his policy?" Daisy asked.

Daph extracted another sheet of paper from a different bag and slapped it on the table. A copy of a filled-in form. "Clive was upfront and honest about the units of alcohol he consumed. He was well under his weekly limits and there were no signs of alcohol-related conditions in the autopsy. Also, there was nothing suspicious about his body that would point to murder or manslaughter. No bruising, scratches or defence marks, no torn clothes, or anything that would indicate he put up a fight before he died. Ergo, he took his own life. Coroner's verdict: suicide." She shoved the form back into the bag. "Sorry, I would let you have a copy but it's confidential. I'm not really supposed to show anyone."

"Oh-kay." Fiona took a seat. "I'm not sure how we can help you."

"Yeah." Partial Sue nodded. "Seems straightforward. The poor fellow was depressed, had a few drinks, locked himself inside his stall and hung himself."

Daph took a deep breath then exhaled slowly. "My client, Tyndale Life, can challenge the coroner's verdict if there is evidence that the forfeiture or slayer rule, as it's known, has been broken. Have you heard of it?"

Without hesitation, Sue rattled off the answer like an audiobook. "A person who is criminally responsible for the death of another person cannot inherit as a result of their criminal actions."

"That's right," Daph said. "I'm impressed."

"You want to prove Scott killed his father, so you don't have to pay out."

"Not me." Daph smiled delicately. "My client wants to establish the truth surrounding his death. I'm merely the conduit."

"Oh, really," Partial Sue snorted. "I heard a rumour that you get a bonus for every claim you discredit — is that true?"

Fiona watched Daph's reaction. She blushed ever so slightly but didn't answer.

"But how could it be murder?" Daisy asked. "You said it yourself. Coroner's verdict was suicide. And Clive's stall was locked from the inside."

"Yes," Fiona agreed. "I was there when they cut the doors open. If it was murder, which I certainly doubt it was, how did the killer get away?"

"Let's just say it's a big payout, and if there's even a slight chance the verdict is wrong, then Tyndale wants to make sure they have all the facts. They understand the coroner's report and the locked stall is a conundrum. However, people can be coerced into taking their own life. I want you to investigate the circumstances of Clive's death. Specifically, uncovering anything unusual leading up to his demise. Threats, blackmail. I want to know everything, no matter how trivial."

Partial Sue folded her arms. "Why doesn't Tyndale investigate this themselves?"

Daph took a moment to answer. "Tyndale is a big household name. It's not a good look for them to be hounding a man who's just lost his father to suicide. That's where I come in."

Fiona's brow furrowed. "But you're asking us to investigate? Why aren't you doing it?"

Her voice and demeanour became cold and forthright. "I'm extremely good at what I do. A professional. And part of being a professional is knowing when to enlist the help of others. Experts like yourselves. You three are Southbourne locals. Know the area. Are trusted by the people of this community. You can get them to open up far better than I could."

Fiona sighed. "This isn't the sort of case we take on. For one, I'm not convinced it's anything but suicide. And secondly, Tyndale just wants to disprove the coroner's verdict, so they don't have to pay out. That's not really what we do. We're definitely not pinning a murder on Scott just so your client can protect its profits."

"Okay," Daph sighed, "forget Scott for the moment. What if the killer, whoever it may be, is still out there, with their trotters up? Fooled everyone and made it look like a suicide in the cleverest way possible. A locked room. If there's a chance that's how it happened, wouldn't you want to explore the possibility? Figure out how they did it?"

The ladies didn't say anything.

Daph leaned forward. "How about this — you investigate with an open mind. Gather all the evidence you can and pass it back to me. If you find that there's nothing suspicious, and it is what it is, as the young people like to say, then that's the conclusion I'll give Tyndale. It was a suicide. But if you uncover evidence that Clive was murdered, then I'll tell Tyndale, and you can report it to the police."

"Okay, this is sounding more promising," Fiona said.

Daph grinned. "Then let me sweeten the deal." She pulled out another sheet of paper and slid it across the table. It had a figure scribbled on it, a very big one.

The three ladies gasped.

"That's a lot of money," Partial Sue spluttered.

"It's what I'm authorised to offer for your services. Split it between you or donate it to the homeless dogs, or both. I don't mind."

The ladies looked at one another, already agreeing.

"As long as you stand by what we find," Fiona said, "whether it suits Tyndale or not. Then we have a deal."

Daph clapped her hands. "Music to my ears." She took back the sheet of paper and slotted it in with all the others. "Now, there can be no mention of Tyndale's name in your investigation. I'll give you my number and I'd like updates any time there's a breakthrough. Now, one last thing. I've heard that you're very good at making tea." She grinned impishly.

Partial Sue got to her feet. "I'll put the kettle on."

CHAPTER 5

Reflections of Southbourne's pretty Christmas lights twinkled in the wet, gritty pavements. Rush hour was in full swing as the ladies hurried up the road dodging puddles along with Simon Le Bon, who was one of those dogs that didn't like getting his paws wet.

As they passed each shop locking up for the night, disgruntled owners turned their "open" signs around to "closed" after another fairly dismal day of trading. Retailers, especially the independent ones, relied on Christmas to make up the bulk of their profit. If it wasn't for this time of year, they'd simply break even and go out of business. She could only imagine the terrible stress they were under. Inching ever closer to Christmas, one Groundhog Day of gloomy sales after another.

Up ahead, the post office came into view, its bright red sign still lit up, blushing in the darkness. They were hoping to catch Scott Preston before he finished for the day. The post office counter closed at five but, like most post offices these days, it was part — only a very small part — convenience store, which stayed open until six selling essentials, mostly bread, milk and booze.

Scott needed to be questioned before anyone else. Not because that's what Tyndale Life or Daph Richardson wanted but because it was the most logical place to start. He was the biggest suspect in all this, the one who stood to gain most from his father's demise. But that didn't mean he did it or that he would be the only suspect. However, this would all be completely academic if they couldn't figure out how his father could have been murdered. They had an impossible puzzle to solve.

"A locked-room mystery!" Partial Sue rubbed her hands vigorously. "I am partial to a locked-room mystery. I've always loved them in crime fiction, and now we've got one of our own, right on our doorstep. Anyone got any ideas how it was done?"

Daisy shook her head.

"I haven't the foggiest," Fiona said. "His stall was locked up tight. No way in or out. I saw it myself; it is what it is."

"You sound like a teenager," Partial Sue remarked.

"Sorry," Fiona apologised. "Daph said it back in the shop. It's one of those expressions that's easy to pick up but sort of meaningless at the same time."

"I wonder if she's got teenagers," said Daisy. "By the look of her, I bet she's always running around after them."

"I think she's one of those eccentric types," Partial Sue replied. "So focused on her job that everything else takes a back seat, including her clothes. Did you see them? And I thought we were scruffy."

"Speak for yourself," Daisy replied.

"Well, I liked her," Partial Sue continued. "Not like the stuffy claims investigators I'm used to dealing with." Which inferred she'd had run-ins with plenty before, possibly due to the integrity of her insurance claims being questioned.

Fiona didn't comment. Her eyes were cast down on the saturated pavement.

"Are you okay, Fiona?" Daisy asked.

"Yes, I'm fine. I'm just wondering what we're going to say to Scott. It feels awful what we're doing after what he's been through. We can't exactly wade in saying, 'Oh, we think you killed your father and made it look like suicide to get your hands on his life assurance, although we have absolutely no evidence or idea how you did it.' I'm wondering if we should be doing this at all."

Partial Sue sidestepped a puddle. "I don't know what to say either. But the shop could really do with the money Daph's offering. And I need a new toaster. I'm using the grill at the moment and can't get the timing right. Keep burning my toast."

"Well, we'd better decide fast," Fiona said. "Because we're nearly there."

"Why don't we just ask him how he is?" Daisy suggested. "Tell him that we're just checking in on him, then see how the conversation goes. He's bound to open up."

"Yes, that's a good idea," Fiona agreed. "Start off gently, then we can gradually bend it towards the events leading up to Clive's passing. I still feel wrong doing this, but at least it will be less traumatising for the poor man."

She pushed the post office door open, and the three of them stepped inside. The light was harsh, not designed for ambience but for checking amounts, filling in forms and getting details right. A smattering of tinsel troubled the shelves here and there, more of a nod to Christmas rather than the deep festive dive of Dogs Need Nice Homes.

As expected, the post office counter at the back was shut up tight, but the retail one at the front was still open for business. Scott stood behind it, towering over an older lady he was serving. A man in overalls queued behind her, a bottle of red wine in his fist, one leg jittering impatiently.

Scott stooped over, bringing his height closer to the lady's. "How can I help you today?" he asked warmly.

"Am I too late to buy a stamp? I really need to send this off to my grandson." She waved a white envelope in the air. "It's a birthday card. He's one of those awkward December babies, poor thing. Everyone combines his birthday and

Christmas present into one. But not me. I think that's rotten. I always put twenty pounds in his card then send him another at Christmas."

Scott's face dropped. "Er, you know, it's not a good idea to send money through the post."

She waved away his concerns. "Oh, it's fine. I've been doing it for years."

"Well, the post office is shut but I can sell you a book of stamps. We have them in four or eight."

"But I only want one." The woman became downcast.

The man behind fidgeted on the spot, clearly wanting to get home so he could crack open the bottle and start his evening with his feet up and a glass of wine in his hand.

"Well, I'm not supposed to break books of stamps, but as long as we keep it a secret between us." Scott winked.

The man relaxed, sensing this was nearly over.

"Oh, thank you so much," the lady said. "But will one stamp be enough? I get confused with all these new rules. You used to stick a stamp on a letter and that would be that. Why did they have to change it?"

"One stamp will be fine," Scott reassured her. "Would you like me to explain how it works, so you know for next time?"

"Oh, yes please."

The man in overalls huffed, clearly thinking this might take a while. Scott had a reputation for his patience and consummate customer care.

As if answering the man's prayers, Scott's wife Angie appeared and signed on to the other till. Like Scott, she was tall, in her thirties with an athletic build and short cropped blonde hair, and equally warm and friendly. "Shall I take that for you? So you can get on your way."

Hope restored, the man brightened. "Oh, yes, thank you."

Angie pointed at the racks of food and drink. "You know, you can get another bottle for half price," she informed him.

"We have a deal on at the moment, and its two for one on large bags of crisps."

"Really? That sounds good. Been a long day." He disappeared off to secure a second bottle and perhaps some snack food.

Once both satisfied customers had paid and left, the couple came out from behind the counter to greet Fiona, Daisy and Partial Sue. Everyone in Southbourne knew Scott and Angie, and Scott and Angie knew almost everyone in Southbourne. The post office was the heart of the community, and they were an extremely obliging couple, as trusted and as helpful as the day was long.

With the pleasantries over, Fiona braced herself for what might become a tricky conversation that would undoubtedly turn awkward. She needn't have worried.

"I'm glad you've popped in," Scott said. "I wanted to have a word with the three of you."

"You do?" Partial Sue didn't hide her surprise.

Scott looked at his watch. "It's nearly six o'clock. Ange, would you mind locking the front door just so we can talk without being disturbed?"

"Sure," Angie said.

Fiona was curious to know why he wanted to speak to them. "What's on your mind, Scott?"

When his wife returned, Scott took a deep breath. "I know this is going to sound strange, especially as you were there and saw what I saw, but . . ." He paused for a moment. "I don't believe my dad killed himself."

CHAPTER 6

The three ladies stood in stunned silence. In the brief moment they had been waiting in the shop, Fiona had lined up a couple of conversation starters to gently ease into things. Nothing clever, just simple small talk, polite enquiries into how Scott was doing and the usual offers after a bereavement: *If there's anything we can do*, et cetera. Then she would perhaps employ a series of subtle segues, ramping up the gentlest of inclines to the real reason they were there. But Fiona had not expected Scott to pre-empt their investigation with a theory of his own.

"Wh-what makes you think that?" she stuttered.

Scott leaned against the counter and shook his head. "I just know. He wouldn't take his own life. I'm sure of it. He loved life."

"How was he before he died?" Daisy asked, gently.

"His usual cheerful self, happy-go-lucky. Well, except he was buzzing a lot more than usual."

"How come?" Partial Sue asked.

"He'd just finished his first week at the Christmas market and loved it. He liked people, my dad. Being a stall-holder was right up his street. Okay, it wasn't as busy as he'd hoped, but there were plenty of people for him to chat to. He was definitely more chipper than usual."

"Some people will often cover up their unhappiness by acting jolly." Fiona knew a thing or two about depression, having suffered from it on and off since retiring.

Scott shook his head again. "I've heard that before. But my dad has always been like that, ever since I can remember. Always the life and soul of the party. Always looking for the next new experience around the corner. You know, once the Christmas market was over, he'd planned on signing up as a film extra. Was really excited about it. That's how I know he wasn't suicidal. He wouldn't make plans for the future if he was going to kill himself. It just doesn't make sense."

"Did he have a proper job?" Partial Sue asked. "I mean, surely he couldn't pay the bills with a seasonal market stall and walk-on parts in films."

Scott folded his arms. "He bought and sold stuff on eBay. That was his main bread and butter. It gave him loads of free time to indulge in other pursuits, like the Christmas market. The only thing he didn't like was the hours sitting alone at a laptop. He liked being around people. I think that's what prompted him to rent the stall at the last minute — that and the reduced price Malorie was offering. It was a bit spontaneous, but that was Dad all over. He could be very impulsive."

"What was his reputation like on eBay?" Fiona was hoping to uncover a possible suspect, perhaps a disgruntled buyer.

"He had a 100% seller rating."

"How come he didn't sell his stuff on the stall?" Partial Sue asked.

"He didn't think people would want to buy second-hand items on a Christmas stall, so he opted for hot chocolate. Not the best hot chocolate in the world — it was just out of a tin — but once the sprinkles, marshmallows and cream were added, he knew people wouldn't be able to resist wandering around with something warm and sweet in their hands."

Now the difficult part. Fiona steadied herself. "How were things between you before he died?"

Scott hesitated, swallowed hard, then batted away a tear. Angie was at his side, curling an arm around him. "It's okay, Scott. It's not your fault."

"I know, but it still feels like it is." He looked up through two bloodshot eyes. "We had a bit of an argument the Friday night before he died. He called in at our house, full of the joys of spring — or Christmas, I should say." Scott gave a painful snigger. "After his first week on the stall, he was jabbering non-stop about how much he was enjoying it. Overflowing with festive spirit. He'd popped in to see if I wanted to come to the pub with him. He was a regular at the Countess of Strathmore on a Friday night, and sometimes I'd join him. But not that night."

"Why was that?" Daisy asked.

A fresh tear streaked down Scott's face. "I was annoyed with him. Christmas is our busiest time, and though numbers are down in the store, it hasn't affected the post office. We rely on his help before the big day. He comes in part-time, but not this year because of the market stall. We didn't know how we'd cope. I snapped at him. Said some things I didn't mean, and now I really wish I hadn't." He bowed his head and began to sob.

Angie drew him closer, soothing his pain. "It's not your fault. It's not your fault."

Scott eventually sniffed back the tears. "I don't believe he killed himself, but I still feel like I'm responsible for all this."

"Now that's not true," Angie reassured him. "You've had lots of arguments in the past. The pair of you were like chalk and cheese. You like things nice and ordered and he was a free spirit, liked being spontaneous. But you always made up in the end."

Daisy offered Scott a tissue. "From what you've said, it doesn't seem like your dad would take his life over a little disagreement. Not if he was enjoying life so much."

Fiona felt desperately sorry for Scott. No matter how a person dies, the ones left behind always feel guilt and shame — if only they'd done this or that, things would have been different. She had come here wanting to gently nudge the conversation in the direction of Clive's assurance money, to quiz Scott on motive and gauge his reaction. Perhaps now wasn't the right time. Besides, her gut was telling her that Scott was probably innocent. Unless he was an expert at turning on the waterworks, the man in front of him appeared, to all intents and purposes, like someone who had just lost his father in the most unexpected and inexplicable way.

Scott rallied a little. "Sorry, it's all very sad and confusing at the moment. It's like I'm carrying a planet on my back."

Fiona thought it best to cut their losses for now, and maybe revisit Scott and Angie when things weren't so raw. She didn't want to overwhelm them, not this early on in the investigation. "We should go, and let you grieve."

"No." Scott straightened up, suddenly alert and full of purpose. "I want you to investigate his death."

Fiona's mouth guppied open and shut, shocked at his request. But that wasn't all. An emotional situation had turned into an awkward one. A conflict of interest. They had already been hired by Daph, but they couldn't exactly tell him this, as they'd been sworn to secrecy.

But was it really a conflict of interest? Both Scott and Daph wanted the same thing. To find the truth surrounding Clive's death. Perhaps the ladies could appease both parties without either of them knowing.

"Would you find out what really happened to him? Please?" Scott begged.

Daisy and Partial Sue fired surprised expressions in Fiona's direction, which quickly turned into panic. She sent them back what she hoped was a look of comfort and encouragement. In actual fact, there might be an opportunity to extract more from the conversation, which she had been prepared to leave to a later date. "Yes, we would be happy to look into it."

"I sense a 'but' coming," Angie said.

"We need more than a feeling to investigate," Fiona replied. "Especially with the elephant in the room — the market stall locked from the inside. It's a big stumbling block. From an outsider's perspective, everything points to suicide. Do you have any evidence that foul play was involved, or perhaps some other information that might be relevant to the case?" Fiona was hoping to swing the conversation towards life assurance and hefty payouts, to see how the couple would react.

Rather than baulk at this, Scott's eyes became more intense. "Yes, yes, I do."

This wrongfooted Fiona for a beat. She was sure Scott's reaction to his father's death was emotional rather than rational. Unless it was all an act.

But the sub-postmaster looked more sure of himself than ever. "You witnessed it. We all did when we finally got the stall open."

Fiona wondered what she had missed, unless he was referring to his own delayed reaction when the stall doors were finally opened. Apart from that, the scene had been pretty straightforward. Grisly but easy to read. A man who'd successfully hung himself. "I'm sorry. What did I witness?"

Angie gently nudged Scott. "Fiona wouldn't have noticed anything unless she knew Clive like we did."

"Noticed what?" Partial Sue jittered, eager for them to spill the beans.

"My dad was untidy," Scott explained. "I could show you his flat if you don't believe me. Boxes and clutter everywhere. But even before he started eBaying, he used to collect things. Shoved them in every available space. That messiness followed him wherever he went."

Fiona's eyes briefly alighted on Partial Sue, who was also a fellow hoarder.

Angie agreed. "I loved Clive, but he was a mess-making machine. If he'd pop in to see us, even if it was just for five minutes, somehow our living room would be chaos after he left. He'd always manage to knock something over. Pull things out and not put them back."

"My dad sent me this picture on the first day of the market." Scott produced his phone and revealed a selfie of Clive grinning proudly in front of his stall, donned in a thick fleece and woolly hat. Behind him, the counter was stacked with columns of upturned disposable cups, swaying so high they were in danger of toppling over. Next to the shiny water boiler were glass jars of sprinkles, marshmallows and other delights, randomly placed around the counter, and the fateful wholesale tin of hot chocolate he'd supposedly stood on. In between it all, chocolate powder and toppings had spilled everywhere. "He hadn't even served his first customer yet and look at the state of it. But on the morning we discovered him, everything had been . . ."

"Tidied up." Fiona finished off his sentence.

"Exactly!" Scott said. "It'd all been put away in the cupboard below the counter. He'd never do that!"

She felt her stomach tumble. All this time, the evidence had been hiding in plain sight — well, behind cupboard doors. Unless Clive had suddenly developed a penchant for neatness, someone had been in that stall with him, murdered him and made it look like suicide, then, for some inexplicable reason, decluttered the place.

CHAPTER 7

The ladies hurried along the pavement at a rate of knots with Simon Le Bon leading the way. The case had interested them before, but now the revelation of Clive's spick-and-span stall, contrary to his messy personality, had them well and truly intrigued. Something was definitely amiss. Enlivened by this new information, they seized the moment and headed straight for the pub, not to congratulate themselves with a drink but because the Countess of Strathmore was where Clive had sipped his last pint.

"It still doesn't answer how a killer could get in and out," Daisy panted, not quite managing to keep up with Partial Sue's blistering pace. "Unless they could walk through walls."

"Yes, I know," Partial Sue replied. "That's the appeal of a locked-room mystery. An impenetrable puzzle in more ways than one. However, there's one thing we can be sure of — the crime scene was staged."

"Yes, someone tidied up after themselves," Fiona replied.

"But why would a murderer worry about putting everything away?" Daisy asked. "Unless they were a neat freak, like me."

"There was probably a struggle," Partial Sue explained excitedly. "Things got knocked over, and that would undoubtedly point to murder. So the killer squared everything away before they left. But they overdid it. And now we're onto them."

"But there wasn't a struggle," Fiona said. "Remember what Daph said? No marks on the body, and no indication that Clive had fought for his life."

"Perhaps it was a gentle fight," Daisy suggested.

"How can you have a gentle fight?" Partial Sue asked.

"I need to stop and catch my breath," Daisy spluttered, coming to a halt. Fiona and Partial Sue joined her, taking a well-earned breather. At least it had stopped raining, but the air was cold and damp, their hearty breaths clouding in front of them. Simon Le Bon used the respite to sniff around a nearby lamp-post.

When Daisy had recovered, she voiced another problem with the case, to add to the many others. "What I can't understand is how come the police weren't bothered about the unusually tidy stall? Scott said he told them about it."

"Normally they would be," Fiona said. "But in the face of such massively compelling evidence — no signs of a struggle, and the stall bolted from the inside — it becomes insignificant. Like you said, a killer can't walk through solid walls. Leaving only one reasonable conclusion: Clive took his own life. Also, the tidying is easy to explain away. Suicide is not a normal state of affairs. People act out of character. He might have been procrastinating until he'd worked up the courage."

Partial Sue had another thought, angling towards foul play. "Well, if someone did kill him, they obviously didn't know him well. Otherwise, they wouldn't have cleaned up his stall. They would've realised it would stick out like a sore thumb."

Fiona shook her head. "But they didn't need to know him to realise that. Surely they'd have noticed the state of it before they killed him. Why didn't they leave it a bit on the messy side? Why go to all the effort of putting everything away? It doesn't make sense."

Under the street light, Partial Sue's eyes glinted with possibility. "Or maybe they did know him intimately and wanted to point the finger at someone else. Maybe Scott did it and tidied up to take the attention off himself. So he could use that as an alibi. He's even got the photographic evidence of his dad's messy stall on his phone. Fishy, if you ask me."

"But Scott *is* a tidy person," Daisy countered. "He'd only be pointing the finger at himself if he did that."

"Unless someone did it to frame him," Partial Sue replied. "But if that was the case, why go to all that trouble to make it look like a suicide?"

Fiona decided it was the right time to air her suspicions. "You know, Scott did something strange when we found Clive dead in his stall. We all gasped, but Scott just stood there. He didn't respond. Not straight away."

"That sounds quite normal to me. He was stunned. Rabbit in the headlights." Daisy popped a Polo in her mouth and offered the packet around. "And it's not fishy to have pictures of your father on your phone. But even if Scott did do it, why involve us? As far as he's concerned, he's got off, er, scot-free."

Fiona sighed. "You're right. Maybe we've got this all wrong. Scott's innocent and just wants to find his dad's killer. It's as simple as that. Or he's in denial. I've heard that's very common with grieving loved ones in these situations. He can't accept that his dad would kill himself."

Daisy sighed. "I can't imagine how difficult that must be. You'd be desperate for any verdict apart from that one. But changing it to murder's not much better, and wouldn't that affect his life assurance payout?"

Partial Sue shook her head. "No, Tyndale would still have to pay out — unless Scott was involved, of course."

Fiona became downcast at how complicated things had got this early on. "I'm not sure how this all fits together yet, but one thing is certain. We need to take a look at that stall. If there is a killer involved, how did they escape?"

"Maybe they're a magician," Partial Sue suggested.

Daisy shuddered. "I don't like magicians. Or clowns. They can't be trusted." But she had other worries on her mind. "Are you sure it's okay, working for both Daph and Scott? We're not going to get in trouble, are we?"

"It's highly unprofessional," Partial Sue said. "But we're not professionals, so it doesn't matter."

"But we're getting paid by Daph."

"It's a donation. Well, apart from my toaster."

"As long as we don't mention anything to either side," Fiona said, "I'm sure we'll be fine. Come on, let's see what we can find out at the pub."

A few minutes later, the Countess of Strathmore came into view, its sign creaking ominously as it swung back and forth in the December breeze. The bizarre image of a pug with a napkin tied around its neck glared down at them. Just one of the many dogs owned by the local eccentric eighteenth-century noblewoman, who was rumoured to dine with her pooches as if they were dinner guests.

As they stepped inside, the warm atmosphere embraced them, a heady mix of alcohol and friendship, clinking glasses and chattering lips. Adding to the intimacy, the pub's low ceilings were held up by thick ancient timbers, adorned with crimson-berried holly wreaths and sprays of mistletoe. Iced cookie decorations in the shapes of Christmas puddings, stars and stockings hung from the ceilings, nearly brushing the tops of the ladies' heads. In one corner, a fire crackled and popped. Daisy nearly exploded with delight as the table next to it suddenly became available. "Oh, oh! We have to grab that table by the fire."

Fiona hated denying her the most sought-after spot in the pub, especially at this time of year. But they weren't here to be Christmassy. "I'm afraid we can't. We need to prop up the bar, so we can question the landlord."

Daisy didn't complain but gazed longingly as they sashayed past the empty table, glowing in the inviting firelight.

Last time Fiona was here, she didn't remember there being so many spare tables. Though the place had a healthy buzz, it wasn't full by any means. Another victim of the sinister cloud that hung over Southbourne.

The landlord smiled, happy to see customers as the ladies perched themselves on three bar stools. "What can I get you?"

"I'll have a gin and tonic," Fiona said.

"Make that two, please," Daisy added.

"Hmm." Partial Sue eyed up the wooden hand pumps, standing to attention along the bar. "I am partial to a real ale. What would you recommend?"

The landlord gestured to one at the very end, its badge showing Santa collapsed in a heap at the bottom of a chimney. "This is our festive guest ale, Hearth Pint. Got a lovely smoky texture."

"I shall have a pint of that, if you please."

After the landlord had poured their drinks and Fiona had paid, she asked, "How's business?"

The landlord forced a smile. "Oh, can't complain. Bit down on last year. Usually can't move for Christmas parties and works dos, but as you can see, some people are giving Southbourne a wide berth."

"Is that because of the stalker?" Daisy asked.

"Yeah, and the death of poor old Clive Preston hasn't helped. You know, he was in here the night before he died."

"Was he?" Fiona was expecting to prise the information out of him, but the landlord was quite keen to share a bit of gloomy gossip.

The landlord leaned in, resting his elbows on the bar. "He'd had a bit of a bust-up with his son before he came here. You know Scott, runs the post office with his wife, Angie. Nice fella. Clive was always having bust-ups with him."

"Really?" Fiona feigned ignorance. "What did they argue about?"

"All sorts of things. Mostly trivial stuff. Trouble was, they were different people. Scott's a steady Eddie, set in his ways, while Clive's the opposite, always looking for new experiences. I think Scott was worried that his dad would blow all his money."

"Was Clive well off, then?" Partial Sue asked, taking a large slurp of her pint. "Mm, that does taste smoky."

The landlord smiled. "Glad you like it. Some people can't get on with it. They say it tastes like a pint of ash."

"So, was Clive well off?" Fiona brought the conversation back on topic before it descended into a debate about real ale.

"I wouldn't say well off. He didn't drive around in a Maserati or anything, but he did okay. I think Scott was more worried that if his dad lost everything it would be him and Angie who'd have to pick up the pieces and put him up. It's almost like their roles were reversed. Scott was the parent and Clive was the child."

"What had they been rowing about before Clive came here?" Daisy asked.

"Something about him not helping out in the post office. Clive told me he'd never promised he would. Scott just assumed it because he does every year. I think that annoyed Clive. Then again, I suppose he should've told them he was doing the Christmas market, but then it was a last-minute decision. He liked being impulsive."

Fiona took a little sip of her G&T. "But would Clive really take his life over an argument?"

"It would've surprised me. Whatever Clive and Scott argued about, they would patch things up afterwards. Clive could shrug things off pretty quickly. Well, that's how it appeared to me. But you never know what's going on in someone's head, do you? Maybe all their quarrelling had built up over the years and that was the tipping point." The landlord cautiously glanced left and right, checking they weren't being overheard. "But that wasn't the only thing that rattled Clive that night. He had a bigger disagreement — in here."

"What happened?" Fiona asked.

"Like I said, Clive never stayed down for long. After getting the argument with Scott off his chest, he wanted to celebrate the first week of the Christmas market. So he bought everyone a round."

"Did he do that often?"

"He'd buy people rounds, but that was the first time he did it for the whole pub. As you can imagine, it went down well on a Friday night. Except for two people who'd been giving him the stink-eye since he'd come in."

"Who were they?" Daisy asked.

"Trisha French and Doug Fielding. Trisha owns the pottery painting place, Clay Slayers, and Doug runs Southbourne Shoe Repairs."

Fiona didn't know Trisha French, but she certainly knew Doug Fielding. Everyone did. Behind his back, he was referred to as Downward Doug, because any conversation, no matter what the subject, would quickly spiral into a dark well of misery. People put up with his degenerating glumness due to the indispensable nature of his business. If you needed a heel repaired, a spare key cut or, bizarrely, a less-than-impressive trophy bought and engraved, you had to endure the dismal, while-you-wait company of Downward Doug.

"Their places are on either side of the garage, opposite Clive's stall," the landlord continued. "They'd been drinking since five, but they didn't look happy. Were deep in conversation all night."

"Do you know what they were talking about?" Partial Sue asked.

The landlord shook his head. "I couldn't hear. But it looked serious. So Clive wanders over, gets talking to them. Next second, they're raising their voices, getting shirty with him. To cut a long story short, they accuse Clive and the other stall-holders of taking their business away. They tell him they don't want the Christmas market, or his stall, outside their shops. Then they get up and storm out."

"How was Clive after that?" Fiona asked.

"A bit shaken, I can tell you. Thing is, Clive got along with everyone — well, apart from his son now and again — so it was a bit of a shock to get all this bad feeling thrown at him, especially seeing how much he enjoyed having the market stall."

"Did he have much to drink that night?" Partial Sue asked.

"Only his usual three pints."

Fiona remembered Daph had stated that the amount of alcohol in his system equated to about four pints, according to toxicology. She wondered where the fourth pint had come from. "Just three?"

"Yeah, he always had three pints. Unlike Scott, he was a small man. Couldn't really handle any more than that. He'd stretch out his drinks until closing time. Sat in his usual spot, sipping away where you're sitting now. He liked being there so he could chat to people at the bar."

"What would happen if Clive had more than three pints?" Fiona asked. "Would he get violent or abusive?"

"God, no. Not Clive. More booze would just make him sleepy. He'd start nodding off at the bar."

Fiona was keen to find out where this extra pint had originated from. "Would he ever go on to another bar?"

The landlord shook his head. "Not that I know of. He'd want to go straight to bed."

Fiona got a tingle down the back of her neck. A fizz of possibility. Somewhere between leaving the pub and heading back home, Clive had downed another pint. Where had he been drinking? More importantly, who had he been drinking with?

Had he encountered Trisha and Doug along the way home? Had they hounded him some more, berating him until he felt he had no choice but to take his own life?

CHAPTER 8

Daisy carefully poured each of them a cup of tea while Fiona slid mince pies onto plates, topping each one with a sizeable dollop of brandy butter. Partial Sue snatched up her tea with wild abandon and took a big slug. Letting out a contented sigh, she leaned back in her chair but stopped short of plonking both feet up on the table. "Well, this seems pretty cut and dried to me. Doug and Trisha spend an evening in a downward spiral of drink, blaming their lack of income on the Christmas market. When, lo and behold, in walks the cause of their misery: a stall-holder. But not just any old stall-holder. Clive's showing off, flashing his cash and buying a round for the whole pub, rubbing their noses in it. Can you imagine how they feel? Confirms all their misplaced suspicions that the market is siphoning money from honest shop owners. Their hackles are up. Fuelled by alcohol and bitterness, they do something rash and kill him."

"But how did they get out of the locked stall?" Daisy reminded her before Partial Sue got any smugger.

Partial Sue straightened up. "Doug cuts keys all day. He probably knows how to pick locks like you, Daisy."

"There was no lock to pick," Fiona reminded them. "Unless he could move a heavy bolt with his mind, there was no way he could get out of a stall that's locked from the inside."

"Okay," Partial Sue said. "The theory might need some finessing, but the motive is sound."

Daisy still wasn't convinced. "I'm not sure of the motive either. Having a moan over a pint or two is one thing — it's Doug's favourite pastime — but killing someone is a whole different ball game."

"Yes, but they'd been drinking since five," Partial Sue replied. "Alcohol and anger does not a good combination make. Reasonable people end up doing unreasonable things. Or miserable people, in this case."

"Still doesn't answer how they got out of a locked stall," Daisy pointed out through a mouthful of mince pie.

"It's not necessary for them to get in or out of the stall," Fiona said. "Like Daph said, someone can be coerced into suicide. What if they waited for him outside, then badgered him all the way home. Accusing him of stealing their income, calling him a thief, taking the food out of their children's mouths. All sorts of nasty guilt-tripping. Clive's already a bit fragile after his argument with Scott. There's no locked-room murder mystery, just a big, nasty shove towards suicide."

Daisy screwed up her face. "I can't see it myself. If someone accused me of all sorts of horrible things, I'd be upset, probably cry, but I don't think it'd be enough to make me do you-know-what."

The doorbell chimed. With the gusto of an opera singer, the Wicker Man swept through the door, letting in all the cold air. "Deck the halls with boughs of holly, fa-la-la-la-la, la-la la-la . . ." Catching sight of the ladies' dour expressions, his *fa-la-la-la-la's* swiftly faded away. "Clearly not in Dogs Need Nice Homes. Tell me, what ails you?"

"Oh, nothing, Trevor," Fiona replied.

Trevor was known as the Wicker Man because he purveyed old-school wicker furniture. He would also tug the dust sheets off antiquated words and phrases, and take them for a spin like a classic two-seater sports car on a Sunday morning. "Is my advent a tad unseemly?"

"We're just discussing a case," Daisy reassured him. "Come, sit down and have a cup of tea and a mince pie."

He also had a knack for showing up just as the tea was being poured and cake appeared. "Don't mind if I do. Oh my, and you have brandy butter. The most beguiling temptress." He poured himself a cup and helped himself to a mince pie. "Now, tell me. What game is afoot?"

"We're looking into the death of Clive Preston on behalf of, erm . . ." Daisy stuttered, realising it was probably best not to mention either Daph's or Scott's name.

"On behalf of justice," Partial Sue stepped in.

The Wicker Man clasped his hands together, prayer-like, mustering his sincerity. "May Clive rest in peace. But surely an investigation is surplus to requirements? The poor chap did himself in."

"Did you know him?" Fiona asked.

"Oh yes. Known him for donkey's years."

"So you think he killed himself?"

"Well, there can't be any other explanation, can there? His stall was locked from the inside, unless the laws of physics have changed since I wore breeches and carried a satchel."

Fiona wasn't buying into the walking-through-walls explanation either, but she did think foul mouths rather than foul play were to blame. "Was he easily influenced? Did he worry about what people thought of him?"

The Wicker Man nearly choked on a mince pie. "Clive? Not on your nelly. He was headstrong. Did whatever took his fancy. Skin on the thick rather than thin side. Whatever demons drove him to the noose must have been inside his noggin to start with."

"Have you heard of any shop owners accusing stall-holders of stealing their income?" Fiona asked.

He hesitated before answering. "There have been rumblings."

"What sort of rumblings?" Partial Sue asked.

"A few people expressed ill will, you might say."

"Who in particular?" Fiona already had a couple of names in mind.

The Wicker Man sobered up somewhat, dropping his Dickensian merchant act. "I'm not supposed to say, but there are a couple of well poisoners, if you take my meaning."

Partial Sue fixed him with two stark eyes. "Who?"

He glanced away, unable to meet her gaze. "You haven't heard this from me. Downward Doug and Trisha from Clay Slayers."

No surprises there, thought Fiona. "And what form did this ill will take?"

"Oh, nothing serious," he was quick to add. "You know, a little remark here, a little aside there. Doug's pretty miserable about everything, but he's joined forces with Trisha, and they've been spreading this rumour to the other retailers that the Christmas market is a big festive money leech."

"They haven't mentioned anything to us," Daisy said.

The Wicker Man's awkwardness intensified. He shifted uneasily on his behind.

"What?" Fiona asked.

"Tell us," Partial Sue demanded.

He winced as he spoke. "Well, it's because you're a charity shop."

"What's that got to do with it?"

"They don't think you have the same struggles as regular shops." He cringed as he spoke. "Making a profit and all that."

"We have to make a profit," Fiona informed him.

As a charity shop with volunteers and tax breaks, sure, things were a little easier, but they still had to pay the bills and make money to fund the vital work of the Dogs Need Nice Homes charity. Otherwise, they too were at risk.

Daisy became offended. "That's discrimination, that is."

"Okay, I agree." The Wicker Man attempted to assuage their discontent. "But you can understand their reasoning. Everyone's losing money."

Partial Sue wasn't having any of it. "Yes, but the reason takings are down is because of the stalker and now Clive's unfortunate death. It's not the Christmas market. If Malorie hadn't organised it in time, no one would be coming to Southbourne and things would be a lot worse."

"I know, I know. I'm just saying what others are thinking."

The shop went quiet. A moody, affronted silence. When it became too uncomfortable to bear, the Wicker Man attempted to restore peace. "May I offer you a sop of knowledge to quell your woes?"

"Go on," Partial Sue said.

The Wicker Man cleared his throat. "Doug and Trisha expressed their dislike of the Christmas market from the moment it was announced. However, the second Clive died they ceased their noxious utterances." He raised his right eyebrow to signify the profound status of this revelation. "Methinks this pair has a guilty conscience." The eyebrow returned to its regular position but was immediately drawn into an exaggerated wink.

Fiona questioned the significance of this information. Anyone with a shred of human decency would naturally be riddled with guilt if the person they'd been at odds with suddenly passed away, especially in such regrettable circumstances. Nevertheless, Trisha and Doug would have to be questioned, no matter how uncomfortable it would be for them.

CHAPTER 9

As they trooped up the road towards Clay Slayers, Fiona assumed that pottery painting would be Daisy's domain. As an expert miniaturist and doll-house wrangler, she had the steady hands of a midnight pixie helping out a beleaguered cobbler. Her house was also littered with china figurines, carefully curated and arranged in collections of woodland animals, puppies, regency maidens and vagabond minstrels, but definitely no clowns or magicians. From every shelf and windowsill, they stared out with big, innocent, glazed eyes. So it was quite a shock when their fair-hearted friend made an unexpected confession.

"You know, I've never been to a pottery café. I'm quite excited. Well, apart from the fact that it might be owned by a potential murderer."

"You surprise me," Partial Sue remarked. "I thought it would be right up your street."

"I'm so busy with painting furniture for my doll's houses that I've never got round to it."

Turning the corner into the side road, Clive's stall was still conspicuous by its absence. A large flat area of pavement stood empty in front of the two shops that sandwiched the entrance to the garage.

Heads bowed, the ladies examined the area briefly, wondering if any sort of clue might emerge. But there was nothing to see apart from smooth, flawless tarmac and a few flattened splodges of discarded grey chewing gum. Simon Le Bon grew impatient, so they abandoned their search and headed into the pottery café.

Daisy immediately gasped at the walls of shelves, stacked floor to ceiling with neutral, unsullied pots, jugs, plates, objects and animals, all waiting for someone to splash colour on them. "Oh, it's wonderful! We have to have a go."

Fiona had to admit the thought of sipping tea and dabbing paint on a bowl with friends would be a most agreeable way to spend an afternoon, apart from art not being her strong suit. She could imagine her finished creation turning into a dog's dinner, in which case, she could actually use it for her dog's dinner, bequeathing it to Simon Le Bon as his food bowl. She glanced down at her little terrier, who for once stood his ground, nose twitching away, overwhelmed by the odour of clay.

Partial Sue brought them all back down to reality. "I don't get it. Why should I pay good money to paint plates and cups when I can just buy them already done from Homesense?"

"Because it's fun," Daisy countered.

"Fun? Sounds like work to me. I might open a café with sinks instead of tables where people pay to do washing-up."

An odd pairing of noises echoed from down a hallway at the back. A clicking and a smacking. As the strange duet grew louder, Fiona realised it was the approach of clip-clopping heels and the slapping of lips, presumably from a mouthful of chewing gum. Another big assumption was about to be smashed like a Christmas tree ornament in the house of an energetic two-year-old. In her mind, Fiona had pictured the owner of Clay Slayers to be a fairly whimsical soul — not that whimsical, seeing as how she had led the charge against the Christmas market with Doug, of all people, but certainly someone of the bohemian persuasion, dressed for the practicalities of running a craft café. Maybe a long smock dress with a paint-splattered apron and hair up in a loose, messy bun.

However, Trisha appeared to have stepped right out of the mid-eighties, specifically a tacky nightclub from that garish era. She sauntered or rather rustled into the café, due to the shiny nature of her puffy, wide-shouldered purple dress. It was as if she had been swathed in a giant Quality Street wrapper. Her hair had been piled up big and improbably high, and stiffly held in place by the application of a great deal of hairspray, giving her the appearance of a human bottle brush.

"All right," she greeted, her bright red lips smacking away, pulverising the gum in her mouth. "Wanna paint somethin'?" She examined her colourful talon-like fake nails while waiting for an answer.

"Oh, yes please," Daisy gushed.

Partial Sue held up a hand. "Er, no. We're not here to paint. We'd like to ask you a few questions."

She stopped mid-chew and eyed the ladies cautiously, batting her vast fake eyelashes like a couple of Venus flytraps. "What about?"

Fiona smiled. "We've been asked to look into the death of Clive Preston, privately as it were, and wanted to talk to you about the night before he died."

"I ain't done nothin'."

"We didn't say you had." Partial Sue edged closer. "But you and Doug Fielding spoke to him that night."

"Maybe we did. Maybe we didn't."

"Someone saw the pair of you arguing with him," Fiona said coldly. "Can I ask what that was about?"

Her shoulders slumped, or would have, if said shoulders hadn't been reinforced with copious padding. "Look, I'm sorry about what happened to him. I really am. But it's nothin' to do with me or Doug."

"Okay, fine," Partial Sue said. "But we'd just like to know what you said to him."

Trisha folded her arms. "I can see where this is going. You think we drove him to suicide."

"Why don't you set us straight?" Daisy said.

Trisha thought for a moment, literally chewing it over, jaws grinding away. Eventually she sighed. "We'd had another bad week, decided to shut up shop early and go to the pub. Halfway through the evening Clive comes in and buys the whole pub a drink. Everyone crowds round the bar, but he looks over and notices we're not taking him up on his offer. We try not to catch his eye, but he comes over to us and is all like, 'Why ain't you drinking?' So, I say we're fine, thank you very much. But he won't leave it alone. Keeps on at us. 'Come on, have a drink,' he insists. But we say no — nicely, like. Then he gets all offended. Starts saying, 'Is my money not good enough for you?' Provoking us. I mean, his stall's outside our shops. He knows who we are. But he's trying to get a rise out of us. Me and Doug ignore him. Then he starts accusing us of badmouthing him."

"Is that true?" Partial Sue asked. "Did you badmouth him?"

Trisha winced. "Not really. Well, sort of. But we hadn't singled him out or nothin'. We were against the whole Christmas market. Wanted people to avoid it and use the local shops instead. We've really been struggling and were worried it was only going to make things worse."

"Then what happened?"

"We got up and left."

"So you're saying Clive started the argument."

"Yeah, but calling it an argument makes it sound like it was a two-way thing. He was having a go at us. If I didn't know better, I'd say he'd come in looking for trouble."

"But he bought everyone a round of drinks," Partial Sue pointed out. "That doesn't sound like someone looking for trouble."

Trisha shook her head. "He set us up. Clocked us the second he walked in. Had a filthy look on his face. Then he decided to buy a round for the pub, probably knowing we'd refuse. Which gave him an excuse to kick off. Make us look like the bad guys."

"And you think he did that because of the things you were saying about the market?"

"Maybe. But he knew we'd been against it right from the start. Nothin' new. And lots of other shopkeepers feel the same way, not just us. I'm sorry he died, but I think it would've turned out the same whether we'd been in the pub or not. Whatever was bothering him, he wanted to kick off at someone, and we happened to be in the firing line."

Fiona decided to enlighten her. "Apparently, he'd fallen out with his son before he came to the pub."

"Really?" Trisha raised her plucked eyebrows. "What, Scott in the post office?"

The ladies nodded.

"That explains a lot. Must have had a hell of a falling out to make him . . ." She made a noose-tightening action and a choking sound that Fiona didn't think was appropriate.

"Well, that's what's puzzling," Partial Sue replied. "Apparently, they were always falling out. Always going at it hammer and tongs, only to make up the next day. Business as usual for father and son."

For once, Trisha didn't have anything to say. The silence gave Fiona time to think. The picture she was forming of Clive in her head was of a gregarious man, a little on the brash side, certainly not oversensitive and definitely not easily intimidated by a bunch of disgruntled shopkeepers. In fact, according to Trisha, he'd been the aggressor on the night he died. Whatever had driven him to suicide, it was neither his son, nor Trisha and Doug. Of course, they had yet to question Doug, but Fiona felt there was some other reason behind his demise that they had yet to discover.

Before they left, Fiona asked, "Do you have CCTV?"

Trisha looked puzzled. "Why would you wanna know that?"

"I was just wondering if it might have captured Clive going into his stall on that fateful night."

Trisha snorted. "Nah, we don't have cameras. There's nothin' in 'ere worth nicking. Just a bunch of plain old plates and paint. Who'd want them?" She produced a forced cackle.

Fiona thought her response a little odd. Most shop owners she'd met in Southbourne thought their enterprises, regardless of their size or what they did, were the best thing since sliced bread, and used every opportunity to boast about them. If she didn't know better, she'd say Trisha resented her own business.

CHAPTER 10

The ladies wandered past the entrance to the garage that separated Clay Slayers from Southbourne Shoe Repairs. A cacophony of high-pitched whirrs interrupted Fiona's train of thought, not helped by Partial Sue's incessant theorising about how Trisha was the most unlikely person to run a pottery café, and if there was some conspiracy at play. Fiona had to agree.

"Yes, she does seem at odds with her own business. Did you notice how she derided it at the end? Strange for someone who's also complaining that it's not making enough money."

"Did you see that hair?" Partial Sue remarked. "I haven't seen hair like that since the *Top of the Pops* Christmas special 1985."

"I quite liked it," Daisy replied. "It had plenty of body."

"Body?" Partial Sue baulked. "You could hide a body in that hair, it was so big."

Daisy had more day-to-day concerns on her mind. "How does she keep that flashy frock from getting covered in paint?"

Eagle-eyed Partial Sue supplied the answer. "Didn't you see the sign? It said, 'Customers must wash up after themselves. Clean pots, brushes and wipe down the tables.' She's not daft. She keeps her hands clean and gets other people to do her dirty work. See, it's not a million miles from what I said. Paying to do someone else's washing-up."

Fiona pointed out the flaw in her business idea. "Except with your idea you don't get anything at the end of it."

"You do. A nice stack of clean pots and pans to be proud of."

"I'd quite like that," Daisy said. "But then I do like cleaning. Maybe you could give out a certificate. A different colour depending on how much washing-up you've done."

Partial Sue embellished her idea. "Or coloured belts like you get in karate."

A black belt in washing-up didn't seem the most illustrious accolade. Before the ladies had a chance to ponder this hygienic grading system, they became distracted by the animatronic cobbler in the window of Doug's shop. The little craftsman had a mesmerising effect. With an inane grin on his face, he ceaselessly hammered the sole of a shoe.

"They always have these in the window," Partial Sue remarked. "But the hammer never seems to hit the shoe. I don't know why, but I find that really irritating."

Daisy shivered. "I've never liked these puppet shoemakers. Reminds me of Mr Rednock, my maths teacher."

"Come on, let's see what Doug can tell us." Fiona pushed open the door and was immediately hit by the stench of chemicals, glues and solvents. Doug had his back to them and was bashing away on an upturned shoe, not unlike the animatronic chap in the window, except he was definitely making contact, judging by the racket.

Partial Sue locked on a display hanging on the far wall — a selection of large house numbers in various bright colours for sticking on wheelie bins. "I've always wondered where you get these. My neighbour keeps on taking my bin by mistake. Drives me mad. I have to nip out at the crack of dawn to get it back in before she half-inches it."

"You know, I might get some as well," Fiona said. "Mine's always getting mixed up with my neighbour's, who never cleans hers. I always get her filthy one that smells of fish."

Partial Sue didn't reply, possibly because, like Fiona's neighbour, she never cleaned her bin either.

"I might get some too," Daisy joined in. "I mean, I've already got numbers on mine, but I wouldn't mind some more just to be on the safe side."

They selected their giant adhesive digits and took them to the counter.

Douglas Fielding, a small-framed man with a balding head and wearing tatty brown overalls, ceased his hammering and turned to eye them through a pair of lopsided bifocals. He didn't offer a hello or greeting of any kind. "Did you notice any prices on these?" He nodded to the numbers, wiping his hands on a rag.

The ladies shook their heads.

He tutted and disappeared under the counter then re-emerged with a well-thumbed catalogue, thick enough to prop open a barn door, its frayed edges browned with dirt. Flicking through page after page of prices, he alighted on one, briefly shook his head and flicked further on, repeating the exercise several times until he reached the end. At this point, he went back to the beginning and started again.

Fiona shot Partial Sue and Daisy a look, wondering if this was worth the effort just for some sticky numbers.

"You know what?" Douglas grumbled. Fiona hoped he would say something like, *Let's just call it a pound a piece*, but no such luck. "I've got the wrong price list." He tutted again and disappeared back down below, rummaged around then reappeared with another similarly smudged and battered book that thudded onto the counter. The painful process began again.

Fiona decided to utilise their waiting time with a little prod to see how he'd react. "So, what do you think of the Christmas market?"

Douglas ceased his tedious price searching, thought for a moment and then said, "I like it."

Fiona wondered if they were in the right place. "You do?"

"Oh, yes."

She eyed him carefully, attempting to detect any hint of sarcasm, but he seemed genuine.

Doug continued. "People like Christmas markets. They're pretty, aren't they? Liven things up a bit."

This was not the response they were expecting. Fiona glanced over at her friends, who appeared just as confused as she was. "Er, yes, they do indeed. Everyone likes a Christmas market."

"Not like this place." He frowned as he reverted into full Downward Doug mode, glancing about his drab surroundings. "It's miserable getting keys cut and shoes repaired. Nobody says, 'Oh, it's a lovely day, let's go to the shoe repairers.' They just want to get in and out with their shoes or keys, or to buy an umbrella. They only associate my shop with miserable things — broken footwear, being locked out, or rain. That's why they never hang around for a chat."

Well, this was more like the Doug they were expecting. Fiona wondered if anyone had told him it wasn't grudge purchases that forced customers to make a swift exit, but rather the person offering them.

Partial Sue attempted to steer the conversation in a more optimistic direction. "What about people who buy your trophies? That's a happy experience, surely."

But Downward Doug was a master of looking on the dull side. "People who buy trophies are the unhappiest of all. They never get to win them. Someone else gets all the glory."

Fiona needed to put them back on track before Doug dragged them into a verbal abyss. "But you like the Christmas market being here."

"Yes, I do. Although, it's a love–hate relationship. I don't like the money it's taking from us shop owners."

"But surely you're not in competition with them?" Partial Sue said. "There's no festive ye olde shoe repairers stall."

Doug glared at her with his world-weary face, as if this was the most stupid thing he'd ever heard. "That doesn't matter. My takings are down. Right from the start, me and Trisha have been against it, and so have the other shopkeepers. Well, maybe me and Trish have been a bit more outspoken, but it's a feeling shared by everyone."

It suddenly struck Fiona what an odd couple he and Trisha were, appearance-wise. At opposite ends of the fashion spectrum, it was as if Trisha had been conceived in lurid Day-Glo and Doug in sepia. But then common causes could unite the most unlikely of allies, especially disgruntled ones. Both of them disliked what they did for a living. Misery certainly does love company, whatever it happens to be wearing.

"But isn't the lack of customers down to people being put off by the stalker?" Fiona felt like a broken record.

"That's true," Doug replied. "But the Christmas market has made it worse. Just like me and Trish warned it would."

Partial Sue's accountancy brain kicked in. "So, let me get this straight. If I were to plot a graph of your takings from the start of this year, I'd see a dip in sales from January onwards when the stalker first appeared. Then I'd see another dip when the Christmas market opened."

Doug stumbled over his response. "Er, ye-es. I suppose."

His uncertainty told Fiona everything. Presumably, like most of the shopkeepers in Southbourne, his dislike of the market was based on emotional rather than empirical evidence.

"Tell me about the night before Clive Preston died," Fiona asked. "You and Trisha were in the pub. Had an argument with him, so we've heard."

Alarm flickered in Doug's eyes. "What's this about?"

"We're investigating the circumstances around Clive's death," Daisy said.

"Who for?"

Daisy blushed, so Partial Sue answered. "That's confidential."

"We spoke to Trisha, and we'd like to hear your side of it." Fiona thought this would be a good opportunity to see if their stories matched.

Doug hesitated for a moment, sizing them up. Presumably, he was wondering if he could avoid her request, but then that would only make him look guilty. He reluctantly answered, "We were having a drink. Taking advantage of happy hour. It was anything but happy. We were fed up after another rubbish week. Then Clive comes in being all flash, buying everyone drinks. We refused and he started accusing us of all sorts of stuff. That we'd been telling people not to use his stall because his hot chocolate wasn't very good."

"And did you?" asked Partial Sue.

"No, not at all. I have no idea what his hot chocolate tastes like. Never touch the stuff. Me and Trisha would never single out his stall. We were against the whole thing."

"Then what happened?" Fiona asked.

"We did the smart thing and left. I can tell when someone can't be reasoned with. He was on a mission to pick on someone, and it happened to be us."

"Where did you go after that?"

"Straight home, of course."

"You didn't wait for Clive outside and follow him home?" Fiona goaded him. "Or maybe you followed him to another bar and waited for him outside."

Doug screwed up his face. "Why would we do that?"

"Because he'd just accused you of spreading lies about him in front of the whole pub. Your resentment must've grown after you left, and you decided to give him a piece of your mind."

"Or something stronger," Partial Sue added.

Doug's anger flared. "What do you mean by that?"

"You tell me," said Partial Sue.

Doug swept up the adhesive numbers off the counter, marched over to the display and stuffed them back into their little slots. He turned to face the ladies. "I'm going to have to ask you to leave. I'm not putting up with your accusations."

"We haven't accused you of anything," Daisy protested.

"No, but you've heavily implied it. I had nothing to do with his death. I'm innocent. And it was a suicide, remember? Now, if you would please leave." Doug strode over to the door and held it open.

The ladies didn't argue as they headed for the exit. Fiona quickly glanced around, checking for CCTV of any kind. Shoe repairers weren't a high priority for shoplifting, and she couldn't imagine Doug splashing out on anything that was superfluous, judging by the utilitarian nature of his store. As far as she could tell, the place was surveillance-free.

The ladies left minus their wheelie bin numbers, but with something far more valuable. Doug had just made himself their number-one suspect.

CHAPTER 11

They regrouped on the pavement outside, eager to discuss Downward Doug's incriminating behaviour. But before anyone had a chance to utter an opinion, Fiona thought it would be wise to usher them along, out of earshot of his shop. Discussing a suspect directly outside his place of business, no matter how he'd behaved, would not be appropriate. They really should've waited until they were safely ensconced in their own shop. However, like a five-year-old on a long car journey who needed a pee, Partial Sue couldn't hold it in much longer. So they stood just inside the entrance to the garage to shield their chatter from Doug next door.

"He's got a guilty conscience, that one," Partial Sue declared. "No doubt about it."

"I don't know," Daisy said. "I couldn't really tell if he had a guilty conscience or if he was just being a misery guts. I kept thinking of that song, 'Don't Bring Me Down' by the Electrolyte Orchestra."

"I think it's the Electric Light Orchestra," Fiona pointed out. "But did you notice something odd about his language during the conversation?"

Partial Sue and Daisy both stared at her nonplussed, perhaps wondering if he'd slipped in random swear words they hadn't been aware of.

Fiona enlightened them. "Initially, when he talked about the Christmas market and the business in the pub, he kept saying, 'Trisha and me, Trisha and me.' Plural. But as soon as he spoke about Clive's death, he reverted to singular: '*I'm* not putting up with your accusations. *I* had nothing to do with his death. *I'm* innocent.' In rushing to deny it, perhaps he made a Freudian slip."

"You know, I never noticed that," Partial Sue remarked. "He's definitely got something to hide. Do you notice how quickly he wanted us out of his shop?"

Daisy strengthened the theory further. "Now you mention it, there was something else I noticed. When we spoke to Trisha about Clive's death, she was sorry for what had happened to him. Offered her condolences, sort of. But we got no such sympathies from Doug."

"Now that is interesting," Fiona said. "He wasn't sorry for Clive's death. Maybe he was working alone and Trisha had nothing to do with it." She tugged on Simon Le Bon's lead as he sniffed a patch of oil. "Well, we've definitely made some breakthroughs today. I'll text Scott and Daph separately later. Tell them what we've learned about local traders resenting the Christmas market. But I'll keep it vague, leave out any names until we know more."

"I'm sure Scott already knows," Partial Sue said.

"I'm not sure," Fiona replied. "The post office is a public service. He might have been kept out of the loop like we were, especially as his dad was working for the enemy."

"That's true," Partial Sue conceded.

"I bet he doesn't know about the argument in the pub the night before Clive died," Daisy said. "He would have told us."

"It's interesting," Fiona replied. "According to the landlord, Trisha and Clive started it. But Trisha and Doug said that Clive started it. Provoked them."

Their chat was interrupted by a broken-down car heading towards them. It was being pushed by the mechanic who'd hacksawed into Clive's stall on that fateful morning. He had one nitrile-gloved hand shoved against the driver's-side door pillar, while the other hand reached in through the open window and steered. His son pushed from the rear, his hands planted on the tailgate. Together, they manoeuvred the car up the drop kerb and across the wide pavement, heading towards the entrance to the garage.

The ladies automatically moved to one side to let them past.

"Need a hand?" Fiona asked.

"Nah, we're good, thanks." The mechanic glanced at Fiona, recognition sparking across his face. Once the car was inside the large workshop and the handbrake engaged, he trotted back out, smiling warmly. "Hey, I remember you. You were there when we found Clive."

"That's right," Fiona replied.

He shook his head sorrowfully. "That was shocking. What an awful thing to happen."

"Yes, I know. Terrible. Absolutely terrible."

The fledgling conversation stalled, the subject matter not exactly conducive to small talk.

"I'm Tony, by the way. Tony De Costa." He stripped off his gloves and offered a clean hand to shake.

Fiona shook it, introducing herself, Daisy and Partial Sue, who also shook his hand.

"It's Scott I feel sorry for," Tony said. "Finding his dad like that, and just before Christmas. I wouldn't wish that on my worst enemy."

The ladies all nodded in agreement, releasing painful sighs.

Fiona seized the opportunity to gather some investigative information. "So what exactly happened that morning, before I showed up?"

Tony folded his gloves and shoved them in the back pocket of his overalls. "Well, me and Joe — that's my son — opened up as normal at eight o'clock. We start early, as people want to drop their cars off before work. Anyway, round about eight thirtyish, I hear this banging coming from out on the pavement. Normally I don't hear anything outside if the garage door is shut. But it was open, as we had to get a car inside. So I came out and saw Scott trying to break into the stall. Shoving his whole body against the doors. He looked desperate and a few passers-by had stopped to help him. They weren't having much luck, so I went over and asked what was going on. He told me his dad was locked inside. I looked at the stall but it wasn't locked. I'd seen them padlocked up at night on the outside. I didn't know they could be bolted from the inside. So I get down on my knees and peer into the tiny little gap between the doors. Sure enough, I can just make out the bolt slid across. So I run back into the workshop and grab my electric hacksaw. The lead's not long enough, so I tell Joe to bring the extension. Then we head back out and, well, the rest you know."

"Well, it was lucky you were here," Fiona said. "To get the doors open."

Tony grimaced, his face paling. "I still haven't got over the sight of Clive in there. Been giving me sleepless nights."

"You poor thing," Fiona said. "Is there anything we can do?"

Tony produced a weak, quivering smile. "I'll be fine, honestly. Just got to man up."

That was the traditional solution to men's emotional problems — bury them deep and get on with it. Never show any weakness, because admitting you're vulnerable somehow diminishes your masculinity.

"There's nothing wrong with feeling upset," Partial Sue reassured him. "Perfectly natural. Especially about something so traumatising."

Tony bowed his head. "Yeah, I know. I'm getting better at dealing with it as time goes on."

"You should speak to someone." With her own unresolved issues, Fiona was well aware that she should take her own advice. But for some reason it was always easier to help other people deal with their problems rather than her own.

Tony didn't reply and swallowed hard, clearly uncomfortable at the thought of talking about his feelings with strangers.

"If you need someone friendly to talk to, just pop into Dogs Need Nice Homes — we're always there and we're very good listeners."

Raising his gaze towards Fiona, his eyes softened. "Thank you. I might just do that."

"Our door's always open," Partial Sue added, but his eyes lingered on Fiona.

"How is your son?" Daisy asked.

"Joe's fine," he replied abruptly. "Didn't see anything. I made sure he kept out of the way."

"That's good."

Tony shifted on his feet and glanced anxiously back to the workshop. They were going to lose him if Fiona didn't act fast.

"Did you speak to Clive much when he had his stall here?"

"Yeah, of course," Tony replied. "We'd have a quick natter every morning. Bit of small talk."

"Did you resent his stall being outside?" Partial Sue asked bluntly.

Tony's eyes narrowed. "Resent it? Why would I resent it?"

Fiona attempted to soften the line of questioning. "We've heard that some local shop owners don't like the market. Believe it's affecting their sales."

Tony shrugged. "It doesn't really bother me. That's not to say I don't sympathise. I know retailers are struggling. But we're in a different line of work. Doesn't affect us. MOTs and car repairs haven't slowed down just because a load of Christmas stalls have appeared. In fact, I'm a big fan of the market, especially the bratwurst stall. But it's not good for the middle-aged spread." He smiled and patted his stomach.

At that moment, Tony's son wandered up, clutching a car part. He didn't make eye contact or acknowledge the ladies. "Dad, they've sent the wrong starter motor."

"Oh, okay. I'll be there in a minute," Tony said.

The teenager was the spitting image of his father. Same angular face, same thick black hair, except he was carrying a lot less weight and was taller and ganglier, his overalls sagging on his scarecrow-like frame.

"Are you looking forward to Christmas?" Daisy asked, as if he was at junior school.

Joe grunted and regarded her in that way that young people often do, as if anyone older than twenty-one were an alien species. He hunched his shoulders, turned and dawdled back into the garage.

"So, is it just you and Joe working here?" Fiona asked.

Tony nodded.

"Did either of you notice any odd behaviour around Clive's stall before he died?" Fiona asked. "Any arguments? Raised voices?" She was hoping he might have witnessed either Trisha or Doug exchanging unpleasant words with Clive.

Tony eyed her suspiciously. "Wait, are you three investigating his death or something?"

Fiona nodded. "For an interested party."

Tony's face became a mix of puzzled expressions, each eyebrow taking it in turns to rise and fall. "Hold on, you were there. Watched me cut through the bolt. You saw he'd killed himself. What's left to investigate?"

This was becoming a recurring question, one they'd have to keep answering patiently and circumspectly. She could understand people being mystified by their enquiries. An investigation seemed counterintuitive — surplus to requirements, as the Wicker Man had put it — when the overwhelming evidence clearly pointed to suicide.

Fiona attempted to gloss over his concerns. "It's more of a dotting i's and crossing t's exercise. You know, a formality."

This answer appeared to satisfy him. "Oh, I see. Well, to answer your question — no, I didn't see or hear anything you'd class as odd. Just a guy outside selling hot chocolate."

"Did you try any?" Daisy asked.

Tony shook his head. "Nah, not my thing. I'm a tea man."

"Good answer," Fiona enthused.

He smiled back and then glanced at his watch. "Which reminds me, I need to put the kettle on."

"Shouldn't Joe be making tea for you?" Fiona asked.

"You haven't tried his tea." Tony winked at her and turned to leave.

"Sorry, just one last question," Fiona asked. "Do you have any CCTV?"

Tony pointed to the heavy sliding metal door, supported by well-greased wheels. "Nah. No need. Once that door's shut, nothing's getting through it. Bulletproof, it is. Now, if you'll excuse me." He started to walk away then hesitated. Turning back to them, he cautiously glanced left and right, then spoke quietly. "Look, this is probably none of my business, and I don't want to drop anyone in it for no good reason, but after what you said about shopkeepers losing money, you might be interested to know that Trisha and Doug's places are both up for sale."

Fiona juddered at this new revelation. The pair already had a motive for murder, a perceived drop in profits. However, it had been superseded by a heftier one. Anything that got in the way of them selling their businesses and perhaps putting their feet up for the rest of their lives would certainly be a threat that they'd need to deal with. Especially if it stood outside, had a wooden pitched roof and sold third-rate hot chocolate.

The ladies exchanged thrilled glances. This had been a very lucrative morning's work.

CHAPTER 12

Back at the shop, Daisy launched straight into a brand-new theory she'd been itching to share since they returned. "That mechanic's got a thing for you."

Fiona blushed and nearly spilled tea over herself. "Don't be daft. Anyway, he's obviously married."

"I didn't see a wedding ring," Daisy said. "But I did see the way he was looking at you. Sue, back me up."

"Come on, Fiona. His eyes did linger on you — more than once."

"Rubbish. He's half my age."

"He is not," Daisy countered. "He's what, late fifties? And anyway, age doesn't matter. It's how you feel. I think it's nice, flattering."

Fiona couldn't deny there was some sort of connection there, and she did get a tingling feeling when she thought about Tony, but she wasn't about to admit it to these two. "If we could get back to the matter at hand, i.e., the revelation about Trisha and Doug?"

Partial Sue was happy to oblige. "It all makes sense now." She drained her tea, then wiped her mouth with the back of her hand, as if she'd just finished a tankard of ale. Judging by the contented expression on her face, everything balanced perfectly in her accountant's brain. A perfect answer with no remainders and no pesky recurring numbers to spoil things. "We thought Trisha and Doug were miffed because they believed their profits were being sabotaged by the Christmas market. Except they were a bit more outspoken than the other shop owners. But now we know why. They have a bigger stake in the game. They're desperate to sell, and having Clive's stall outside on the pavement was getting in the way of that."

Daisy nodded enthusiastically. "Doug's miserable. Hates what he does. Probably can't wait to retire. And running a pottery café doesn't seem to be Trisha's cup of tea at all. Maybe she wants the money so she can travel to far-flung places."

"What, like the eighties?" Partial Sue giggled. "But Daisy's right. Imagine you're looking forward to getting shot of your business and enjoying life. Then Clive's stall turns up outside, putting off potential buyers."

"And remember, they kept quiet about selling up," Daisy added.

"Yes," Partial Sue agreed. "Because they knew it would make them look guilty."

Fiona wasn't about to get swept up in their enthusiasm. "I can see how this makes a lot of sense, but it also makes no sense at all."

Her colleagues' faces dropped. "What?" they chorused.

"Well, for starters, how long have their businesses been for sale?"

Daisy got on her phone and began searching. The result came back quicker than Fiona expected. "Both businesses are advertised on the same website, but it doesn't say."

"How much are they on for?" Partial Sue asked.

"Doug's business is forty thousand and Trisha's is thirty-five. Both have a turnover of around two hundred grand a year. Hey, that's not bad."

"What's their profit?" Partial Sue asked.

"Doesn't say," Daisy replied.

Partial Sue snorted derisively. "Turnover is vanity. Profit is sanity. Sales is for show. Profit is for dough."

"What does that mean?" Daisy asked.

"People like to boast about their turnover," Partial Sue explained. "Because it sounds big, but it doesn't mean anything. Your turnover could be huge but if your expenses are also huge, your profit's going to be tiny. Profit is what really counts in business."

Fiona leaned in to examine Daisy's screen. "The fact that they haven't disclosed their profit says a lot. Their businesses aren't financially attractive. Not going to be snapped up by some money-hungry investor. I'd guess they've been on the market for a while."

"All the more reason to get rid of Clive and his stall," Daisy replied. "To make them more attractive."

"Clive's stall was a temporary inconvenience at best," Fiona replied. "If your business had been on the market for a while, would you really do something so drastic when you knew it would be gone in a few weeks? More importantly, if you wanted to make your business attractive, would you create a crime scene right in front of it?"

"Well, technically it wasn't a crime scene," Partial Sue pointed out. "Clive took his own life."

"Okay, fine," Fiona replied. "But that spot will be remembered as the place where someone lost their life. The stigma of a dead body attached to it. That's only going to make selling more difficult."

"Maybe they didn't think it through," Daisy remarked.

This was also very possible. It wouldn't be the first or last time that someone had killed without thinking of the consequences. Still, Fiona couldn't accept that Trisha or Doug would go to such lengths to remove a problem that would be gone by the New Year. As for "thinking it through", if this pair had the smarts to pull off an ingenious locked-room murder, she was sure they'd have had the foresight to realise what effect it would have on the sales potential of their businesses. Fiona had made up her mind. "I think it might be the opposite of what you think. If you're trying to sell, a dead body outside is the last thing you'd want. I think this gives Trisha and Doug a cast-iron alibi."

"What about their dislike of the market?" Daisy asked.

"Rightly or wrongly, they believed it was affecting their profits. And as Sue's just mentioned, profit is king in business. It's the first thing a potential buyer will look at. If theirs isn't good enough to post on a sales website, you can bet they'd be quick to point fingers. But it still leads us back to the same place. Would they really commit murder right outside the very businesses they were trying to sell?"

Her question hung in the air, the silence uncomfortable and all-consuming. Though Fiona thought her logic was sound, she was aware that what had started off as a promising lead this morning had flipped around and been sent packing in the opposite direction. Trisha and Doug couldn't have had anything to do with Clive's death. Unless they were incredibly stupid and the worst businesspeople she'd ever met. Of course, that was also a possibility. Doug maybe. He didn't know the price of his own stock and the place desperately needed a makeover, but not Trisha. Although an unlikely candidate to own a pottery café, she did seem to have her head screwed on. Fiona would keep the pair on her mental list of suspects, but way down at the bottom, together with Scott. Trouble was, she had no one filling the slots above them.

CHAPTER 13

After Fiona's unfavourable deduction, no new theories emerged, and the rest of the day plodded along, shuffling ponderously until it turned into a quiet and uneventful afternoon — apart from a lot of forced sighs, mostly originating from Partial Sue's direction. Fiona could tell her colleague desperately wanted Trisha and Doug back on the table as suspects but they didn't have any evidence, let alone theories, to back it up. So she resorted to laborious exhales of air, possibly in an attempt to provoke Fiona into further discussions. Fiona would happily entertain any thoughts she had, but until she produced something tangible, rather than a load of huffing and puffing, then there was nothing more to say.

Fiona was glad that the day had finally reached its end. She forgot the investigation for the time being and locked it up tightly behind the sturdy door of the shop, where it would stay until they picked things up in the morning. Though it was early days, she needed a break. A chance to put the detective work on pause and give herself a bit of mental recuperation. Although, if she was being truly honest, it had nothing to do with the investigation. She didn't like it when they didn't see eye to eye. Disagreements were, of course, inevitable and all part of the debating, discussing and scrutinising process of detective work. However, on this occasion, Partial Sue had taken it personally, and it felt as if the pair of them had fallen out. She hoped her friend would be in a more agreeable mood tomorrow and they could put it behind them. But for now, she desperately needed some alone time. A book in her hands or perhaps the TV remote control for indulging in some boxset therapy.

First, she treated herself to a plate of comfort food — a hearty serving of sausage and mash, drenched in homemade gravy. She saved some bits of sausage for Simon Le Bon, tossing them in his direction as he waited patiently by her feet, mesmerised by the promise of meaty treats. When they were all gone, she slotted herself in her usual spot on the sofa, the upholstery almost hugging her as it moulded around the familiar shape of her body. Simon Le Bon curled up beside her like a furry little comma. She settled herself in for the evening and was about to switch on the TV, but her phone had other ideas. It buzzed angrily in front of her, rattling across the coffee table. She wanted to ignore it but couldn't help a surreptitious glance at the screen.

She groaned. The investigation had followed her home and sneaked in under her defences: it was a message from the landlord of the Countess of Strathmore. As with everyone she questioned, Fiona left her contact details, accompanied by the usual "just in case you remember anything". Normally, no one ever did. She snatched up the phone.

> *Scott's here drinking alone. Shop owners here too. Bad atmosphere. Nothing's happened. But think words will be exchanged. Words you might want to hear.*

> *I'll be there ASAP.*

> *If it kicks off, I will have to throw them out or call the police or both.*

Please hold on until I get there.

So much for the quiet night off, but she couldn't miss this. If it did kick off, as the landlord put it, she'd want to witness what was said and, more importantly, step in and act as peacemaker, unless the landlord threw them out first. In which case, she'd be acting as go-between on the pavement outside. Not exactly how she pictured her evening. Hopefully it wouldn't come to that. If words were exchanged, both parties might keep things civil. She could keep a low profile, observe from a safe distance and eavesdrop on the conversation, carefully noting down anything of any relevance. But who was she kidding? Alcohol and bad feelings usually resulted in raised voices and shaken fists, or worse.

Fiona pushed herself off the sofa, slipped into her shoes and shrugged on her coat.

Hopeful that an unscheduled walk was about to commence, Simon Le Bon circled her feet, his pert, swishing tail bringing up the rear.

"I'm afraid not, sweetheart. I have to go to the pub and there might be things said that aren't for a young dog's ears."

Sensing the tone of Fiona's voice, the little terrier's tail ceased its metronoming. He stared at her with guilt-tripping eyes then resigned himself to defeat and climbed onto the sofa.

The pub was well within walking distance, but time was of the essence. Fiona grabbed her keys and jumped in the car. A couple of minutes later, she pushed open the doors to the local drinking establishment and was immediately confronted by a prickly atmosphere. The landlord stood defensively in front of the bar, attempting to look relaxed, his arms by his side. But his shoulders betrayed him. They were hunched, poised and ready should he need to spring into action. Catching Fiona's eye, he nodded towards a small group gathered near the fireplace.

She spotted Trisha first, her high hair acting like a signal flare. Doug stood beside her along with half a dozen others, who Fiona assumed were fellow shop owners, who had semi-circled themselves around Scott. With a drink in his hands, he was listing slightly to one side. She wondered how many he'd had. He didn't look particularly worried that he was outnumbered. Perhaps the drink had furnished him with enough alcoholic armour to not sense the threat. But from her brief, initial assessment, it appeared as if the group had ganged up on him.

Fiona knew first impressions could be wrong, so she surveyed the rest of the pub to gauge the gravity of the situation. Similar to her last visit, the place was busy but not full. Empty tables were dotted here and there. However, instead of patrons enjoying a joyful pre-Christmas evening out, they sipped their drinks quietly, keeping their heads low with one eye cautiously on the gathering near the fireplace.

Fiona circled around the opposite side of the pub, edging her way towards the bar to get an update from the landlord.

She sidled up to him. "Anything happened yet?"

"No, nothing. It's all fairly civil."

Fiona relaxed. "Oh, good."

"But I've done this job long enough to know when something's about to go off. One word taken the wrong way and it's shots fired."

Fiona didn't like the sound of his colourful language. "Er, and then what happens?"

"I pull out 'The Pacifier'." He made air quotes. "That usually ensures people behave themselves."

Fiona wondered if this was a baseball bat or a length of scaffolding he kept behind the bar. "Is that some sort of weapon?"

The landlord spluttered, "Goodness, no." He reached in his pocket and pulled out his phone. "I start filming them. Nobody likes being posted on YouTube losing their rag."

Though true, in all the videos of that sort Fiona had had the misfortune of seeing, filming only seemed to aggravate people more. Although she suspected that the landlord's motives were less to do with calming the situation and more to do with gathering video evidence of any altercations. "I don't suppose you filmed Clive on the night before he died?"

"No, it never came to that."

"Do you have CCTV?" Fiona realised she should have asked him this the other day.

"Only by the front door. I really should get some inside, then I wouldn't have to bother using my phone. But it's expensive."

"Could you send me the footage of the night before Clive died?"

"Of course. But there's not much to see. Just him coming and going."

"It'd be helpful, nonetheless. I'm going to get a bit closer so I can hear what they're saying."

"Good idea — but don't get involved," the landlord warned. "If it starts going south, stay out the way and let me handle it."

"Right you are." Fiona threaded her way around the tables towards the gathering. The fact that she had to move closer to hear them was a good sign. Their voices were still at an amicable level — a discussion rather than an argument. Although their body language said otherwise, the group surrounding Scott like a pack of hyenas. Just as she got within earshot, the landlord's words came true.

"I'm not accusing anyone of anything!" Scott suddenly snarled, slurring his vowels.

The whole pub went quiet at his outburst. At the same moment, Tony De Costa and his son walked in. Dressed in civvies, the two mechanics had the contented expressions of a pair of men with an evening of festive drinking ahead of them. Fiona regarded Tony, who looked particularly dapper out of his greasy overalls. They exchanged fleeting smiles. But his pleasant demeanour quickly fled when he clocked the odd silence pervading the whole place, not to mention the peculiar confrontation near the fireplace.

Scott didn't notice the intrusion and continued his rant. "I know for a fact that some of you had an argument with my dad in here the night before he died. And I want to know who!"

Fiona's heart turned to a hard block of ice as she realised this was all her fault. She'd separately texted Daph and Scott earlier to update them both. She hadn't thought anything of it and had left out specific names, feigning ignorance on purpose. But now her stomach twisted with regret as she realised how naive she'd been. It was obvious that Scott would come here for a showdown. How could she have been so foolish?

A compact man dressed in a fleece emblazoned with wolves offered his condolences. "We're sorry for your loss, but we weren't here that night."

"None of us were," someone else said.

Doug and Trisha shrank slightly.

"So who was it then?" Scott demanded. "I'm sure you all gossip to one another. Look, if you don't tell me, I'll just ask the landlord, but I'd rather hear it from you first hand. Give you a chance to tell your side of the story."

Half a dozen shoulders shrugged, except for Trisha's and Doug's. Scott may have been tipsy, but this didn't escape his attention. "You two." He glared at them. "Was it you?"

Trisha and Doug said nothing.

Scott took a step closer. He stared at the assembled shop owners one by one. "I'm not stupid. I've heard that you think the Christmas market is stealing your profits." He turned his attention back to Doug and Trisha. "My dad's stall was right outside your shops. Didn't like him being there, I bet. Did you kill him?"

"Now steady on, that's out of order," the man in the wolf fleece protested. There were grumbles of assent.

Trisha scowled. "We didn't do nothin'."

"We didn't kill him," Doug said. "I'll admit, I don't like what the market's doing to our profits. But we had nothing against your dad. We were against the whole thing, right from the start. We all were. Everyone with a shop is struggling to make ends meet and it's just made things worse for us."

There were nods of heads and murmurs of agreement from the others.

Doug continued. "You can't go around accusing people of murder."

"Why not?" Scott hissed.

"Firstly, because it's slanderous if you don't have any evidence. And secondly, your dad killed himself, if you remember."

"And whose fault was that?" Scott asked. "As for evidence, his stall was right outside your shops. And you just said you don't like the market. Bit of a coincidence that he's the one who winds up dead."

Fiona had heard enough. She stepped into the fray. "Scott, let's not do this right now. Why don't I give you a lift back home?"

"Ah, Fiona. Just the person." Scott regarded her through half-lidded and somewhat bloodshot eyes. He pointed in the direction of Trisha and Doug. "Was it these two who were trash-talking my dad the night before he died?"

"Hey!" Trisha snapped. "We never did that. He picked a fight with us. And from what we've heard—" she glanced at Fiona briefly — "you fell out with him before he came here."

"Yeah!" Doug joined in and jabbed a finger in Scott's direction. "How do we know it wasn't you that drove him to suicide?"

The whole pub went silent again, everyone collectively groaning inside.

Scott's face became sullen. Wounded.

Doug swallowed hard.

Scott placed his drink down on a nearby table then swung a hooking fist at the key cutter. He missed him by miles, over-rotated and twisted himself into a heap on the floor. Quickly scrambling to his feet, he swayed a little as he became upright again, then reloaded his right arm for another pop. In the swiftest of pincer movements, the landlord and Tony De Costa swooped in from opposite sides, grabbing Scott's arms and pinning him against the wall.

"That's enough of that!" the landlord cried.

"Let me go!" Scott attempted to break free from his restrainers.

"Don't let him near me!" Doug cowered. "He's a danger to the public."

Still holding onto Scott, the landlord turned to Doug. "And that's enough from you lot. Stop provoking him."

"Provoking him?" Doug's anger flared. "He just accused me and Trisha of murder."

"Yeah," said Tony, "and you just accused him of driving his dad to suicide. Swings and roundabouts."

Doug fell silent, chewing the inside of his cheek. Eventually he offered a quiet apology. "I'm sorry, Scott. That was out of order."

Every head swivelled in Scott's direction to observe his reaction, which was difficult to read. His eyes were blank and watery, as if Doug's words hadn't registered with him yet. His features shifted a little, contorting into a mixture of pain and confusion.

Everyone stared at him expectedly, befuddled by his odd expression. Except the landlord, who knew that look well. "He's going to be sick."

Fiona had never seen him move so fast. With Tony's help, they railroaded Scott through the pub and onto the pavement outside. Thankfully its thick, sturdy doors slammed behind them, muffling the worst of it.

Not knowing what to do with themselves, the shopkeepers hung around, dishevelled and downcast, their heads drooping in shame. And quite rightly so. Although Fiona probably reserved the largest slice of guilt for herself. If she hadn't been so quick to share information with Scott, none of this debacle would've happened.

As she headed towards the doors to check on Scott, the whole pub descended into a muddle of hurried gossip, apart from Tony's son Joe, who seemed more preoccupied by his phone screen.

CHAPTER 14

"It's not your fault." Partial Sue poured the tea, not paying much attention to whether it was going into Fiona's cup or not. "You simply texted Scott with an update. None of us thought it would have that effect."

"That's right." Daisy whipped out a cloth and was already mopping up the spilt tea.

Fiona sighed. "Thank you, but I feel it was amateurish on my part. I'm extremely careful about what I say to people during an investigation — to avoid situations like this. Well, I'm not doing that again. If he asks, I'll keep my cards close to my chest."

"Well, he did ask us to look into his dad's death," Daisy said. "He has a right to know."

"Yes, I suppose. But I need to be more sensitive about what I share. I basically sent him and Daph the same message — separately, of course. Next time I'll edit his version to remove anything too triggering."

"I suppose it's all triggering," Partial Sue remarked. "If you've just lost your dad in suspicious circumstances."

Fiona took a sip of tea. "Yes, good point. Then maybe we hold fire until we have something concrete."

"What about Daph?" Daisy asked. "Should we keep sharing with her?"

"That's different. She doesn't have an emotional stake in this." Fiona's phoned pinged. She pulled it out and examined the screen. "Oh, the landlord has sent me the footage of Clive's last night in the pub."

Daisy and Partial Sue rapidly scuffed their chairs around the table for a better view.

Fiona opened the video file and pressed play. The view was from the pub's one and only camera above the front doors, pointing down at an angle.

"Just one camera?" asked Partial Sue.

"I'm afraid so." Fiona fast-forwarded to the time stamp of quarter past five, when they were treated to the sight of Trisha and Doug entering the pub, backing up their story of leaving work early. Scrolling on, more people entered as late afternoon became early evening, until at eight thirty the haunting figure of Clive passed beneath the camera's lens. Fiona paused the video and enlarged the image with her fingers. From the steep angle, it was difficult to read Clive's expression or his general demeanour. Just another punter going in for a Friday night pint.

Fiona's breath hitched in her throat as she stared at the frozen image. She wondered if Clive already knew his fate, had made up his mind to end his life and was having one last session in the pub. Or perhaps circumstances from that point on had exacerbated an already precarious situation. Created a perfect storm in Clive's head, giving him no other option but to take his own life. Or had someone taken it from him? Murdered him in the cleverest way possible. One that could only point to a verdict of suicide.

Fiona wound the footage to 9.29 p.m., when they caught a fleeting glimpse of Trisha and Doug bundling out of the pub, clearly in a hurry to get away. The pair made a hard right and were gone.

"They're in a hurry," Partial Sue commented.

Fiona replayed it. "Yep, they certainly look like they've just had a quarrel with someone."

Fiona continued the footage, watching various people enter and leave, until at precisely one minute past twelve, Clive emerged. His movements were slow and deliberate, lethargic but not drunken by any stretch of the imagination.

"Look, he turned right as well!" Partial Sue jabbed Fiona's phone screen. "Same direction as Trisha and Doug!"

Fiona halted the footage and replayed it several times, hoping that it might reveal a clue. Nothing emerged of any significance, although Partial Sue didn't think so.

"He went the same way as Trisha and Doug. There's something in that."

Fiona wasn't convinced. "There are only two ways he could go. Left or right. It's fifty–fifty he'd go the same way."

"Yes, but there's a possibility they waited for him."

"They'd have been waiting a long time," Daisy pointed out.

"Yes, nearly two and a half hours," Fiona said. "Wouldn't they be worried someone would notice them hanging around?"

"Well, they obviously didn't wait right outside the pub," Partial Sue replied. "Maybe down the road, along his route home, in a bush, waiting to pounce."

Daisy was sceptical, mostly because of style issues. "That's a long time to wait in a bush, especially with Trisha's big hair. Hedges and big hair do not a good combination make."

Partial Sue huffed, annoyed that her theory was being systematically dismantled. "Okay, well, maybe just Doug acting on his own, then."

Fiona gave it a fatal blow. "But even if he did, somehow he's got to persuade Clive to go with him to his stall, without using force. Then make it look like suicide, again without using force, then leave him hanged inside, escaping through a locked door, bolted from the inside."

Partial Sue hesitated, some rapid mulling over going on inside that head of hers. "Okay, let's hear your theory, then," she said defensively.

Fiona chose not to bite and instead decided to distract her with another puzzle. Not that they needed any more — they were already up to their necks in bewildering conundrums. "So, we know from the toxicology report that Clive had the equivalent of four pints of beer in his system before he died. Yet the landlord informed us that Clive had his usual three pints that night. So between leaving the pub and going home, he had a fourth pint somewhere."

Daisy began thumbing her phone, dazzlingly fast.

Partial Sue screwed up her face, possibly giving into a smidgeon of petty revenge for Fiona disparaging her own theory. "Okay, and then what happened?" She folded her arms.

"Well, I don't know. That's what we need to find out. But if he stopped off at another bar along the way home, we need to know who he came into contact with. What was said, et cetera."

Daisy ceased her thumbing and gave the other two a mournful look. "Every bar and restaurant in Southbourne shuts at either eleven thirty or before that. The Countess of Strathmore is the only one that stays open until twelve."

"So where did that extra pint come from?" Fiona asked.

"Maybe he went home first," Daisy suggested. "Needed another drink for what he was about to do."

"Or he could've had a drink before he went out," Partial Sue said. "That's very popular with the young people. They call it 'pre's'. Saves a lot of money. Smart idea, if you ask me." Anything that saved money was a smart idea in Partial Sue's world.

"It does sound like a good idea." Fiona sighed. "But whether he drank at home before or after the pub is neither here nor there. I was hoping it would give us another lead. Another place to investigate. But if everywhere was closed, it's a dead end."

Daisy released a painful groan. "Oh, no."

Fiona and Partial Sue regarded their friend, who appeared as if she'd just sat on something pointy.

"What is it?" Fiona asked.

Daisy flipped her phone around and played them a video that had been uploaded on a social media platform, entitled "Postmaster vs key cutter". It was a snippet of last night's events, specifically Scott throwing an unsuccessful punch at Doug and twirling himself into a heap. The brief footage had been edited so it played on a continuous loop. Slapstick sound effects accompanied Scott as he repeated his calamitous swing again and again and again.

CHAPTER 15

Daisy gasped. "It's already had twenty views. Poor Scott's going to be so embarrassed. As if he hasn't got enough to deal with."

Twenty views may have been a pitiful number in social media terms, hardly viral, but by Southbourne standards it was epidemic proportions. Soon the whole community would know about Scott's drunken attempt to knock out Downward Doug, which, to be fair, a few people would've been happy to see. But Daisy was right. This was the last thing Scott needed. Dealing with the death of his father was hard enough. Harder when it was a suicide, and to make matters worse, everyone knew about Scott's loss, giving him a very public cross to bear. He didn't need the additional burden of humiliation and ridicule. Something had to be done. Fast.

At first, Fiona thought the landlord had posted it, seeing as just before it happened he'd revealed his fondness for videoing bad behaviour with the intention of shaming the culprits. But the footage was taken from the opposite side of the pub. Plus, at that moment, he would've been rushing towards Scott to prevent him from having another pop at the key cutter.

She peered at the corner of the page and spotted the name of the little weasel who'd posted it. "SpannerBoy2006. I think I have a good idea who did this."

"Who is it?" Daisy asked.

"Let me enquire first before I start accusing anyone." Fiona got to her feet and put her coat on, ignoring Simon Le Bon's pleas for a walk.

"Shouldn't we come with you?" Partial Sue asked. "In case things turn nasty?"

"I doubt that will happen, and it might look like we're ganging up on them if we turn up *en masse*. Besides, it's just a hunch."

Though her answer was sincere, if she were being completely honest there was an ulterior motive for going alone that she decided not to share.

Fiona left the shop and made her way towards the Christmas market, but just before reaching it she turned into the little side road where Trisha and Doug had their shops. However, it wasn't either of them she'd come to see.

Passing the pottery café, she headed into the wide entrance of the garage, sidestepping its greasy puddles. Beyond she could see a car up on the ramp while Tony battled with a stubborn exhaust beneath it.

"Hi, can I speak to you for a minute?" she asked.

"Can it wait? I'm in the middle of something." Red-faced and flustered, Tony twisted his head around. As soon as he realised it was Fiona, his features relaxed and quickly transformed into a smile. "Oh! Hi, Fiona."

He stopped what he was doing and turned to face her. "How are you doing?"

"I'm fine, thank you." Fiona beamed. "How are you?"

"All the better for seeing you," he smirked.

Fiona suppressed a blush. "Do you know someone who goes by the name of SpannerBoy2006 on social media?"

"Yeah, that's Joe. Why do you ask?"

She pulled out her phone, tapped the screen and showed him the footage. "This was posted yesterday. I'm sure I don't have to tell you the effect it will have on Scott at this delicate time."

Tony watched a few loops of the video, until he absorbed its true awfulness. "Joe!"

At the sound of his less-than-pleased father, Joe's gangly frame appeared from behind a VW Polo jacked up on one side and missing its front wheel. As he bounded towards them, his baggy overalls billowed out as if he might take off.

"Did you do this?" Tony shoved Fiona's phone in front of him.

Joe squinted at the screen. Swallowing hard, his face went pallid.

"You need to take it down. Right now."

Joe fished out his own phone, his hands fumbling as he attempted to remove the video.

Tony handed Fiona's phone back. She examined the screen. The post went blank and a no-entry symbol appeared together with an annotation: *video not available*. "It's gone."

"Okay, good," Tony replied. "Remember what I've told you — think before you act."

Joe nodded and scuttled off to his wheelless Polo. Tony turned to Fiona and rolled his eyes. "Sorry about that. It was good of you to tell me. It would be terrible for Scott if everyone saw that. But I'm selfishly thinking of what they'll say about me. Joe posted it, but it'll be me that gets it in the neck. Mostly from his mum. We divorced three years ago, but that won't stop her from giving me an earful. He lives with her but works with me. I think she wanted more for him than fixing cars. So did I. But what else was he going to do? If it was up to him, he'd be posting stuff on his phone all day. That's all him and his mates do. They want to be 'influencers'." Tony made air quotes. "I told him he needed a proper job. He could work with me until he's made it as an online superstar. Sorry, I'm sure you don't want to hear the trials and tribulations of a single dad."

"Oh, it's quite all right." In Fiona's mind, what Joe did wasn't right by any means but, as far as she could tell, he was just being a typical teenager. Obsessed with posting content, they were always online but not always aware. "Kids do silly things — not that I think Joe is silly," she was quick to point out.

Tony laughed. "He has his moments, believe me. Let me buy you a bratwurst from the Christmas market for your trouble. Bit of brunch."

"Aren't you busy?"

"I can always make time for a bratwurst." He grinned devilishly.

"Well, if you insist."

"Follow me." Tony stripped off his gloves and chucked them to one side. "You won't regret it. They're amazing."

They crossed over the road, drawn by the intoxicating smell of sizzling German sausages. Although she had already eaten a hearty breakfast, Fiona's stomach rumbled. It also popped with butterflies.

As they approached the bratwurst stall, an aproned woman was out the front, on her haunches with a dustpan and brush, huffing and puffing as she scraped up a mess of broken glass.

"Everything all right, Alina?" Tony asked.

Alina rose to her feet, careful not to spill any debris. "Oh, yeah. Some idiots pelted my stall with beer bottles last night." She tipped the glass into a nearby bin.

"Does that happen a lot?" Fiona asked.

Alina hesitated, the dustpan in one hand and the brush in the other, as if she were a low-budget monarch holding a sceptre and orb. "Er, sometimes."

"Who do you think did it?" Fiona asked.

Alina shrugged. "Drunks, probably." She hurried into her stall, stowed the dustpan and brush away, then washed her hands. Turning to the front counter, Alina snatched up some large, weapon-like tongs and rapidly turned over a row of giant sausages sputtering on a metal grill. She tutted to herself, as their charred undersides were revealed one by one. "And now these have started to burn."

"That's okay. I like mine well done," said Tony.

"Me too," Fiona said. "Nothing worse than an anaemic sausage."

Tongs still in her hands, Alina wiped her brow with her sleeve. "Are you sure? I can cook another batch."

"They look fine from where I'm standing. We'll have two bratwursts in rolls, if you please."

Alina didn't argue and plucked a couple of sausages from the grill, which bowed under their own weight as she slotted them into awaiting bread rolls. "Sauerkraut?"

"Yes, please," Fiona replied.

"Always," Tony said.

She handed them the finished articles. Tony accepted his with a gluttonous grin, but Fiona eyed hers worryingly. Feeling its heft, she doubted she had the appetite to finish the whole thing. However, after one mouthful her fears were allayed. She wouldn't be able to stop even if she tried. "Oh my. This is so tasty."

"Told you." Tony took a mammoth bite then groaned with delight. "Oh, that hits the spot."

"Alina, these are amazing," Fiona said, resisting the urge to talk with her mouth full. "I can see why Tony loves your stall."

"Oh, thank you so much." Finally, a smile graced Alina's face. "Tony is our biggest customer."

"Yeah, I have to be careful, or I *will* become your biggest customer, literally."

Alina relaxed under their continual barrage of praise for her bratwursts, so much so that she began revealing her culinary secrets. "You have to use a good quality sausage, of course, but the trick is soaking them in beer first — just a mild one, otherwise it overpowers the flavour. And then I always grill them over charcoal, but you have to keep an eye on the heat, which is what I did wrong just now."

Fiona finished up her food and wiped her mouth with a napkin, "Well, you could have fooled me. That was delicious. I'm going to recommend you to all my friends."

Alina clutched her hands to her chest. "Oh, that makes me so happy."

Now that Alina had been disarmed by compliments, Fiona decided to broach the subject that was really on her mind, being careful to tread lightly. "So, how are you finding it here?"

"It's okay, I suppose." Her response was less than enthusiastic.

"And how are the other stall-holders?"

She brightened. "Oh, I already know them. We tend to do the same events throughout the year. Summer fairs and festivals. We all show up in the same places."

"That's nice. So it's like a little club."

Alina nodded enthusiastically.

"And was Clive part of that club?" Fiona asked.

The question threw Alina momentarily. She stared at Fiona curiously, as if wondering how she should answer. "Yes, I suppose so. I mean, none of us knew him, but we welcomed him into the fold, as it were."

"And did he like it here?" Fiona asked.

Alina answered without hesitation. "He loved it. He'd come and chat every morning before opening up. Always had a smile on his face. Even though he was stuck out on a limb, over the road, I think he loved the camaraderie of the market."

"I'm guessing you all look out for one another."

"Oh, definitely. Isn't that right, Ed?" Alina called out to her neighbouring stall-holder, a small man in a very large pompom hat, who was bent over, cleaning the large circular griddle on his crêpe stall.

He straightened up and cupped a hand to his ear. "What's that?"

"I said we look out for one another," Alina repeated.

"Oh, yes, absolutely," Ed replied. "Stalwarts, we are."

Fiona smiled. "I like that — stall-warts. Very clever."

He looked at her puzzled then his face cracked into a smile as he realised his unintentional pun. "Oh, yes. Stall-warts."

"So how did it feel after he died?" Fiona knew this would be a triggering question, but that was her intention.

"How do you think it felt?" Alina snapped. She immediately regretted her outburst. "Sorry, I didn't mean to get angry, but it was traumatising for us."

"Still is." Ed had sidled over to join in the conversation.

"We've lost one of our own," Alina continued. "In the worst way possible. Even though we hadn't known him that long, everyone liked Clive. We felt terrible. He must have been going through some truly awful things and none of us spotted it or did anything to help. So much for our little club."

"Don't be too harsh on yourselves," Fiona said. "Even those closest to him didn't spot anything amiss." She paused. "How do you get along with local shop owners?"

Ed shrank, the question clearly distressing him. Alina briefly glanced at Tony, seeming to wonder if this was some sort of trick question. "What do you mean?"

"Are they friendly, like your fellow stall-holders?"

"They don't talk to us," Alina replied abruptly.

Fiona remained silent, hopefully leaving a space for Alina to embellish her answer, but she didn't provide any further details. She bowed her head and nudged bratwursts around the grill.

Fiona persisted. "Has there been any bad feeling towards you?"

Alina didn't answer.

"Is there something on your mind?" Tony asked her. "You can tell us."

"There's nothing to tell," Alina replied quietly.

"Sorry, but it doesn't sound like it," Tony remarked.

Alina sighed and put her tongs down. "Okay, yes. They've had it in for us from day one. At first, it was a few filthy looks, a bit of sneering, a few nasty things muttered under their breath, but then it got worse."

"Like what?" Fiona asked.

"Like smashed bottles and people peeing up stalls late at night."

"But like you said, couldn't that be just drunks?" Fiona suggested.

"Jeff's woodcraft stall got covered in flour," Ed said sheepishly.

"Yes," Alina replied. "Actually, that one backfired on them. It looked quite nice, like it was covered in snow."

"That's not drunks staggering home," Tony remarked. "Who goes out drinking with a bag of flour on them?"

Fiona remembered seeing the white-powdered stall on one of her morning walks to work and had just assumed it was all part of the festive decorations. "When you said shop owners were muttering things under their breath, can you remember who?"

"Definitely those two next to Tony," Alina said. "That Trisha and Downward Doug."

"To be honest, they all do it," Ed added. "We just don't feel welcome here, especially after what happened to Clive."

"You don't think that's what drove him to suicide, do you?" Tony asked.

"Who knows? Probably didn't help," Alina replied. "But if it is shop owners doing this, they haven't let up since Clive died. Our stalls are still getting vandalised, as you can see."

"Does Malorie know anything about this?" Fiona asked. "I mean, she organised the Christmas market. It's her responsibility."

Alina jabbed her sausages, which responded with angry spits. "I've never met her. Never seen her. Well, apart from when this place first opened."

Ed glanced around conspiratorially. "When I first applied for this pitch, the strict criteria on the application said that stalls would only be granted as long as they didn't conflict with local businesses."

"Yes," Alina agreed. "I remember that. Our stalls were fine, but Little Bo Bean's application was turned down."

"What, because of the name?" Tony joked.

Alina didn't see the funny side of it. "No, because Bo sold coffee and she'd be treading on the toes of Southbourne's coffee shops. The application form said there could be no exceptions. No doubling up of existing businesses. No Christmas clones."

"Malorie wanted to avoid any bad feeling between stall-holders and shop owners," Ed added.

"That didn't work out too well," Tony said.

"So then why was Clive allowed to sell hot chocolate?" Fiona asked.

Alina pointed her tongs at Fiona. "Exactly. If you ask me, that's just asking for trouble."

Something didn't add up. Malorie was normally a stickler for the rules, especially ones she'd made up herself. She had a reputation for enforcing her iron will as far as her sphere of influence would allow, which these days, thankfully, was limited to organising the local dog show and managing the Southbourne Community Centre. The poor retired souls who frequented the latter were subject to her strict but superficial rules — her centre-wide ban on skimmed milk was legendary. However, in the case of the Christmas market, Fiona could fully understand why she'd created such a rule. It made sense to maintain harmony among shopkeepers and stall-holders by ensuring their trades didn't overlap. Which begged the question, why had Malorie ignored her own regulations and allowed Clive Preston to open up a hot chocolate stall, of all things? And had this little oversight somehow been the cause of Clive's demise?

CHAPTER 16

"So how was your date?" Daisy had been gently pressing Fiona for details ever since she had returned from the market, inadvertently letting it slip that Tony had bought her a bratwurst. A fact that she sincerely regretted sharing now.

"It wasn't a date."

"Well, I think it's really sweet," Daisy beamed. "We're happy for you."

"Thank you," Fiona replied then swiftly backpedalled. "I mean, there's nothing to be happy about. Nothing's going on."

"Could've fooled us," Partial Sue smirked. "You walked in through that door like a sixteen-year-old."

"I did not." Fiona blushed, confirming everything they were inferring.

Partial Sue raised an eyebrow. "Denial is not just a river in Egypt."

Fiona quickly changed the subject before her whole head became the colour of beetroot. "Do you want to hear what I learned at the Christmas market?"

"Fire away," Partial Sue said.

"I discovered something very intriguing. Why didn't local shop owners complain about the Christmas market?"

Partial Sue's face contorted into a mask of confusion. "From what we've heard, that's all these people have been doing. Complaining since day one."

"Yes, but not to Malorie they haven't," Fiona said. "She's the cause of all their misery. The Christmas market was her idea. Her baby. She's the driving force behind it. Yet, as far as I know, no one's gone knocking on her door to voice their complaints. So why single out a lowly hot chocolate seller when the real culprit's sitting pretty in the community centre?"

"Some people — well, most people — are frightened of Malorie," Daisy said, speaking from experience.

"That's true," Fiona agreed. "I suppose Clive's an easier target to take out their frustrations on. It's easier to punch down than up, and Malorie's definitely someone you'd have to punch up to."

Partial Sue was slowly warming to the idea. "That's if anyone could manage it. Malorie would give them a bloody nose before they got close enough. But it does makes sense. She's the architect behind this, so their anger should be directed at her."

"But here's the rub," Fiona said. "Malorie had a rule that no stall could sell the same products or services as a local trader. It was on the application form."

"So why did she allow Clive's hot chocolate stall?" Partial Sue asked. "Hot chocolate's sold up and down the length of Southbourne Grove."

"Exactly." Fiona gave a wry smile.

"You don't think Malorie was responsible for Clive's death?" Daisy gasped.

"I'm not sure," Fiona replied. "But she could certainly nudge things in the right direction. Get a disgruntled local trader or, more likely, café owner to do her dirty work for her."

"For that to be true," Partial Sue said, "Malorie would need a motive."

"That's true," Fiona agreed. "And it's what we need to find out."

Had Clive and Malorie's paths crossed? Had he wronged her in the past? In her mind, Fiona gave a dismissive shake of the head. Apart from Sophie Haverford, Malorie fell out with just about everyone who spent more than five minutes in her company. She spoke her mind — and there was nothing wrong with that in theory, except her words, usually swathed in coarse-grade sandpaper, had a habit of rubbing everyone up the wrong way, leaving a trail of grazed and bloodied egos in her path. She was a thick-skinned, keep-calm-and-carry-on type of person who didn't give a fig about what people thought of her. So it was unlikely that she'd have been worried about Clive. He'd have been just another person in a very long line of people she'd offended.

However, one thing was sure. Malorie had flouted her own strict decree of no Christmas clones. What had caused that? For someone whose life was dictated by rules and dogmatically making others follow them, it would have taken something big. Something she almost certainly didn't want anyone knowing. Which would mean prising it out of her.

"Crowbars at the ready!" Fiona thought aloud.

Partial Sue and Daisy shared a worried look.

CHAPTER 17

Girding their loins and just about anything else they could gird, Fiona and Partial Sue pushed open the stiff metal doors to Southbourne Community Centre. A flat-roofed carbuncle of salmon-pink brick, it stood as a shameful seventies reminder of how not to do architecture. It was big, brash and unapologetic, not unlike Malorie herself, who led her little kingdom from an office in the back, although some people referred to it as her lair.

Daisy had sensibly offered to stay behind with Simon Le Bon, as she always did when a trip to see Malorie was on the cards. The woman intimidated her, as she did everyone, but that wasn't the main reason for her absence. Malorie had a habit of roping anyone within a five-metre radius into volunteering for things that they really didn't want to do. Being a nice person, Daisy found it hard to say no, and last time she'd encountered Malorie, she'd found herself clad in her floral wellies early one Sunday morning, wading through the brackish water of a stream around the back of Matalan, pulling out discarded shopping trollies. Before they left, Daisy warned that they wouldn't get out alive without Malorie enlisting them for something or other.

In contrast to the centre's brutalist exterior, inside was a warm cauldron of seasonal conviviality. It must have been Christmas jumper day, as everyone was adorned with colourful festive knitwear. To Malorie's credit, the place was buzzing. People sat at tables playing board games, writing Christmas cards, knitting jumpers (presumably more festive ones) or just having a natter over a cuppa and generous wedges of Christmas cake. Festive favourites played over the crackling PA system and a portly Christmas tree sat in the corner, its branches straining under a myriad of decorations. Someone must have ordered the wrong size (possibly Sophie Haverford), as a suspended ceiling tile had been removed to accommodate its soaring top, which disappeared into the pipe and ductwork. Fiona couldn't tell if there was a star or a fairy up there, but she was sure whoever was responsible for the sizing error had got an earful from Malorie.

A small woman appeared in front of them, dressed as Santa's helper, sleigh bells sewn onto the tip of her hat and the ends of her curled-up felt booties. She thrust a tray, wider than herself, in front of the ladies, piled with unkempt mince pies. "Can I tempt you?" she smiled.

Partial Sue was straight in there. "Don't mind if I do. I am partial to a homemade mince pie or two." She slipped a couple off the plate. One for now and one for later. Santa's helper spotted her palming the second mince pie into her pocket and did not look impressed.

Fiona declined, still full from her bratwurst. "We've come to see Malorie."

The small woman shuddered, her bells giving a worried tinkle. "Er, do you have an appointment?"

"We never need an appointment," Partial Sue replied, mid-chomp. "We usually just rock up."

Santa's helper stared at her as if she was trying to work out a difficult sum in her head. Possibly because Partial Sue had used the phrase "rock up", but more likely that someone had dared to request an audience with her lord and master without prior arrangement. "She's not receiving visitors at the moment."

Fiona knew engaging in a discussion with one of Malorie's minions would get them nowhere. "I'm afraid it's a matter of urgency." She sidestepped her and headed to the back of the community centre, weaving around the seated people. Partial Sue followed closely behind, still munching her mince pie.

Santa's helper gave chase, tray in hand, sleigh bells urgently jingling as she trotted after them. "I must protest!"

"Nothing wrong with protesting," said Partial Sue. "That's your God-given right."

Heads raised at every table as the strange trio passed. Activities halted as puzzled faces followed the bizarre but sedate foot-chase unfolding before their eyes, complete with comedy sound effects.

Fiona and Partial Sue reached the kitchen, heading for the door at the back where Malorie kept her office.

"You can't go in there. It's not safe," Santa's helper fretted, as if they were entering the land of Mordor. Behind the door, like the engine room of a vast coal-fired ocean liner, volunteers sweated and toiled with hardly an inch to spare, hunched over flour-strewn counters, stirring and kneading, flitting this way and that, draining steaming pots into colanders while orders were yelled with the urgency and precision of a special ops mission.

"Sprouts are on. Sprouts are on."

"Yorkshire puds standing by."

"Who's minding the meat?"

Fiona threaded her way through the manic workspace, Partial Sue and Santa's helper huddling close behind. The trio made good progress until a vast oven door was flung open in front of them, blasting them with searing heat.

A woman clad in oven gloves pitted with burn marks thrust both hands into the furnace-hot oven and tugged at two trays of sizzling pigs in blankets. Smelling utterly divine, it took all of Partial Sue's willpower not to pluck one off and pop it in her mouth as the woman swung the trays past them with wild abandon. To avoid being burned, the ladies backed away as an industrial-strength food mixer went off behind them.

Quickly course-correcting, they narrowly missed a man transporting a fresh crop of teas. It was like running the gauntlet on the TV show *Gladiators*, by way of *Great British Bake Off*. He glared at Santa's helper, still clutching her tray of mince pies, and chided, "You're going the wrong way." Before she had a chance to reply, the tea man had chicaned around his coworkers and disappeared.

Dodging several more culinary calamities, the ladies finally made it to Malorie's door.

Santa's helper made one final, desperate attempt. "Please don't go in there."

"Don't worry, we'll say we took you by surprise." Fiona knocked once then pushed the door open.

Malorie sat on her throne-like studded leather wingback chair behind her vast desk, covered, as it always was, in a mountain of paperwork. But rather than anger — her usual default setting for anyone, whether she liked them or not — she appeared exhausted, stressed even. A woman under pressure, overworked maybe, or perhaps carrying the weight of a guilty conscience.

CHAPTER 18

Santa's helper pushed in front of Fiona and Partial Sue, nearly spilling her cargo of pastries. "I'm sorry, Malorie. I tried to stop them," she exclaimed.

Malorie rolled her eyes. "It's okay, Lynn. I'm used to dealing with these two."

"Sorry, sorry, sorry." Lynn retreated out of the office, bent over her tray, bowing in deference.

"What do you want?" Malorie demanded. "I'm very busy."

Fiona replied with equal curtness. "We're here about Clive Preston."

"What about him?"

"He passed away in one of your market stalls—"

"Yes, yes, I don't need reminding. It was awful. Now, what's this about? You'd better not be investigating that poor man's death."

"You granted him his stall," Partial Sue said.

Malorie swore. "You are investigating his death, aren't you? Let me remind you that he took his own life. There's a clue in that sentence. Took. His. Own. Life. Case closed. Now stop making trouble."

Fiona ignored her broadside of verbal aggression. "Why did you break your own rule and grant Clive's stall when you knew it would conflict with local traders?"

Malorie expelled a heavy lungful of air and leaned back in her chair. She rubbed the bridge of her nose and closed her eyes. When she opened them again, they had become tortured and drained of energy. "That market has been nothing but trouble. Long before poor Clive Preston took his own life. Do you know how hard it was to get it off the ground? How much hassle and red tape I had to go through?"

Fiona went to speak but Malorie held up a hand to silence her. "I knew it had to be done. Southbourne needed a shot in the arm with the threat of the stalker hanging over it. Think what it would be like without the market. Place would be a ghost town. But it was bloody exhausting, and no one's thanked me, or said, 'You've saved Southbourne from Christmas oblivion.' Then after the suicide . . . Well, let me tell you, next year someone else can do it. But to answer your question, I didn't grant Clive Preston a stall to sell hot chocolate. I laid down strict instructions. As you rightly said, no Christmas clones. No doubling up of local businesses." Malorie reached down and opened a filing cabinet in her desk, then walked her fingers along a row of hanging files until she snatched out a piece of A4 and placed it in front of the ladies. It was a brief and simple form, dominated by an *APPROVED* ink stamp and signed by Clive at the bottom.

Malorie jabbed at a line halfway down. "I authorised Clive Preston to sell didgeridoos. I have no idea why anyone would buy a didgeridoo at Christmas, but there you go. The important thing was no shops in Southbourne sold them. However, he couldn't get them supplied in time. Instead, he started selling hot chocolate without my knowledge or authorisation."

"So why did you allow him to continue?" Partial Sue asked.

Malorie sighed heavily. "I was exhausted by that point. Still am. Had Christmas market fatigue. My resistance was low and, much to my regret, I let it slide."

This was a new side to Malorie. Normally she was a dependable bastion of fortitude, resistant to slings and arrows, bricks and breeze blocks, and just about anything that could be thrown at her. Fiona had never seen her look so beaten and downtrodden. She was only human after all, and everyone had their breaking point. Maybe the market had been it, and Fiona had to remind herself that someone had died on her watch. Crushing for even the most stoic of characters. However, Fiona couldn't let her sympathies get in the way.

"How do you think local traders felt about that?" she asked.

"To be honest, I couldn't care less. I'd had it up to here. Everyone criticised the market. None of them were grateful, and apart from Sophie Haverford, no one supported me. Although even she managed to cock up ordering the stalls. I gave her one job to do. Anyway, I'd had enough by then, so I didn't bother pulling up Clive for selling hot chocolate."

"Okay, fair enough," Fiona said. "But didn't you think café owners would be provoked by that, possibly into doing something rash? I mean, they're under a lot of pressure at the moment, just trying to keep the lights on."

"You'd have to ask them."

"We will," Partial Sue said. "Right after this."

"But one thing I will say, local traders are all the same. Whether they own boutiques, greengrocer's or cafés, they're all a bunch of whingers. Always finding something to moan about. But that's all it is. Moaning doesn't make someone a killer, which brings me to my next point. The elephant in the room. Clive's stall was locked from the inside. If malice is involved, how did the killer get out?"

"Er, we're still working on it," Fiona replied.

Malorie harrumphed. "Last time I checked, people can't walk through walls. My advice to you, stop ignoring the obvious, and let sleeping dogs lie. Give Clive some dignity."

Partial Sue was about to bite, but Fiona got there first with a mollifying reply. "Yes, point taken. You're quite right." She wanted to appease Malorie because they needed more information from her, of a personal nature. "But can I just ask if you knew Clive before all this happened?"

Malorie rolled her eyes. "Didn't you hear what I just said?"

"We'll let sleeping dogs lie once we have an answer," Partial Sue replied.

"No, I didn't," Malorie huffed. "I knew of him. Seen him a few times, helping out in the post office at Christmas. He's well-known around here and hard to miss. Loud, jovial type. Not like his son Scott, whom I've known for a long time. He's a nice chap and has my utmost sympathies."

"So you hadn't crossed paths at all? Had a falling out at any point?"

Malorie sent Fiona a daggered look. "I did not fall out with Clive because I did not know him."

Her words were convincing, and Malorie had a reputation for being nothing if not a straight shooter. For now, Fiona would take her word for it, unless they found evidence to the contrary, of course. But it was highly unlikely. She moved on to her final question. "Do you know that the Christmas market is causing bad will to all men, women and everyone in between? There's hassle between stall-holders and shop owners? Stalls are getting vandalised and—"

"Yes, yes. I know." Malorie's freckled cheeks reddened as she became more incensed. "Mark my words. It ends tonight."

Partial Sue and Fiona edged back at the force of Malorie's uncompromising tone. Fiona plucked up the courage to ask, "Er, how will you manage that?"

Malorie didn't bite her head off but calmly outlined her plan for achieving harmony and peace, through brutal castigation. "There's a carol service this evening at the bandstand after the market shuts. I've told all stall-holders, shopkeepers and everyone else to be there — on pain of death. I'm going to give them the verbal equivalent of bashing their heads together. There'll be no more nonsense after I've finished with them."

Fiona didn't doubt it for one second. Malorie struck terror into everyone, and her words were as hard as granite and just as impactful. Woe betide anyone who didn't comply. "We'll be there."

"Good." She rose up and moved around to the front of her desk. "Now, we've got Christmas dinner today and it would make me very happy if you two—"

"Oh, I'm sorry, we can't stay for dinner," Fiona replied. "But it's kind of you to offer."

"I wasn't going to." Malorie retrieved two large boxes of Christmas crackers stacked beside her desk and handed them to Fiona and Partial Sue. "But I would like you to help lay the table, in return for the information I've provided. Cutlery's in the first drawer on the left outside. Now, chop-chop. They'll be dishing up soon."

Fiona and Partial Sue had no other option but to accept the task they'd been given. It was a fair trade-off and, besides, Daisy did warn them this would happen.

CHAPTER 19

A subdued debate ensued, as Fiona and Partial Sue made their way to the next port of call. Subdued because it was tinged with embarrassment, due to an oversight to which neither of them dared admit. They should have realised it right from the start, and it was blatantly obvious if one followed the logic — which the ladies had done. However, like a flicked rubber band, their line of thinking obeyed certain laws but was prone to flying off in any given direction.

In this particular instance, they had been well aware of the rivalry between stall-holders and shop owners, but this had distracted them from a more specific and more likely rivalry. One originating from a subset of local traders who had more reason to take umbrage to Clive's stall because they also sold hot chocolate. In other words, café owners.

"I can't see it myself," Partial Sue remarked. "Even just saying it sounds daft — Clive was murdered because of hot chocolate."

"It does make sense, though. Cafés sell hot chocolate. He sold hot chocolate. He was treading on their toes. Affecting their business. They took him out of the picture."

"Is hot chocolate that much of a money spinner? I can't see anyone resorting to murder just because they sold a few less cups of the stuff over the festive period."

"I think you've answered your own question. Surely, Christmas is when hot chocolate sales are highest."

"I've never liked hot chocolate." Partial Sue wrinkled her nose in disgust. "On the rare occasions I've had one, it's either too strong and bitter, or weak as dishwater because they put too much milk in it. They always muck it up because they're not used to making it, because they don't sell it that often."

Fiona was acutely aware her argument needed bolstering. She opted for a different angle. "You know, come to think of it, that night in the pub when Scott was surrounded by local traders, none of them were café owners."

"Well, that proves my point," Partial Sue said. "They weren't bothered about the market or Clive's stall."

"Or they're keeping a low profile because they're the ones responsible for his death."

"Well, let's see what Fran has to say about all this." Partial Sue pushed open the door to Beans & Blossoms, and they were immediately greeted by a heady, beguiling mix of pungent coffee and freshly cut flowers. Beans & Blossoms, as the name suggested, was a café and a florist, and the two had been so perfectly blended that it was impossible to tell where one started and the other ended. You could sip shots of espresso and steaming lattes surrounded by dazzling floral displays and delightfully perfumed air. Guaranteed to lift the spirits, it was also a very savvy marketing trick. Customers who'd popped in for a caffeine fix often found themselves leaving with a vibrant bloom in their hands.

Fran, the larger-than-life owner, stood behind the counter, putting the finishing touches to a hefty Christmas wreath the size of a life ring, awash with berries, pinecones and baubles. Originally from Czechia, she was decked in a green apron with her jet-black hair pinned up in random places. The second her small, piercing arctic-blue eyes caught sight of the ladies, she came straight out from behind the counter, all warm smiles and open arms. "Fiona! Sue! It has been too long. Come, come. I have a special table for you." In her sturdy Velcro sandals, sported whether it was boiling hot or bitterly cold, Fran led them over to the table in question, which was indeed special. For it was the only one free in the bustling café. Her face dropped. "But where is the lovely Daisy?"

"She's back at the shop. Minding the fort."

"Oh, this is a shame. I like to see all three of you together. It is like *Sex and the City* without Samantha."

Partial Sue's face lit up. "That's interesting you should say that, because Fiona here has—"

Fiona kicked her foot. Partial Sue looked annoyed that her gossip had been curtailed.

"What she was about to say," Fiona said, "is that we're gasping for one of your famous flat whites."

Fran stared at them, confused, then beamed. "Of course. Coming right up." She headed back to the counter, collecting spent coffee cups along the way.

"Why did you kick my leg?" Partial Sue demanded.

"You know why. You were about to tell her about me and Tony."

"I wasn't."

"Well, what we're you going to say then?"

"Okay, well, maybe a bit. Sorry, it just came out. I'm just happy for you."

"Thanks, but there really is nothing to be happy about. Nothing's going on."

"That's exactly what people say when something *is* going on."

Fran returned with their drinks, two steaming hot coffees in her trademarked spotty mugs. "There you go, ladies."

After thanking her, Fiona asked, "So, Fran, how's the run-up to Christmas been?"

"So busy. I love Christmas but there is much to do."

Partial Sue didn't beat around the bush. "Has the market affected business at all?"

"No, not really. As you can see, not a spare table."

"What about the other cafés?" Fiona asked.

Fran hesitated. "They aren't having it so well as us."

"Oh, has the market taken sales away from them?"

"We are lucky," Fran replied. "People like coffee. People like flowers. But other cafés are not so lucky."

Fiona was acutely aware that Fran had avoided answering the question. "Can I ask, those other cafés, did they resent the hot chocolate stall in the market? Did it affect sales?"

The florist's face contorted into shock. "You mean the one where that poor man died?" She blew out through her teeth. "No. I mean, God rest his soul, but did you try his hot chocolate?"

Fiona and Partial Sue shook their heads.

Fran winced and shielded her words with the back of her hand. "His hot chocolate was like something scraped from a puddle. But other cafés, they have bigger problems."

"Problems? What sort of problems?" Partial Sue asked.

"Do you know how many cafés there are in Southbourne?" Fran asked.

Fiona and Partial Sue shook their heads again.

"Eighteen. Eighteen! How can such a small place have so many cafés? More open all the time. Two last year and three more this year. Each time one café opens, other cafés lose money. We are okay at the moment, but if this keeps going on, I think we'll suffer too."

"Is there resentment towards these new café owners?" Partial Sue asked.

Fran put her hands on her hips. "You know, people who run cafés are nice people. Hospitable. They have the brave face, as you say. But soon I think their politeness will turn to anger."

"But nothing has happened yet. No angry words?"

"Not yet, but who knows? Excuse me. I must now serve someone." Fran sped off, weaving around the tables to take an order.

Partial Sue leaned in. "Well, that puts the kibosh on café owners being annoyed with Clive's hot chocolate stall. They've got bigger fish to fry. The ever-increasing number of competitors opening."

Southbourne's ongoing obsession with having more cafés than it knew what to do with had firmly overshowed any threat posed by Clive's humble little stall. Struggling proprietors would hardly be worried about a temporary third-rate hot chocolate seller when permanent competitors were springing up all around them.

Fiona sighed. "Yep, I think you're right."

The pair sat in defeated silence, sipping their coffee as yet another promising lead turned into a red herring, slipped from their hands and swam away. The mood between them would have rapidly deteriorated had it not been for Fran appearing, clutching one of her branded polka-dot coffee mugs filled with a cute posey of flowers.

"This is for your shop. It's my new product. Flowers in mug."

"Oh, what a lovely idea," Fiona exclaimed.

"It's actually a clever idea." Fran lowered her voice, pointing to the logo on the side. "Flowers die, but the mug stays. Advertises business." She cackled.

"How much do we owe you?" Fiona asked.

"It's on the house. This will remind you to come back." Fran handed the pretty ceramic ensemble to Fiona.

"Thank you, Fran. That's very kind of you."

"Even though it's a totally cynical marketing ploy," Partial Sue added.

The trio of ladies laughed, although Fiona felt far from happy as she contemplated another setback in the investigation. She loved visiting Beans & Blossoms. It made her happy and always lifted her spirits, but she was reluctant to return to this bright, joyful place. She didn't want her spirits lifted. Not yet. Not until this case had moved forward and improved.

CHAPTER 20

In the UK, outdoor events and weather have a nasty habit of not playing ball with each other. The moment anyone decides to arrange anything, you can bet the laws of attraction will conspire to do whatever it takes to send a spiralling weather system towards said date. With summer events, at least there's a half-decent chance you'll get the right weather, but at Christmas, it never matches festive expectations. The problem is that we've all been brainwashed by a million Christmas cards. Conditioned by scenes of solitary robins perched on snow-covered branches and villages nestled in fields of white. The reality never lives up to the ideal.

Okay, so maybe expecting snow for an open-air carol service was a bit much, but a crisp, cold starlit night with people's breath clouding in front of them would do. Instead, a keen, moist southerly breeze dashed off the sea, forcing its way down Fisherman's Walk and through the crowd assembled beneath the bandstand. The mild salt-laden air snuffed out candles and pushed the temperature into double digits, so on the off chance a stray snow flurry did show up, it would immediately turn to drizzle.

At least the fairy lights glowed overhead, although they appeared distinctly ominous, swaying in the breeze, accompanied by the creaking and groaning fir trees from which they hung. Fiona worried the whole lot might come down on their heads, showering them in coloured glass, branches and pine needles.

To distract herself from this potential disaster, she glanced around and spotted many a familiar face. It appeared that Malorie's instructions, or rather demands, had been heeded by most of Southbourne without question. On the left, she spotted Trisha and Doug, flanked by their fellow shopkeepers, while on the right, stood a slightly smaller contingent of stallholders including Alina and Ed. The two groups eyed each other warily, not doing a particularly good job of hiding their animosity. So much for peace on earth and goodwill to all men. Thankfully, the members of the community centre and the general public, together with Fiona, Partial Sue and Daisy, formed a defensive Maginot Line between the two factions.

Up on the bandstand, decked out in red tunics, a six-piece brass band readied themselves, mostly fighting with their sheet music, attempting to secure it to their music stands as they were jostled by the wind.

Malorie stood in front of them all like a dictator, slowly surveying the assembled mass from the bandstand. Her eyes vigilantly scanned the crowd, mentally taking names before she started banging heads, noting anyone foolhardy enough to not heed her invite — including Fran and the other café owners, who were conspicuous by their absence. Why had they stayed away, knowing it would incur Malorie's wrath? Fiona received a small hit of adrenalin as her café owner theory rekindled itself. Was there some conspiracy going on? Before her imagination had a chance to take flight, she was reminded of the unequivocal evidence they'd heard from Fran earlier today. Café owners weren't worried about the Christmas market, or Clive's hot chocolate stall. They were more worried about their ever-increasing number and dwindling profits. Probably why they'd stayed away *en masse*, so they didn't have to see one another and be reminded of their collective problem. Either that, or they wanted to distance themselves from the market-stall-slash-shop-owner's feud. Or, possibly, after a day of standing on their feet waiting tables, the last thing they would want to do is spend the evening standing and singing in the damp night air, even if it would put them in hot water.

The Wicker Man appeared next to the ladies. "Happy Yuletide, one and all."

"Oh, Trevor, you made it," Daisy gushed.

"Do you jest?" he replied. "When Malorie doth summon, one does not decline." He slipped a hip flask from his coat pocket and sneaked a quick draught, then offered it around. "Nip of whisky to keep out the cold, anyone?"

"The cold?" Partial Sue exclaimed, tugging at her scarf. "I needn't have bothered wearing this. I'm boiling. But I won't say no." She necked the liquor and gave a delightful shiver. Daisy and Fiona declined the offer.

"So where's Sophie, then?" the Wicker Man asked. "She never misses an event like this."

"Never misses a chance to show off, more like," Partial Sue grumbled.

"Oh, now that's a tad harsh," the Wicker Man replied. "She has a penchant for people, that's all." He always took Sophie's side, was perhaps the only one who ever did, apart from Malorie. Deferential to her elite social standing, there was more than a touch of admiration for the self-styled PR maven. But Fiona was beginning to think it went beyond that, and he had a small crush on her. If he did, sadly, the feeling wasn't reciprocated, as she barely acknowledged his existence. Not that this was anything personal. By and large, Sophie believed everyone in the entire country was beneath her, except perhaps Kate Middleton.

"Ah, 'tis Gail, she'll know." The Wicker Man spotted Sophie's sweet but long-suffering monosyllabic assistant buzzing between people, distributing leaflets. "Gail, Gail," the Wicker Man called.

On hearing her name, she made a beeline for the little group, then immediately shoved a sheet of paper in their hands.

Fiona examined hers. "Oh, carol sheets."

"'S'right," Gail muttered.

As with any printed material for a community event, it was a hastily prepared mixture of randomly placed clip art — holly, snowmen and Santa — mingled with local companies that supported the event, their logos doing nothing to enhance the festive tone: Dave's gutter cleaning, Tuckton 24-hour plumbers and What's the Crack mobile screen repairs. The only one that had a tenuous link to Christmas was Clay Slayers, accompanied by Trisha's brief and direct sales pitch: "Paint stuff at Xmas". Fiona wondered if Trisha had taken the ad to show her support, as a pre-emptive gesture to possibly appease Malorie, knowing that she was one of the major reasons for the divide between stall-holders and shop owners.

"Gail, wherefore art Sophie?" the Wicker Man asked.

Gail shrugged then continued on her way, handing out carol sheets.

Malorie thumped the microphone a couple of times to get everyone's attention, far too hard than was really necessary, making everyone jump. It sounded like the approaching footfalls of an ogre. All mouths fell silent, all eyes on Malorie.

"Welcome, everyone. I'd like to thank you all for coming to this year's open-air carol service. Before we get into any hearty Christmas singing, I want to have a minute's silence for Clive Preston, who sadly lost his life at the end of November. He was one of our stall-holders and may he rest in peace." Before bowing her head, Malorie glared in the ladies' direction, clearly signalling her dislike of their investigation.

Everyone fell silent. When the respectful minute was up, Malorie's mood had not improved. Her lips tightened and her eyes narrowed. She gripped the rail of the bandstand in front of her, preparing the crowd for a telling-off. "Now, there's something else that needs to be said. I don't like saying it but I'm afraid I have to smack some collective wrists. I've heard there's been some animosity between stall-holders and local shopkeepers. An us-and-them rivalry. I don't care who started it or who did what, I'm not interested. But I will say this — it ends now. All of you, stop squabbling like a bunch of children or I swear there'll be trouble. Do I make myself clear?"

A few half-hearted murmurs circulated around the crowd.

"I said, do I make myself clear!" Malorie barked.

"Yes, yes!" everyone cried, eager to please her in case she rained down fire and brimstone on their heads.

Malorie's demeanour instantly switched, her voice filling with sweetness and light. "Now, our first carol of the evening is 'Ding Dong Merrily On High'."

The band struck up, however, the singing that followed didn't match the perky, jovial tune. Voices were nervous and distinctly subdued after the dressing-down Malorie had given everyone. It must have been too much for some people, as a few of them slipped away while Malorie concentrated on her hymn sheet. Fiona noticed Trisha was one of them.

By the time the singing had ended, Malorie was brimming with positivity. "I think you'll all agree, what a perfect, rousing way to get our service started." However, she wasn't about to let the lacklustre effort go unchecked. "But I think we can all do better next time. I really want to hear those voices!"

Collective feet shifted uneasily, spurred by the pressure of meeting Malorie's exacting demands.

"Now, my dear friend Sophie Haverford would like to say a few words about harmony and peace. Where is Sophie?" Malorie peered around, attempting to locate her.

Without warning, the band started up, surprising everyone, including Malorie herself. Enigmatic and soaring, the tune was infuriatingly familiar, and danced just beyond everyone's recognition, judging by the contorted faces all around.

"What's this music?" Partial Sue asked. "I'm sure I've heard it before."

"Me too," Fiona agreed. "But it doesn't sound Christmassy."

A commotion from behind interrupted their conversation. The crowd parted as a figure in a burgundy velvet hooded cloak swished through their midst, then swept up the stairs of the bandstand. The wind caught the edge of the cloak, billowing it out dramatically. Malorie stepped aside as the figure strode up to the microphone. The hood was thrown back to reveal a wildly grinning Sophie made up to the nines. Her hair remained perfectly bobbed despite just having had a hood over it. She raised her arms wide and triumphant while the band continued the cryptic melody, as if embracing the crowd's adoration, which was largely non-existent. Most people were regarding her with what could only be described as curious befuddlement.

"Just who does she think she is?" Partial Sue grumbled.

"I know that music. It's Enya's 'Orinoco Flow'," Daisy declared, joining in with the irresistibly catchy chorus.

"Oh my gosh, you're right," Partial Sue said.

The penny dropped for Fiona. "Sophie has her own *walk-on music*?"

Partial Sue screwed up her face. "Aw, that's completely ruined that song for me. Now I'll think of Sophie whenever I hear it."

The three ladies stared at the woman whose pomposity knew no bounds. Malorie stood off to one side watching the whole bizarre show, an equally bewildered expression on her face. Fiona wondered how someone as down to earth as Malorie could be friends with such a mountainous ego swathed in a cape.

The band ceased playing, but Sophie kept her hands aloft, glorifying herself. "Yes, yes. It's me. I know I need no introduction, but just in case you've been living under a rock for the past — oh, I don't know — for ever, I suppose you could say I'm the beating heart of Southbourne. A bright light followed by everyone. Not unlike the star the wise men followed to find baby Jesus." She lifted the microphone from its cradle and paced up and down, as if this were a Ted Talk. "In many ways, I resemble our Lord and Saviour. Selfless and driven to help others. You may recall, my recent Make Southbourne Safe Again campaign has rid our neighbourhood of the Southbourne Stalker. There hasn't been an attack in months, so yay for me. That's the power of my personal PR. It's like kung fu but with words — word fu, if you will."

"More like word salad," Partial Sue grumbled under her breath.

Sophie continued, "It's the reason why I've worked with so many world leaders and celebrities, throughout my career. However, my real gift is that I can still relate to you — the ordinary people." Her arm swept in a wide arc, gesturing to the crowd below her. "Why, just the other day, I met with an old friend who works at a hospital. Private one, of course. She was giving me a breast screening and we reminisced about the old days — you could say, ahem, it was a trip down mammary lane." Sophie paused, waiting for the laughter which never came. Sophie repeated the punchline, a surefire sign that the joke hadn't landed.

"What is she doing?" Daisy asked.

"Attempting humour, I think," Fiona remarked.

"I wonder how long it took her to come up with that one," Partial Sue said.

The Wicker Man suddenly forced a laugh louder than was necessary, to show his solidarity. He was the only one who did.

Sophie giggled to herself, unfazed by the lack of laughter. "But seriously, folks, the point I'm making is this, we need to make the most of every moment—"

Sophie's clumsy foray into life coaching was interrupted by the arrival of a breathless and panicked man who stumbled into the midst of the crowd. "Someone's . . ." He took a great gulp of air. "Vandalised one of the market stalls." Resting his hands on his knees, he nodded to the opposite end of Fisherman's Walk. "Near the ornamental pond."

"What!" Malorie roared, thundering down the steps. "Show me."

The man had no more time to catch his breath, as Malorie forced him to march back the way he came. Others began to follow, joined by Fiona, Daisy and Partial Sue.

"Wait, but I haven't finished yet — I have a great story about me meeting the Dalai Lama."

Upstaged by vandalism, Sophie's attempts to stem the flow of people failed miserably. Soon the whole crowd moved like one giant snake towards the far end of the Christmas market, eager to see what new calamity had befallen it.

CHAPTER 21

Despite Malorie's best efforts and her nothing-to-see-here routine, dozens of people swamped around the stall. She had gone straight to Defcon 3 and blew her top, but even her anger had its limits and was no match for mob mentality, fuelled by insatiable curiosity.

The ladies couldn't get close enough to give the stall a thorough examination, although Daisy managed to snap off a few jostled shots by holding her phone above her head. They took themselves off to one side to examine the photographic evidence.

All three of them gasped.

The doors of the stall had been daubed in red paint, spelling out a vile message: *Go back where you came from.* Now, this could have been interpreted as a hideous act of racism were it not for the fact that the stall-holder was from Ringwood, a pretty little forest town about ten miles away.

"Who would do such a thing?" Daisy exclaimed.

"Doesn't that stall belong to the sweet old gent who does the caricatures?" Partial Sue remarked.

"You're right." Although, from what Fiona had observed, all the likenesses were essentially the same face, at the same angle, with the same smile. A repeated template he could draw with his eyes closed, except he'd modify each one with different hair, and perhaps the addition of longer lashes if it were a female. Had this provoked the act of vandalism — was it a dissatisfied customer, annoyed at his cookie-cutter approach to portraiture? More likely, it was another provocation in the ongoing local traders vs stall-holders rivalry. The timing couldn't be more perfect and ironic, seeing as Malorie had just delivered a speech intended to put an end to such hostilities. She was still having no luck holding back the throng of controversy-hungry onlookers. "All of you stop!" she bellowed. "Vacate the area immediately!" More people appeared to be arriving by the second thanks to the volume of messages being hurriedly thumbed into phones.

"We need to give that stall a proper examination without all those bodies around it," Fiona said.

"We could shove them out of the way," Partial Sue replied.

Daisy shuddered. "I don't think that would go down well. Maybe it would be better to come back tomorrow, when no one's here."

"I agree," Fiona said. "Plus, it will be light then. Let's call it a night and regroup in the morning."

The ladies went their separate ways, heading back home, but Fiona made a detour, taking a short-cut to the late-night petrol station. She was out of teabags and there was absolutely no way she could face getting up tomorrow without anointing the start of the day with a refreshing cuppa. She might even treat herself to a KitKat. Not for the morning, of course, but for when she got home. Buying something for Simon Le Bon might also be a good idea, otherwise he'd give her the cold shoulder for not taking him to the carol service. She felt guilty for not including him, but all the people and music would've unsettled the little dog, especially with the unexpected hullaballoo afterwards.

At that moment she desperately wished she had her little furry companion by her side. The back roads were eerily quiet, apart from the moist breeze troubling the branches of the trees overhead, but Fiona became aware of footsteps behind her, matching her pace.

Some distance away, they began to gradually increase, closing the gap between them. Though the night was mild, a cold sliver of fear slipped down Fiona's back. Adrenalin spilled into her veins, instinctively forcing her walk into a hurry. Panting, she dashed across the road. She had no idea why. Weren't you supposed to walk in the middle of the road, if you feared someone was going to attack you?

She berated herself for thinking such a thing. Or was she too frightened to admit it? Denying the dark truth tugging at the frayed edges of her nerves — that the Southbourne Stalker was pursuing her. But surely not.

It was relatively early, not even nine o'clock. Did stalkers strike this early? Did they have a schedule they stuck to? Was there any need when there was a perfectly quiet street and an obliging victim stupid enough to walk along it?

Nice houses scrolled past her with neat front gardens and tasteful lawn ornaments. Surely this wasn't the kind of street where that sort of thing happened, but then the whole of Southbourne wasn't the place where that sort of thing happened. Yet it had. She took comfort in the fact that there were a multitude of windows from which to witness an attack. Glancing sideways, she noticed every one of them was tightly swathed in thick curtains. From previous reports, the stalker struck victims on the back of the head, rendering them unconscious. Minimal noise and no alarms raised, which meant no curtains thrown back. Just a quick, stealthy pop to the head, lights out, valuables taken and stalker gone, all in a matter of seconds.

A beacon of hope appeared at the T-junction ahead, the blessed bright lights of the petrol station beckoning her forward. Her heart soared as she drew ever closer to this safe haven. Its glaring illuminated signage had never looked so inviting.

Just before crossing over, she spun around to check behind her, hoping to catch a glimpse of her would-be attacker. But there was no one. The street was empty. She put it down to paranoia and her overactive imagination getting the better of her. Probably just another carol service attendee making their way home.

As she approached the forecourt, a group of four teenagers — three boys and a girl — were propped against the wall outside, sipping Coke and sucking on vapes, comparing phone screens and snapping off selfies, then randomly bursting into fits of giggles.

Fiona recognised one of them. The unmistakable shape of Joe slotted in the middle, although his body language completely differed from all the times she'd seen him before in the garage. Away from his dad, he was animated, chatty and jovial, cocky even.

As soon as he caught sight of Fiona his banter ceased, and he became the Joe she was more familiar with, bashful and unable to make eye contact. His friends became equally guarded and subdued, the default setting many teenagers adopted whenever an adult was nearby.

"Hi, Joe," Fiona said cheerfully.

"All right," Joe mumbled.

"You okay?" Fiona asked, attempting to make small talk.

He nodded, cringing with embarrassment.

"I'm just picking up teabags," she informed him, although why he would need to know this she had no idea. "Got to have my morning cuppa."

Fiona received no response apart from an awkward shuffling of feet.

"Oh, well," Fiona said. "Tell your dad I said hi."

As she headed into the petrol station, chuckling erupted behind, probably at her expense. Fiona didn't mind. They were just being teenagers, having a laugh and hanging out, free from the gravity of grown-up worry. Good luck to them. Besides, after the fear of thinking she was being followed, it was heartening to see a familiar face, even if it was an awkward one. When she emerged from the petrol station, clutching her tea, chocolate and a chew for Simon Le Bon, the giggling quartet had moved on somewhere else.

CHAPTER 22

The ladies gathered early next morning to get a proper look at the damage, without the distractions of the previous night.

However, in the cold light of day — and it was actually cold this morning — there really wasn't much more to see. The vandal had strategically targeted what would have been the quieter end of the market, as far away from the carol service as possible, just before Fisherman's Walk emerged at the clifftop road. The seventh stall from the end had been selected, just far enough away to be out of sight from any passers-by, although there wouldn't have been many in last night's damp and blustery air.

Simon Le Bon sniffed around the stall, while the ladies stared at the lurid words daubed in red paint across the front.

The graffitied threat had certainly done the trick. The stall-holder had swung by early this morning to pack up his things, which weren't very many. Just some pens, an easel and a couple of chairs, plus samples of his work, which he had hung around the wall of his stall.

"What do you think the police will do?" Daisy asked.

"Nothing, probably," Partial Sue replied.

"Really?" Daisy sounded surprised. "Isn't this a terrible hate crime?"

"Yes, but it's too small for them to be interested in. However, we need to move quickly on this."

"How do you mean?" Fiona asked.

"Well, isn't it obvious? Whoever did this still might have paint on their hands. We go into every shop and café today and check everyone. We could literally catch the perpetrator red-handed."

"What if they washed it off?" Daisy suggested.

"It's worth a shot," Partial Sue replied. "And we should start with Trisha. I saw her slip away last night. She's got access to loads of paints and brushes nearby."

"Yes, but she wasn't the only one to leave," Daisy pointed out. "And her brushes are little. This looks like it was done with something you'd paint a house with."

"But surely we need to explore the possibility. What do you think, Fiona?"

Fiona had become silent, her eyes fixated on the vertical red lines that had dripped from each letter. The words were broadcasting a message to her but not the one intended. "You know what? I'm not buying this. I get the feeling someone's playing us, playing everyone. They want us to be preoccupied by the rivalry, to distract us from the obvious. Malorie mentioned the elephant in the room, and we've mentioned it now and again, but we haven't given it any serious thought."

"What's that?" Daisy asked.

"The locked-room mystery. Or should I say the stall-bolted-from-the-inside mystery. We were excited about it when we first started. The challenge of solving the unsolvable. But since then, we've been distracted by angry shopkeepers and disgruntled stall-holders. Thing is, if we can't solve that, then there is no murder to investigate."

Partial Sue had a different slant on it. "But like Daph said, Clive could've been driven to his fate. And you agreed, people can be coerced into doing anything if the right buttons are pushed."

"Yes, also true. But my gut is telling me all this shop-slash-stall rivalry is a wild goose chase. I mean, we haven't looked into the locked stall at all. I say we give it some thought. See if it's possible then move on."

"It does seem like someone is leading us up the garden path," Daisy said.

Although she'd admitted to being partial to a locked-room mystery right at the start, Partial Sue took some more convincing, but eventually and reluctantly she agreed. To sweeten the deal, Fiona treated them all to one of Alina's bratwursts. She knew nothing would cancel out Sue's grumpiness like a large, chargrilled German sausage, but they'd also need some brain food to attack the impossible conundrum.

As they began to wander back, the monotonous warning of a flatbed truck beeped as it reversed into Fisherman's Walk. It stopped beside the offending stall. The driver jumped out of his cab and started feeding heavy-duty straps beneath it, ready to crane the small wooden structure. The ladies stood and watched and, a few minutes later, the hydraulics whined and strained as the stall slowly lifted off the ground.

Daisy smiled to herself. "I've just had an idea."

CHAPTER 23

Daisy's idea wasn't a breakthrough or even a lead in the loosest sense of the word. Fiona, and no doubt Partial Sue, had hoped that she might provide them with a key to the locked-room mystery or at least some direction. But it wasn't that sort of idea.

After they had wandered back from the market, Daisy had snapped shot after shot of the market stalls, then taken a detour to the model shop to buy supplies. For the rest of the day, they'd sat around the table thrashing out ideas (or would have if they'd had any) while Daisy created a perfect 1:10 scale model of a Christmas stall, faithfully recreated in balsa wood and complete with fully functioning double doors and sliding bolts — one on the outside and one on the inside, just like the real thing.

For the next couple of days, the ladies had used Daisy's impeccable creation as a visual aid to help them fathom how a killer could've got in and out again. They'd examined the model inside and out. Turned it around, upside down, examined it from above, below and all sorts of jaunty angles. They'd studied it up close and from afar, then just stared at it blankly for hours. Despite Daisy's charming and highly accurate recreation, nothing budged where cerebral matters were concerned. It remained a hopeless and ridiculous notion that anyone could pass through solid walls — although, at one point, out of frustration, Partial Sue had wanted to shove her thumb thought the soft balsa wood walls. An impossibility out in the real world. The stalls, though temporary fixtures, were sturdy and well-constructed, made of "tough uncompromising spruce", according to the supplier's website. The ladies had even ventured back outside to the market, using Alina's stall to crash-test the claim — with her permission, of course. Despite their best efforts to push and tug, the wooden walls were impenetrable, just as they had been when Scott had tried to break into his father's stall on that terrible morning.

Back at the shop, Partial Sue had given up on the whole idea and decided to excuse herself from any further discussion. She had slotted herself in the storeroom and began sorting through boxes of donations, while Daisy and Fiona persevered at the round table. Not getting any further, their deliberations weren't helped by customers interrupting them, cooing over Daisy's miniature Christmas stall and asking if it was for sale. This had piqued Partial Sue's interest. She shot out of the storeroom to persuade Daisy to start a business making and selling her models — a cottage industry, which could include model cottages too, if she so desired. But despite Partial Sue's best efforts and an *ad-hoc* business plan, complete with profit projections, scribbled on the back of an envelope, Daisy firmly declined. The model stall was an investigative tool. She wanted to use it to solve the mystery and therefore the crime, not make money from it. So a frustrated Partial Sue had slunk back into the storeroom, huffing in annoyance, as she rummaged through donations and shifted cardboard boxes around.

About an hour later, Partial Sue's rifling suddenly increased in volume. Goods were frantically shoved aside as if her life depended on it.

"I don't bloody believe it!" she exclaimed. Not angrily, but in more of a eureka moment. She burst out of the storeroom holding a metal object aloft as if she'd won the world cup. "I've got it! I've got it!"

Daisy and Fiona gazed at the object nonplussed, wondering just what she had got. It appeared to be a heavy-duty metal hook, the type you might screw into the ceiling to support a punchbag or a hanging chair, except the fixing bracket had no screw holes and was rather on the thick side. Very thick, in fact.

"A hook?" Daisy asked.

"Not just any old hook. It's magnetic. I found it in one of the donation boxes. It's very strong." She demonstrated by holding it close to some metal shelving. The thing was nearly snatched out of her hand as it latched onto a shelf with a loud *thunk*. She then had to use two hands and a great deal of tugging to prise the thing off. It really didn't want to let go.

"I still don't understand," Daisy said.

"I'll show you." Partial Sue exhaled and sat down at the table. Holding it by the hook end, she slowly extended it towards the model. The little double doors of the stall flew open, its miniature ironmongery unable to resist the pull. Daisy held them steady while Sue moved the magnet gently from side to side. The bolt on the outside obeyed as if hypnotised, sliding in and out, and so did the one on the inside, the magnetic field easily passing through the wood.

Daisy gasped. "Oh my! The killer used a magnet to slide the inside bolt across."

Partial Sue couldn't help looking extremely pleased with herself. "That's about the size of it. I can't believe we didn't think of this before."

Fiona had some reservations. "Sue, that's an amazing breakthrough. But we have to be a bit cautious. Passing through balsa wood is one thing, thick pine is going to be another."

Partial Sue stood up. "Agreed. I think we should go back to the market and test this on Alina's stall. And if it doesn't work, we just keep ordering stronger magnets until it does."

Brimming with optimism, they all stood up, eager to put the theory to the test. If manipulating the bolt with a magnet was possible, then so too was murder.

CHAPTER 24

Alina was happy for her stall to be the ladies' test lab once more. But the bright, swelling bubble of optimism the ladies had arrived with suddenly popped and left them all deflated. It quickly became apparent something was wrong. At first, they thought the magnet's field wasn't strong enough to pass through the wood. The inside bolt simply refused to move, so Partial Sue tried it on the outside one without any wooden barrier to get in the way. But there was no attraction whatsoever, even when the magnet was held right next to it.

Abandoning Alina's stall, Partial Sue immediately moved to Ed's crêpe stall next door, testing the bolts on his doors without asking him. Ed frowned at her but didn't engage. Partial Sue had the intense face of someone possessed, who might explode if their mission was interrupted.

Fiona stepped in. "Sorry, Ed. We're just testing a theory."

"Oh, er, that's quite all right." Although he didn't look all right, having his stall hijacked by a magnet-wielding ex-accountant who appeared to become more frustrated by the second, judging by the increased huffing and puffing. But despite Partial Sue's best attempts, both bolts lay idle in their cradles. Like a spoilt child not getting her way, she stamped over to the neighbouring stall, Dragon's Breath, a purveyor of magnificent ceramic mythical creatures — some bigger than Simon Le Bon and terrifying, while others were large-eyed, cute and no bigger than a little finger.

Once more, blinded by her frenzied ambition, Partial Sue neglected to ask permission first.

Quite aptly, the stall-holder, a woman clad in a heavy-weight fleece and fingerless woollen gloves, gave an appropriately fiery response to having her stall accosted. "That'll never work," she snapped.

Partial Sue straightened, indignant. "Why not?"

The stall-holder sighed. "Because the bolts are made of aluminium, a non-ferrous metal. They don't contain any iron and are therefore not magnetic."

Partial Sue made another attempt then stopped. "Are you sure?"

"Positive." She glared.

"Are they all like this?" Fiona asked.

"I have no idea." She folded her arms and knotted her eyebrows. Code for, *Please leave my stall now.*

Daisy didn't take the hint. "Can I ask one more question?"

"If you must."

"How much is that baby dragon, the one bursting out of its shell?"

The ladies left the market with nothing to show for it except Daisy's impulse purchase and a slightly happier stall-owner. On the way back to the shop, Fiona called the stall supplier, New Forest Wooden Buildings, on the off chance that Clive's stall was the exception and had been fitted with a steel bolt. It hadn't. Graham, the owner, informed her that he always specified aluminium bolts because they were less susceptible to corrosion. A handy benefit in the damp south-coast salt air.

But it didn't stop there. To further put the kibosh on the whole idea, Fiona had noticed the bolt's design, unlike the one on Daisy's model, was fashioned with a hooked end.

The bolt couldn't simply be slid across unimpeded. It first had to be flipped through ninety degrees, otherwise the hook would snag on a butterfly-shaped bracket that stood proud of the whole assembly. An extra security feature. Even if the bolts had been made of steel and the killer in possession of the most powerful handheld magnet in the world, it would be impossible to perform such an awkward manoeuvre from outside, with over an inch of wood in the way.

She decided to keep this information to herself, not wanting to add insult to Partial Sue's injury.

No matter how much Daisy and Fiona tried to console her, she remained subdued for the rest of the day. Her big promising breakthrough had amounted to nothing. Apathy taking over, she sat at the till, gazing vaguely at her phone as the hours dragged by.

Not wanting to remind Sue of her disappointment, Daisy sensitively removed the model from the table, placed it in a large bag and hid it away in the storeroom.

Fiona didn't know how to improve the situation. There was nothing that could be said or done. Even the offer of tea didn't appear to move the needle as far as the collective mood was concerned. They needed a new lead, pure and simple. A nice big, hefty one, or the pivotal kind that turned the investigation on its head and exploded with possibilities.

Having been in this situation several times before, Fiona was acutely aware that new leads never happened when she wanted them. If things carried on as they were, with nothing but a petty rivalry to show for their efforts, she could see no option but to invite Daph back and tell her that despite all their best endeavours, they could find no evidence of foul play from Scott or anyone else. Not a bad outcome for Scott. But being avid detectives, it would feel like a hollow, lacklustre end to the investigation.

CHAPTER 25

First thing the following morning, Scott called in to the shop, pushing open the door with a disheartened scowl on his face and a clear plastic bag in one hand. Not even Simon Le Bon's affectionate tail-wagging could assuage his pessimistic demeanour.

Fiona immediately rose from the table. "Scott, are you okay?"

He inhaled deeply and shuffled further inside. "I've come to tell you to stop your investigation."

"Why, what's happened?" Partial Sue asked.

Scott lifted up the bag, which on closer inspection was an evidence bag. It contained a single item — a phone. "I picked this up from the police station this morning. It was Dad's. The police held onto it to see if they could get anything from it."

"Did they find something?" Fiona asked.

Pain rimmed Scott's eyes. His body shuddered.

Daisy gestured to the table. "Come, sit down. I'll make you a cup of tea."

He shook his head and remained standing. "No, thank you. I won't stay. I just wanted to tell you to stop investigating."

"What was it they found?" Partial Sue stepped out from behind the counter.

"A suicide note." His voice was numb and monotone. "It was saved in drafts but never sent."

"Oh no!" Daisy cried. "Scott, we're so sorry."

Scott stifled a sob. "I think I was trying to convince myself he'd been murdered because somehow that was easier to accept than suicide. But now I have to face facts. That he took his own life and I'm to blame. We had that blistering row the night before he died. I must have driven him over the edge."

"I'm sure that's not true." Fiona edged towards him.

Scott backed away. "Please don't be nice to me. I don't deserve it."

Fiona halted her progress. "Okay, but were there any indications in the note your dad left?"

Scott slid the phone from its clear bag, jabbed at the screen a few times and turned it to show the ladies.

They gathered round. The note was brief and to the point:

Scott, I'm sorry. But I can't go on like this.
It's better if I end it now.
I love you and wish you only the best.
Your old man.

Partial Sue didn't mince her words. "That doesn't sound like anything you've done. Seems like he was fighting his own demons."

"So why did he say, 'I can't go on like *this*?' *This* meaning us always fighting and squabbling. He wanted to end it because of what I put him through."

"Well, the word 'this' is very vague," Fiona said. "Could mean anything. I think you're reading too much into it. And you were always having disagreements. Just part of your day-to-day relationship."

"It doesn't matter if you argued," Daisy added. "I argue with my daughter all the time. But I still love her. I'm sure he loved and cared for you, especially if he had life assurance . . ." Daisy suddenly went as red as the setting sun.

This caught Scott's attention. "How did you know about that?"

Partial Sue quickly stepped in with a little white lie. "Daisy meant to say, I bet he had life assurance. We were just talking about it, because Daisy was thinking about taking some out for her daughter."

Daisy nodded sheepishly.

Partial Sue continued, "The point is that people leave things for their kids because they care about them. I bet Clive was no different."

"Well, I was surprised to find that he had life assurance. He must have taken it out when I was little, after Mum died. He probably forgot to cancel it."

"I doubt that," Fiona said. "He wanted you to be looked after, whatever your age, because he loved you. He said so in his text."

Scott's sorrow quickly shifted to anger. "Then why did he do this? Why did he end his life and put me through the worst pain I've ever felt? He could've said something. Anything. I could have helped him. Worked something out. But now he's gone. And it's too late." He slid the phone back in its bag and sealed it up. An exasperated breath escaped through his teeth. "Look, I know you're trying to make me feel better, and I do appreciate it. But right now, I have a lot of anger and confusion to process."

"We can't even begin to understand what you're going through," Fiona said. "But our door is open any time you want to chat, and I really mean that."

"Thank you," Scott replied. "I might take you up on your offer, but please don't worry about the investigation. I'm guessing you didn't find anything."

Fiona shook her head.

"Well, thank you for trying." Scott offered them a weak smile, said his goodbyes and left.

Partial Sue flopped down on a chair. "Poor Scott. But now there's no doubt about how Clive died."

"And no locked-room mystery either," Fiona added. "Because there was never a murder to start with."

Daisy also collapsed in a chair and slapped her forehead. "I'm so stupid. I can't believe I let it slip about the life assurance."

Partial Sue smiled sympathetically. "Don't worry, Dais. It's an easy mistake to make."

Fiona began gathering the cups off the table. "I'll call Daph later and fill her in about the note. I can't face it at the moment. First, I need tea. Who wants one?"

Partial Sue's hand shot up in the air, but Daisy remained strangely still and quiet, her face pensive, her thoughts distant and unreadable.

"Daisy, are you okay?" asked Fiona. "You're not still worried about that slip-up?"

Daisy took a moment to respond. "No, it's not that. I've had something on my mind since the carol service. Something Sophie said. I didn't want to say anything because it was horrible to think about, until Scott showed us the note on Clive's phone."

"What was it?" Partial Sue asked.

"Well, Sophie was going on about making Southbourne safe again, and that there hadn't been an attack in months. She was right. Since the start of January, there's been a stalker attack roughly every two months. We should have had another one in November. But it's gone quiet. What if the reason is because the stalker's dead? The stalker was Clive. He couldn't help himself. Was ashamed of what he was but couldn't stop. The only way to end it was to take his own life."

Partial Sue and Fiona both gasped.

Fiona had to sit down. "Oh dear."

"*I can't go on like this*," Partial Sue exclaimed. "That's what his note said. Maybe that's what he was referring to — his addiction to attacking people late at night."

"And why he could never mention anything to Scott. He was too ashamed." Fiona's head began to spin and her tinnitus squealed as it all made uncomfortable sense.

"Daisy, I think you're on to something," Partial Sue enthused.

Daisy didn't look too excited and wrung her hands nervously, not too pleased that she'd uncovered the macabre connection.

Fiona reminded them that it was still just a theory, and they had no hard evidence, apart from some extremely convenient and significant timing. "We'll never know for sure, of course. If he was the Southbourne Stalker, Clive's taken that secret to his grave."

"And that's where it should stay," Daisy said adamantly. "If Scott finds out, it will kill him."

"But what about all the stalker's victims?" Partial Sue replied. "Surely they deserve justice? To know that their attacker can never do it again."

The ladies had a conundrum on their hands, far worse than any locked-room mystery. A moral dilemma. Should they continue to investigate and discover if Clive was indeed the stalker and posthumously bring him to justice? Or should they let sleeping dogs lie and spare Scott any awful truth about his father?

CHAPTER 26

The rest of the day passed in contemplative silence. Three minds wrestling with the possibility that Clive could have been the stalker and, more importantly, what should be done about it. Fiona was indecisive, the moral centre of her brain stuck in binary stalemate. One second, yes, people should know what he did. Then the next second, not a chance, leave things as they are. Of course, this was all dependent on whether they could find compelling evidence of his guilt. That was one thing the ladies could all agree on — they would do nothing until they had a body of proof the size of King Kong's house.

However, the laws of attraction had other ideas, seeming to have waited until they'd had one planet-sized breakthrough so they could use the increased gravity to send another one hurtling towards them. Although, at first, it didn't seem like a planet-sized anything. More like a pea-sized asteroid that would burn up in the outer layers of the atmosphere.

A timid young lad, not more than eighteen or nineteen, popped his head around the door, then quickly retracted it.

The ladies exchanged puzzled glances.

Making a second attempt at entry, he appeared far less sure of himself than the first time.

"Are you okay there?" Fiona assumed he needed to buy a present for a first-time love interest. They often frequented the shop at this time of year; cash-poor and with not a clue what to buy, they turned to charity shops to make their money go further.

Eyes as wide as saucers, he pushed the door slightly wider and sidestepped in, nearly jumping out of his skin when the bell jangled above him.

"Please come in and have a look around," Daisy encouraged him. "We don't bite."

To strengthen that claim and perhaps sensing the boy's nervousness, Simon Le Bon gave a welcoming wag of his tail from his basket, but this did nothing to assuage the boy's discomfort. As he sidled further inside, his eyes erratically scanned the shop from all possible angles as if surveillance cameras were tracking his every move.

"Can we help you with anything?" Fiona asked.

He mumbled something under his breath.

"Come again?" Partial Sue asked.

"I have information," he whispered.

"Oh, what sort of information?"

He swallowed hard, looked left and right, nervously licked his lips and said, "I saw who murdered Clive Preston."

CHAPTER 27

Fiona studied the boy's face as he sipped his tea, clutching the cup as if his life depended on it. Though he was young, his skin had a pallid, paper-like texture and creases where there really shouldn't be any at his age, with black smudges under his eyes. A worried face, holding onto a secret. Almost certainly a dangerous one.

"Would you like anything to eat? A biscuit or some cake?" Daisy asked.

He shook his head.

"Can I ask your name?" Fiona said.

Terrified, he shook his head again.

Partial Sue was eager to get down to business. "You said someone murdered Clive Preston. But he took his own life." She sounded like every person they had ever questioned in this case — the ladies had joined their ranks ever since reading the note on Clive's phone. "What makes you think he was murdered?"

"B-because of the Southbourne Stalker." The lad winced as he said the name.

The ladies looked at one another, wondering if Daisy's theory was about to become fact. It would be a record for them. The shortest time an idea had been proposed and confirmed — all in the same day.

Fiona didn't beat about the bush. "Was Clive Preston the Southbourne Stalker?"

He anxiously shook his head again.

Partial Sue shifted to the edge of her seat. "Did the Southbourne Stalker kill Clive?"

He hesitated, then slowly nodded.

Partial Sue jumped straight in. "Do you know who the Southbourne Stalker is?"

"No," the lad replied quietly.

"Then how do you know they killed him?" Partial Sue asked.

"I don't. Well, not exactly."

Partial Sue attempted to suppress her confusion. "Er, I thought you said you saw who killed Clive Preston."

"Yes, I did. I mean, sort of."

"Start from the beginning," Fiona said. "Tell us everything that happened."

The lad rocked back and forth in his chair a couple of times, the request clearly rattling him. He took a deep breath, steadied himself, then began. "I'd been at a mate's house playing Xbox. The new *Call of Duty* had just dropped."

"What day was this?" Fiona asked.

"Friday the nineteenth of November. I stayed till about midnight. I can't be sure as my phone died. I forgot to charge it because we were so into the game. I walked back home. Roads were empty. That's why I thought it was after midnight because it's always dead at that time. But as I headed home, I heard footsteps behind me." He gulped hard as he recounted his ordeal. "Someone following me, getting closer, so I crossed over to shake them, but they came after me."

Fiona shifted uneasily in her seat, as she recalled her own similar experience, which had thankfully amounted to nothing.

"I panicked. Did something stupid and ducked into an alleyway . . ." His words faltered and his breaths became ragged.

"It's okay," Fiona said. "Take your time."

He blinked back a few tears, brought his gasping under control, then continued. "Something whooshed past my head. I think he was trying to hit me, but he missed."

"You said 'he'," Partial Sue pointed out. "So it was definitely a man?"

The lad hesitated for a moment. "I think so. But I can't be a hundred per cent sure."

"Okay, then what happened?" Fiona asked.

"He grabbed me from behind. I struggled. We spun around and I ended up facing the opposite way, but I couldn't escape. Thought I was a goner. But then someone shouted, 'Oi, leave him alone!' A man was standing in the entrance to the alleyway, under a street light. He must have passed by and saw what was happening. My attacker let go. I made a run for it, out the way I came, past the guy who'd shouted."

"And that was Clive Preston?" Fiona asked.

"Yeah, well, I didn't know that at the time. He asked if I was okay. But I didn't stop. I was too frightened. But I recognised him a few days later after I'd heard what had happened."

"So you think the Southbourne Stalker killed Clive?" Fiona asked.

Doubt tugged at the lad's features. "Well, I'm not a hundred per cent. I never saw him. But as I ran off, I heard Clive say, 'What are you playing at?' The way he said it, sounded like he knew the guy."

Daisy gasped. "Clive recognised the stalker?"

"I think so."

"If Clive knew his identity," Fiona said, "it would only leave the stalker one option."

"He'd have to kill him to shut him up," Partial Sue added with morbid delight.

The lad's hands shook. "I'm terrified he's going to come after me next. Tie up a loose end."

"But you never saw him," Daisy countered. "And he doesn't know who you are."

"He might do," the lad replied.

"Don't worry," Fiona reassured him. "I think if he did, he'd have made a move by now. But I would urge you to go to the police with this information, especially if you're worried about your safety."

"No!" His head shook rapidly, and he worked himself up into a lather. "No way. They'll want statements and names and things. I don't even know who he is, so what use would I be? And even if they did find him and arrest him, I'd have to go to court. What if he goes free and comes after me? I'd end up like Clive. Please don't tell the police—"

"Don't worry," Partial Sue interrupted him. "We'd never do anything you didn't want us to."

"Can I ask you a question?" Fiona said. "Why did you come to us with this information?"

The lad froze. Now they were getting to the nub of things. He scratched his arm nervously. "Because I was hoping you could catch him. I've been terrified since this happened. Can't sleep or eat. And I know what you're going to say, I should report it. But everyone around here thinks Clive killed himself, even the police. I was worried no one would believe me. Then I heard that the Charity Shop Detective Agency was investigating Clive's death. I thought, if you're investigating that means you don't think he killed himself either. I don't know if what I've said helps, and I don't know who the stalker is, but I swear it's true."

"Oh, believe me, it helps," Partial Sue exclaimed. "More than you can imagine."

"Really?" A small light of hope kindled in his eyes.

"Oh, yes," Fiona reassured him. "Your information has given us, er, a new direction on things."

"Help us catch him and put him behind bars," Partial Sue enthused.

The poor lad sighed with relief, his whole frame sagging. "Oh, man. That makes me feel a lot better."

"Now, a bit of advice," Fiona said. "I know you don't want to go to the police, but I would urge you to see someone. Talk to a counsellor or therapist. You've had a traumatic experience. You should get some help with that."

Concern flared in his eyes.

"Don't worry," Partial Sue reassured him. "It's confidential. They won't tell a soul."

"But it will help you deal with all that nasty stuff in your head," Daisy said. "So you can get a good night's sleep."

He was clearly uncomfortable with this suggestion and began rising to his feet. "I have to go." He bustled towards the door but, before leaving, he turned. "Please catch Clive's killer."

"You can always talk to us, if you need a supportive ear," Fiona called after him.

He dashed through the door and was gone.

Daisy shook her head sorrowfully. "Poor lad. What an awful thing to go through. Do you think he's going to be okay?"

"No, not in his current state," Fiona replied. "He should really get help. Otherwise, he's going to be carrying that trauma around for ever."

"Unless we catch his attacker, who is almost certainly Clive's killer." Partial Sue's face flushed with glee. "Who knew that would drop in our laps? Just when we thought Clive was the stalker and killed himself, the universe throws us a curveball. No wonder the stalker has gone quiet. He's been lying low after killing his one and only witness."

Fiona's brow furrowed. "We really should go to the police with this information."

"Didn't we just promise we wouldn't do that?" Partial Sue said. "Besides, you know what they're like. Once they've settled on a verdict, they rarely want to change it because it makes them look stupid."

"They might in light of new evidence," Fiona replied.

Partial Sue frowned. "We've got an anonymous witness who doesn't want to come forward. We'll need more than that to persuade them to change their minds. I don't think we can rely on them to find this guy. It's up to us."

"But shouldn't we tip them off about the Southbourne Stalker?" Daisy said.

"What would be our tip, apart from we think the stalker is probably a man?" Partial Sue countered.

"Well, he might have been an acquaintance of Clive Preston," Daisy said. "That would narrow their search."

"That's a good point," Fiona admitted. "Trouble is, Clive knew everyone around here. Let's press on with this new lead, but as soon as we have something more concrete, we go straight to DI Fincher and DS Thomas."

"Deal!" Partial Sue became fired up. "This horrible murdering stalker's days are numbered. That much is for sure."

Daisy joined in, adding her own bluster to the mix. "We're going to catch him and put him away. Make Southbourne safe again."

Partial Sue and Fiona stared at her, shocked that she'd used Sophie Haverford's provocative slogan. A campaign designed not so much to help catch the stalker, but to shame the ladies that they hadn't caught him.

"What did I just say?" Daisy asked.

"Sophie's catchphrase," Partial Sue informed her.

"Oh. Sorry."

A big grin split Partial Sue's face. "No need to apologise, because it's true. We are going to make Southbourne safe again."

"Amen," Daisy added.

And with that, the bravado was back, soaring higher than before. Fiona could understand their excitement. After so many setbacks and dead ends, it had felt as if they were chasing their tails. But now they had solid intel on which to base the investigation.

Fiona smiled along with her colleagues, but she didn't share their confidence. The grim reality of the situation troubled her — namely, the calibre of person they were dealing with. After the incident in the alleyway, this individual had somehow managed to soothe Clive's concerns, enough to persuade him to trek across Southbourne, get him inside his stall, murder him without leaving a trace or a single suspicious mark on his body, then escape leaving the door bolted from the inside. What's more, he'd done it all on the spur of the moment, completely unplanned and in the middle of the night without being seen or raising the alarm. One thing was for sure, they were dealing with an extremely cunning and resourceful individual. A cold-hearted and calculating killer, completely unfazed by high-pressure situations. Most terrifying of all, Clive must have trusted him. Whoever could've pulled that off?

A logical name popped into her head. A name that she really didn't want to be there. No matter how much she tried to pluck it from her mind, it kept popping back in. An uninvited guest who wouldn't stop knocking on her door, despite her refusing to answer.

Fiona's phone pinged, pulling her from her thorny deliberations. It was a text from Daph, requesting an update. Her timing couldn't have been more perfect, or awkward, depending on which way you looked at it.

CHAPTER 28

Daph had arranged to pop in first thing the next day. As they waited, Daisy wore a hole in the carpet, anxiously pacing up and down. "What are we going to tell her? Because you know I don't like lying. I always get nervous and blurt out something stupid."

"Relax, Dais," Partial Sue said. "We've got nothing to hide."

"We promised that lad we wouldn't tell anyone what he told us," Daisy answered.

"No, we promised we wouldn't tell the police," Partial Sue replied. "Big difference. We can tell Daph without breaking our word."

"But what if she goes to the police?" Daisy fretted. "She wants to get the suicide verdict changed so her clients don't have to pay out."

"She'll have the same problem as we have," Partial Sue replied. "An anonymous witness who won't come forward. It'll take a heck of a lot more than that to change their minds, which means she'll need us to do more digging."

"Don't worry," Fiona said. "This is probably just a catch-up. Save me having to text her the information. It'll be fine."

Daisy didn't look fine. She could worry herself to death about anything and had been known to return to the supermarket in a panic because she'd put something back on the wrong shelf. "Okay, I'll let you two do the talking."

Twenty minutes later, Daph shoved her way into the shop with fewer bags than before, but still enough to hinder her progress through the door. Squeezing inside, she was eclectically dressed in a khaki bucket hat, a thick multicoloured crocheted poncho and mud-splatted wellingtons. She wouldn't have looked out of place glamping at a rain-soaked Glastonbury. Simon Le Bon greeted her, momentarily sniffing around her bags. Not detecting any signs of food within, he retired to his bed by the till.

Daph immediately pre-empted their drinks offer. "Tea, one sugar, if you please. The bigger the better."

Once they'd furnished Daph with the largest mug they could find and filled it with tea, Fiona carefully outlined their progress.

Daph slurped her drink. "So let me get this straight. This lad had no idea who his attacker was?"

"Not a clue whatsoever," Fiona said. "Didn't see him."

"And you don't know the lad's name?"

Partial Sue shook her head. "Nope. Wouldn't tell us. Didn't want us to go to the police either."

"Do you think he could be persuaded to change his mind?" Daph asked.

"Not a chance," Partial Sue replied. "He's terrified. Can't force someone to be a witness if they don't want to be. Sorry, but I doubt we'll ever see him again."

Daph leaned her chair back on two legs, musing away to herself. "Mm."

Fiona wondered if she was annoyed with them, angry that they didn't press him for a name — after all, his testimony would be key to challenging the suicide verdict. "I know it's disappointing. But we had to respect his wishes to remain anonymous."

Daph was surprisingly philosophical. "It's fine. I understand."

"At least we know there's an extremely good chance that Clive was murdered," Partial Sue said. "He'd discovered the identity of the stalker, and the stalker took him out."

Daph straightened her chair and leaned forward. Her tone dropped an octave or two. "Now, forgive me for what I'm about to say. I'm not trying to sway your opinion, and you'll probably say I'm biased because of my client's stake in all this, but my mind is immediately drawn towards Scott being the culprit. Think about it. He ticks all the boxes."

Fiona hated to admit it, but she'd quietly arrived at the same conclusion.

Daph expanded her theory. "This lad said Clive knew him. Scott ticks that box. Who else could've made Clive listen while he made up some excuse for attacking the boy? He ticks that box too. Who else could've persuaded Clive to go back to his stall? And who else would've known the passcode for Clive's phone, so he could leave the supposed suicide note?"

"He could've used facial recognition," Partial Sue suggested. "After, he'd, er, dispatched the victim."

"Sure," Daph said. "But my point is, Scott's the only person who could've pulled all that off, and he had two very powerful motives for murder — avoiding arrest and money."

Daisy broke her vow of silence. "But Scott said he didn't know about Clive's life assurance."

"He could've been lying to us," Fiona said. "But even if he wasn't, avoiding jail would be a huge motive for murder."

Daisy huffed. "I can't believe he's the Southbourne Stalker and a killer. This is Scott we're talking about. Runs the post office and helps seniors with their pensions, helps you decide on the right postage when you have an important letter to send, pillar of the community and all that."

"What better cover?" Partial Sue offered.

"But would he really kill his own father?" Daisy replied.

"They did argue a lot," Partial Sue pointed out.

That last comment caught Daisy's attention. "Yes, they did. At the drop of a hat, so we've heard. So why didn't they argue in that alleyway? After what Clive had witnessed, surely they would have had a huge bust-up, yet no one heard a thing. No raised voices or curtains drawn back."

"Maybe they kept their voices down." Partial Sue's argument was weak and she knew it.

Daisy ignored her. "But there's something else that doesn't make sense. Why would they go back to his stall?"

"Scott probably suggested it so they could discuss things further," Daph said.

Fiona was starting to see Daisy's point. "Yes, but that's an odd place to have a chat in the middle of the night, don't you think?"

"Maybe Scott wanted to talk over hot chocolate." Partial Sue was really scratching around now.

Daisy screwed up her face. "I might be tempted by that offer. But Clive's just been out drinking. It'd make more sense if Scott tempted him with a stiff drink."

Fiona was reminded of the extra alcohol in Clive's system. Had Scott plied him with another drink or two at some point to soften him up? It seemed likely, although she couldn't see how or where this would've happened as everywhere was shut, unless Clive had beer stashed in his stall.

"Why didn't they go back to Scott's?" Daisy asked.

"He probably didn't want to disturb his wife," Partial Sue said.

"Okay, Clive's then," Daisy suggested. "That would make a lot more sense. They could have had a beer or a whisky, but I can't see Clive agreeing to open up his stall in the middle of the night so they could have a hot chocolate."

Fiona pictured the scene. Well after midnight, father and son standing in Clive's damp, cold stall, resolving their differences over paper cups of hot chocolate. A bizarre image, and quite unbelievable.

Daph didn't seem to be particularly bothered by any of it. "I think we're all clutching at straws here — drinking straws, you could say." She giggled at her little joke then rose to her feet and smiled. "Oh well, keep at it. I think you're going to crack this. I've got a good feeling. Right, I'm off to do some Christmas shopping. Hey, you don't know where I can get one of them ring light thingies? My son wants to start doing podcasts."

"Hardware store," Daisy blurted without missing a beat. "They sell everything there."

Daph thanked them and bustled out of the shop.

"She left abruptly," Daisy said. "I thought we were just getting going."

Partial Sue leaned back and folded her arms. "Well, we didn't have any more hard facts to tell her. We were straying into conjecture. No point hanging around for that."

Fiona agreed. "Especially as we weren't exactly seeing eye to eye."

"Sorry about that," Daisy apologised. "It's just how I feel."

"No, no. Don't apologise. You were making a lot of sense," Partial Sue conceded.

"I thought Daph would be twisting our arms to find out the name of the lad," Fiona said. "But she didn't seem particularly worried. She was fairly laid-back about the whole thing."

Partial Sue supplied the cynical yet realistic answer. "I suppose she gets paid either way. Just needs to demonstrate that she's exhausted all avenues. But I think it's great that she's got confidence in us. Said we're going to crack this. That's a first. Usually, people treat us like a bunch of well-meaning amateurs."

The ladies went quiet for a moment. Despite the recent breakthrough, and Daph's unexpected faith in them, Fiona felt they were still staggering around in the dark, stubbing collective toes on one stumbling block after another. With this new information in mind, they needed a fresh starting point, or perhaps to revisit an old one. "There's one avenue we haven't been down. Actually, that's not true, we've tried going down it, but we didn't get very far — the avenue of the locked-door mystery."

"Oh, not that again," Partial Sue groaned.

"Look, I'm sorry to bring it up, but no matter how much evidence we amass against Scott or anyone else, police will never buy it until we can prove how someone got in and out of a locked stall. Unless we crack that puzzle, it will always remain a suicide."

Daisy and Partial Sue exchanged the same downcast expressions as they contemplated a return to the no-win situation. The button on the blouse that refused to fasten. At the start of this investigation, the locked room had filled them with glee and intrigue, the thrill of solving a unique and beguiling challenge, but now it brought them nothing but dread and anguish.

Daisy resigned herself to the inevitable and got to her feet. "I'll get the model."

CHAPTER 29

To an outsider, or even a customer inside the shop (although they were thin on the ground that morning), it appeared that the ladies were attempting telekinesis. All three of them sat equally spaced around the table, intensely gazing at the model stall, as if willing it to move. They'd put themselves in this meditative state not so much to flex their psychic powers but more as an act of desperation. It had taken them less than a minute to realise they had no new ideas how to solve the locked-stall conundrum. This had left them with only one course of action: stare at the blessed thing in the hope that inspiration might spring from its balsa and wood-glue construction.

The more they stared, the more their minds refused to cooperate. The only serviceable idea they'd fumbled with involved no murder at all, and therefore no locked stall: Clive, in his semi-inebriated state, discovered that Scott was the Southbourne Stalker and was so shocked that his mind couldn't cope. Devastated, the overwhelming shame had driven him to end it all. Flimsy as a wet flannel, the idea didn't track. Surely Clive would have required more time to digest this horrible revelation before doing something so drastic, but it was all they had come up with, and it was now lunchtime.

Partial Sue drew her eyes away from the model and squinted, as if she'd been staring at the sun too long. "You know what? I think the model is the problem."

Daisy's face flushed.

"Sorry, Daisy. That came out wrong. The model's brilliant. Perfect, in fact, and we're lucky to have it. But I think we need to look at the real thing."

"I agree," Fiona said. "We should be looking for genuine clues and we're not going to find them staring at this."

"But the real stall is under lock and key," Daisy replied. "Police won't let us near it."

Partial Sue smiled impishly. "Ah, but it's not with the police. It's not really evidence because they don't believe a crime has been committed. The supplier's got it locked away in storage. Just as a precaution."

"Will he let us look at it?" Daisy asked.

"There's only one way to find out." Fiona pulled out her phone and called New Forest Wooden Buildings. Graham, the owner, was very nice and apologetic but advised her that the stall wasn't open to the public.

Partial Sue frowned. "Great, what are we going to do now?"

"I know someone who could persuade him." Fiona winced a little. "But we'll need to offer her something in return."

Partial Sue cottoned on straight away. "You're talking about Malorie, aren't you?"

"Oh no!" Daisy cried. "She'll have us doing all sorts of horrible activities." Subconsciously, she pulled a wet wipe from her pocket and smeared it around her palms and fingers.

"I can't think of any other way," Fiona said. "I know Sophie ordered the stalls, but Malorie is the force of nature behind the Christmas market."

"Do I have to come?" Daisy sounded about seven years old.

"I think it will take all of us to sweeten the deal," Partial Sue wisely stated.

"Fine," Daisy croaked.

Fiona made the call and, after some haggling back and forth, struck a deal. Malorie secured them a meeting with the supplier but demanded that each of them volunteer for her on one separate day each. Fiona managed to bargain her down to all three of them volunteering on the same day, which would be easier to stomach. Fiona felt rather pleased with herself until Partial Sue pointed out that it was basically the same deal, amounting to the same amount of time, just expressed differently.

Daisy was eager to examine the fine print. "Did she say what we'd be doing?"

Fiona shook her head. "It would be at a time and place of her choosing."

Tremors of fear rocked Daisy. "This is bad, very bad. She'll have us scrubbing out skips, or something else unmentionable."

"I thought you liked cleaning things?" Partial Sue reminded her.

This threw Daisy for a second. "Depends on the venue. Dirty streams, muddy ditches and abandoned brownfield sites full of dumped rubbish are not my cup of tea. I like cleaning kitchens, bedrooms, lounges and dusty forgotten attics. Actually, that last one would be top of my list, as long as it's not haunted by a Victorian orphan."

"So basically, you don't like cleaning outdoors," Partial Sue observed. "Or in haunted attics."

Fiona stepped in before they became too sidetracked. "Well, the important thing is, we're visiting New Forest Wooden Buildings at 4 p.m."

Forgetting her volunteering commitments, Daisy brightened. "Oh, a trip into the forest at Christmas! Wonderful! I wonder if we'll see a reindeer!"

CHAPTER 30

They didn't spot any reindeer because there weren't any in the New Forest, but there were plenty of sika and red deer native to this vast ancient woodland. Although, in the winter twilight they didn't glimpse any of these either. The creatures were notoriously shy, keeping their distance from people or anything manmade, unlike the ponies that roamed wild in the forest and liked nothing better than to stand in the middle of its roads, holding up traffic. Partial Sue was convinced they were smarter than they looked and did it on purpose.

But on this trip, the roads were distinctly pony-free, and they were treated to a majestic wonderland of dark, soaring pines and gnarled oaks. They passed squat red-brick cottages, their Christmas lights popping on and their sturdy chimney stacks sending columns of black smoke into the fledgling night. Of course, it would have been better with a dusting of snow, but you couldn't have everything.

"Oh wow," Daisy commented as they pulled into New Forest Wooden Buildings. It was essentially a handsome farmhouse complete with a courtyard surrounded by stables and outbuildings. Across the courtyard stood a higgledy-piggledy cluster of miniature wooden buildings of all shapes and designs and confectionery colours. Garden rooms, log cabins, summerhouses and humble little sheds were spotlit from every angle and criss-crossed with festive lights from above. "They're so cute and diddy. It's like a little village from *The Wizard of Oz*."

Graham emerged from the farmhouse in a hardwearing flannel shirt with the sleeves rolled up and thick mustard-yellow corduroys. Tall and broad-shouldered, he smiled warmly at the ladies as they exited the car, extending a large hand to each of them. Fiona shook it, her skin reading the braille of calluses across his rough palms.

"Welcome, welcome. Malorie told me you'd be dropping by." He seemed eager to please them. Malorie had that effect on people.

"I love your wooden buildings," Daisy gushed. "They're very pretty."

"Oh, thank you."

"Did you supply all the buildings for the market?" Fiona knew he had but wanted to get down to brass tacks.

"We did. On a rental basis. Although next year we've got an exciting new line of stalls we'll be launching — would you like to see?"

"Oh, yes!" Daisy exclaimed before Fiona had a chance to decline.

They followed him to the right-hand side of the courtyard to a battered sliding door, which squeaked and complained as Graham wrenched it back. He flipped on a row of switches. A formation of fluorescent tubes hanging from chains high above them plinked into life, revealing a vast workshop, pungent with sawdust and cluttered with wood and heavy machinery. In the midst of the mess stood what could only be described as a scaled-down Dickensian shop. Constructed from bare unpainted wood, it was narrower and higher than the average Christmas stall. The frontage was divided in two — a bulging bay window gridded with square glazing bars on one side and a large wooden door on the other. Above this, to give the appearance of a first floor, the design incorporated a generous inclining overhang with a small window and even a swinging sign. A sharply pitched roof, complete with wooden tiles, gave it that authentic *Old Curiosity Shop* look. The whole construction stood off the floor, supported on wooden blocks like the stalls in Southbourne.

"This is just a prototype," Graham informed them. "Christmas market stalls are much of a muchness. Just big garden sheds really. We think this might make a better Christmas experience. It'll be painted, of course."

Daisy couldn't contain herself. "Can you imagine lines of these down Fisherman's Walk? It'd look like a Victorian Christmas card."

Graham smiled. "Not just Fisherman's Walk but town centres everywhere."

Fiona had more practical matters on her mind. "But aren't they a bit small for customers to go in and browse around?"

"Ah, it may look like a shop, but it works in the same way as a stall, just a bit prettier." He tugged at the bay window and the door, which both swung out on hinges, opening up the full frontage of the little building.

The ladies couldn't resist the urge to poke their heads in and have a quick nose. Pungent with freshly sawn pine, the space was similar to a regular market stall, apart from the higher, more steeply angled rafters.

"I think it's much nicer than the ones you usually see," Graham said. "Ours included."

"Oh, yes!" Daisy gushed. "Much more Instagrammable."

"Exactly," Graham replied. "I'm hoping local councils will see it that way too."

Ever the cynic, Partial Sue pointed out a flaw in his business plan. "But couldn't other suppliers just copy your design?"

Concern flared in Graham's eyes. "If I can get there first, I can corner the market in, er, Christmas markets before they have time to react. Please don't tell anyone about this, will you?"

Fiona reassured him. "Not a problem. We're only interested in one stall — Clive's. Would we be able to see it now?"

"Yes, this way."

They followed him out of the workshop and around the back of the courtyard, which was hidden from the public. Several blindingly bright security lights glared into life, illuminating the whole area. This appeared to be the dumping ground for the business — unwanted offcuts of wood, broken machinery, cracked panes of glass and carcasses of wooden buildings in various states of disrepair. On the left stood Clive's Christmas stall, padlocked and tightly encircled by a heavy-duty chain. Another stall stood nearby on the right. Daubed with red paint, it had once belonged to the caricaturist.

"What's going to happen to that one?" Partial Sue pointed to the vandalised stall.

"We'll sand off the graffiti," Graham replied. "Use it again."

Fiona nodded to Clive's stall. "Isn't this supposed to be under lock and key?"

"It is." Graham pointed to the padlock and chain.

"No, sorry. I meant behind closed doors."

"Don't worry. No one knows it's here and it hasn't been tampered with, as you can see."

"Fair enough," Partial Sue said. "Mind if we have a look round it?"

"Be my guest."

The ladies slowly circled it, Daisy snapping off shot after shot. Intermittently, Fiona stooped down and craned her neck, examining every inch of its wooden surface. After several slow circuits it became apparent that there was really nothing to see. Nothing out of the ordinary, no damage and certainly no clues. The stall was completely intact and exactly the same as all the other stalls currently residing in the Christmas market.

"Can we have a look inside?" Fiona asked.

"Well, I'm not really supposed to, but I guess there's no harm in it." Possibly Malorie's bludgeoning influence coming to their aid once more. Graham fished a large bunch of keys from his pocket, flipped through them and selected one to unlock it. He swung open both doors wide, and while the security lights provided plenty of illumination, the ladies switched on their phone torches just to be on the safe side.

"Wow," Partial Sue remarked. "It's a bit of a mess."

The floor was covered in sprinkles and empty cardboard cups, and various jars and tins that had presumably tumbled out of the storage cupboards, whose doors hung open.

"Oh, yes, sorry about that. The police didn't want anything removed. That's the peril of craning a stall onto a flatbed when it's full of stock. The thing sways around a bit."

Partial Sue stepped in, bent down and did a quick recce inside the cupboards and the fridge, then wrenched them back to have a look behind, but came up empty handed. "Was there booze anywhere, do you know?"

"Booze? I have no idea. I haven't seen the inside since I locked it and took it away. Maybe the police swiped it."

Fiona and Daisy joined Partial Sue, crunching their way around the stall. Graham followed them in, keeping a close eye, his head just missing the rafters. With all four of them inside, conditions were cramped, not unlike a lift that had reached its maximum occupancy, which was just as well. Apart from the mess, there really wasn't much to see, just four plain wood walls, a floor and a roof. No evidence or any means of escape whatsoever. Just a simple Christmas stall like all the others.

Nevertheless, while they had the builder and architect on hand, it was worth an ask. "Is there any way someone could leave this stall bolted from the inside?" Fiona asked.

Graham chuckled to himself. "Ye cannae change the laws of physics." His impression of Scottie from *Star Trek* was terrible. Daisy managed a sympathy titter. Graham cleared his throat and became serious. "No way. The construction is simple, but we build them to last." He did a circuit of the stall, banging the inside of the walls and roof with his sledgehammer fists. "See, they're solid."

Silence descended over the ladies. Though they continued to shine their torches this way and that, it was hard for the building to be anything but what it was. Essentially a wooden box with one way in and one way out. They were no closer to solving the locked-room mystery.

As they exited the stall, Fiona spotted the inside bolt, or what remained of it, hanging forlornly from the door after it had been sawn in half. Graham pointed to it. "That's the only way of escaping a locked stall."

As they regrouped outside, Fiona's mind went off on a different tangent. "I understand that this stall was surplus to requirements. How come you didn't just haul it back here?"

"That was Sophie Haverford's doing. She put in the order and we fulfilled it. The contract was non-refundable. I could've taken it back, but they'd paid for the stall and had to use it."

"I take it that Malorie suggested putting the stall in the little side road," Partial Sue said.

"Oh, no. That was my idea," Graham replied. "On the morning I delivered the stalls, Malorie was none too happy with Sophie, I can tell you. At first Sophie tried to blame me, but I had all the paperwork, showed Malorie her emails. It was all there in black and white. I could see the pair of them about to have a meltdown, so I stepped in. Pointed out the wide pavement in the side road adjacent to Fisherman's Walk. I suggested putting it there and that they rent it at a discount."

"And how did they react to that?"

"Malorie still looked annoyed at Sophie and I'm sure she had words with her later, but I think it avoided a full-scale bust-up between them."

"One last question," Fiona said. "Did you know Clive Preston before all this happened?"

Graham shook his head. "Nah, not at all. I don't really know Southbourne that well, stuck out here in the forest. But I've heard a few people tell me that he was well-known around those parts."

"Okay, thank you. I think we've seen enough." Fiona wanted to leave. She had a tingling sensation in the end of her fingertips. Another suspect had just popped up on her crime radar and she wanted to discuss it immediately with Daisy and Partial Sue.

CHAPTER 31

The ladies had been arguing all morning, although they would never admit it. "Heated discussion" would be the preferred definition of the passionate back-and-forth currently reverberating off the shop's elegant, panelled walls. Fiona had put the cat among the pigeons by proposing Graham as a suspect, justifying this with reasons that were more than a little shaky. "All I'm saying is that he was the one who suggested placing Clive's stall in the side road, right outside Doug's and Trisha's shops."

"Yes, but it wasn't Clive's stall at that point," Daisy countered. "It was an empty, leftover stall. He had no idea who would rent it."

"Yes, but he must've known it would provoke Trisha and Doug," Partial Sue replied. "Having a stall right outside."

"How would he know?" Daisy said. "He's not from Southbourne."

"Doesn't matter," Partial Sue replied. "Any shop owner would be annoyed at having a stall outside their shop. If he murdered Clive, they'd be under suspicion, not him."

Daisy folded her arms. "And just why would Graham want to kill Clive?"

Partial Sue fell silent. Fiona didn't have an answer either, or anything resembling a motive, but then a silly idea popped into her head. "He did seem very protective of his Dickensian stall. Maybe Clive found out about it. Threatened to steal his idea. We know Clive was a bit of a wheeler-dealer." It was a weak argument, and she was about to get punished for it.

"If that's true, why did he show us?" Daisy asked. "Seemed like he couldn't wait to show it off."

"Yes, but he could probably sense we weren't the type of people to build and rent out Christmas stalls."

"Speak for yourself," Daisy sounded offended. "I reckon I could have a good stab at it. Well, if it was made of balsa wood and about a tenth of the size."

Partial Sue's eyes lit up with possibility. "Hey, maybe Clive found out about it. Held him to ransom. Said he'd tell other suppliers unless Graham coughed up the cash. So he had no choice but to kill Clive and make it look like a suicide. Think about it. Those Dickensian market stalls are going to take off. Every town's going to want them. Graham's going to be sitting on a small fortune."

"I have to admit, that is a pretty compelling motive," Fiona added.

"Okay, so Graham kills Clive. How did he get out of the locked stall?" Daisy asked. The immovable problem raised its irrepressible head once more, their train of thought slamming into it, sending carriages jack-knifing everywhere. Partial Sue and Fiona fell silent.

Eventually, Partial Sue shrugged. "I dunno. He built the stall. Probably incorporated a special hatch or a secret door."

"But we didn't see anything like that," Daisy huffed. "It was just a bog-standard stall like all the others."

"What if he switched the stalls around before we got there?" Partial Sue asked. "Maybe the one we looked at was really the caricaturist's stall. And the one with paint on was Clive's stall."

"You've answered your own question," Fiona remarked. "We know it was the caricaturist's stall because it had paint on the front."

"Paint on the doors," Partial Sue corrected. "Doors can be removed. Swapped over."

"But the police examined Clive's stall before any of that happened," Daisy pointed out. "On the morning he was found. They didn't find anything. And if such a hidden feature existed, Graham would've had to add it while he was building the thing, long before he knew Clive would try to blackmail him. As a miniaturist, that's what I would've done."

"Well, we don't know when Clive blackmailed him," Partial Sue said. "Could've been long before the Christmas market. Which left Graham no choice but to create a special stall to kill Clive in — one that he could escape from with a hidden door no one could see."

Daisy screwed up her face, as logic and credibility were stretched to breaking point. "But how would he know Clive would rent the leftover stall? Or that there would even be a leftover stall? That was Sophie Haverford's doing."

Partial Sue snapped her fingers. "Unless Graham doctored the order to make it look like Sophie had made a mistake, so he could slip in his modified stall."

Fiona shook her head. "Sophie might've allowed that, but Malorie never would. She'd have gone through all their emails with a fine-toothed comb until she was certain the mistake was Sophie's."

"And would Clive really rent a stall supplied by the person he was trying to blackmail?" Daisy added.

Partial Sue rubbed her chin. "He could've done that as a constant reminder to Graham that he needed to pay up."

"Seems a bit over the top." Fiona sighed. "He could've just sent him a text. Actually, I'll check with Scott, see if there's any contact between the two of them on Clive's phone." Wearily, she pulled out her phone and sent a message to Scott.

If she was being honest, mental fatigue was setting in and she was beginning to regret suggesting Graham as a suspect. All it had done was connect up the wrong dots and create a more confusing picture. Fiona's phoned pinged. "Scott says there's nothing."

"Clive probably deleted them," Partial Sue snorted. "He's not going to leave incriminating evidence on his phone."

"But he did leave a suicide note," Daisy pointed out.

Partial Sue fired back a response. "Which Graham must have put there."

Rather than an investigation this was beginning to sound like a conspiracy theory. One of the more preposterous ones, and Daisy was about to make it even more unbelievable. "Aren't we forgetting something? For this to be true, Graham also has to be the Southbourne Stalker."

"Why can't he be the Southbourne Stalker as well?" asked Partial Sue.

Fiona was ready to admit defeat and put the kibosh on the theory she herself had proposed. "Because for Graham to be the killer, the murder has to be premeditated. However, we know from our young, anonymous informant that it was anything but. Clive just happened to be passing by the alleyway. Pure chance. The murder was a spur-of-the-moment necessity to silence Clive."

Partial Sue wasn't done with the theory just yet. "Maybe it's a bit of both. Serendipity. Clive was blackmailing Graham. Graham wanted Clive dead. Graham was also the Southbourne Stalker. Clive recognised Graham in the alleyway. Graham seized the opportunity to kill Clive. Two birds, one stone."

"That would be a huge coincidence," Fiona said.

"But it's still possible."

"But improbable," Fiona replied. "How does Graham then escape from the locked stall?"

"Through a hidden trap door," Partial Sue replied.

"But there wasn't one," Daisy was quick to point out.

And with that, they'd come full circle once more. The ideas roundabout had spun and thrown them off, leaving them in a heap, exactly where they were before.

"Sounds like one of those parrot thingies," Daisy proposed. "Chicken and egg."

"Oh, you mean a paradox," Partial Sue said. "I don't think so."

"Yes, it is," Daisy replied. "What came first, the murder or the stall? No, that doesn't make sense. What came first, the blackmail or the . . ."

Fiona's head began to spin as the theories entangled themselves like those pesky cables behind her television set. As Daisy and Partial Sue verbally jousted with no one emerging the winner, Fiona closed her eyes in a bid to soothe the ache burgeoning behind them. She started rubbing the bridge of her nose, and her colleagues immediately ceased their investigative banter.

"Are you okay, Fiona?" Partial Sue asked.

"I might have to take a break. My mind's whirring with all this speculation. It's all over the place."

"Like jelly that hasn't set properly," Daisy proposed.

"Yes. That's what it feels like." Fiona shifted her fingertips to her temples, massaging them with both hands.

Daisy sighed. "That's a pity because I did have something else I've been working on. Another conundrum we need to figure out."

"Sorry, Daisy," Fiona apologised. "I don't think my head can take it at the moment."

"What is it?" Partial Sue was desperate to know.

"Oh, just a little observation," Daisy replied. "I've been examining chewing gum."

CHAPTER 32

Fiona and Partial Sue shuffled their chairs around the table, scooching next to Daisy so they could examine her phone screen. With fingers on fast forward, she prodded a social media app, flicked and swiped, until she arrived at a page awash with images of a modern trend that Fiona could never fathom. That desire to post pictures of an item of food or drink that had just been purchased, as if it was a trophy, or a rare artefact that had never seen the light of day. What was the point? To make people jealous? Hungry? Thirsty?

"It's probably nothing," Daisy reassured them. "But I've been on social media. Looking at shots of hot chocolate."

"Why would you do that?" Partial Sue asked with a slightly derogatory tone.

"Because I like looking at them."

"Fair enough."

"I found some bought from Clive's stall," Daisy said.

Gazing at the photos amassed on her screen, Fiona could see the allure. Clive's hot chocolates were little works of art. Handheld festive sculptures of whipped cream, marshmallows and sprinkles with a miniature candy cane popping out of each one at the same jaunty angle. Clive had been nothing if not consistent with his arrangement of sweet condiments. Each image appeared almost identical, except with a different customer's hand proudly holding aloft the recently purchased beverage, with Clive's stall directly behind.

"They almost look too good to drink," Fiona said.

"Some people wish they hadn't," Partial Sue said, "judging by these comments. Listen to this: 'Pretty to look at, pretty nasty to drink.' Or this: 'Very expensive hand warmer. Don't bother.'"

"Yes, Clive hadn't won any fans in the taste department," Daisy added. "But they did make great images to share. I've picked these shots because of the angle they were taken." She enlarged one with her fingers, closing in on the edge of Clive's stall, specifically a splodge of discarded chewing gum on the pavement in front of it.

"Urgh!" Partial Sue baulked at the flattened grimy grey glob.

"I know," Daisy agreed. "At first it made me quite queasy. But I've seen so many of them now, I've got used to them."

"You've been looking at a lot of chewing gum?" Fiona asked.

"Oh, yes, but mostly just this one. I wanted to gather enough evidence to make sure I wasn't seeing things."

"And what is it you've seen?"

"Well, people drop chewing gum everywhere. It's like the pavement's got measles. But they're also a bit like snowflakes."

Fiona couldn't think of anything more diametrically opposed than spat-out chewing gum and snowflakes. One pure, delicate and exquisitely beautiful, the other a disgusting and unhygienic blight on our streets. But she guessed the comparison Daisy was trying to make. "You mean they're all different shapes and sizes."

"Exactly, each one's different. This one here's shaped like your appendix."

Fiona instantly preferred Daisy's previous snowflake comparison. "And why is that important?"

"So it can't be confused with any other piece of gum."

Fiona's headache was on the rise again, her tinnitus too, simmering in the background like a kettle about to boil. She needed Daisy to quickly get to the point. "So what's this got to do with Clive's murder?"

Daisy began enlarging each image. "You can see the gum's in exactly the same place in every picture. About four inches from the edge of Clive's stall." She swiped to the final shot. "This was taken on Friday the nineteenth of December, the last day Clive was alive. Now, compare it to this image, taken after Clive's death but before his stall was removed." Daisy swiped along to a duller and far less joyful shot. The hot chocolate was conspicuous by its absence and the stall was shut up tight. "The angle's a little different, but if I enlarge it, you can clearly see something has changed."

The appendix-shaped gum was now closer to the stall, just an inch away. Fiona gasped. "The stall has moved."

"Yes, it looks that way," Daisy said. "And it must have happened on the night he died."

Partial Sue wasn't having any of this. "Wait a minute. Fiona, didn't you say Scott and a few others tried to break into the stall, bashing it with their shoulders on the morning Clive was found dead. They've probably just nudged it a bit."

"I didn't see the stall move, but even if it did, the direction would be wrong. They were attempting to break into the doors at the front. If it had moved the stall would be further away from the gum. Not closer to it."

Partial Sue maintained her cynical stance. "Okay, maybe a car backed into it. Or one of the cars being dropped off at the garage for its MOT bumped it out of position."

"There's not a mark on the stall," Daisy pointed out. "Remember, we examined every inch of it, inside and out. If a car had gone into it, surely there'd be some damage. Splintered wood, scuff marks at least."

Partial Sue squirmed and fidgeted in her chair as the uncomfortable evidence mounted up. "Okay, so the stall's moved. How does this help our enquiry? As you both keep reminding me, how did the killer get in and out?"

While the slightly shifting stall was a huge revelation, it hadn't actually moved them any closer to a suspect, the identity of the Southbourne Stalker or how anyone could've carried out the murder.

"Okay," Fiona said. "It's a clue. A very big one. We just have to make sense of it, or use it to build a picture of what happened that night. At some point, Clive's stall moved. That has to be significant."

"How or why would the killer need to move the stall three inches?" Partial Sue asked.

"The why we've yet to discover," Fiona said. "But the how, that's something we could find out. We should call Graham, he'd know."

"We already know how he moves his stalls," Partial Sue harrumphed. "He's got that dirty great big lorry with a crane on the back. Slings a couple of harnesses underneath them."

"Yes, but you couldn't use something as big and noisy as that in the dead of night. And what would be the point of going to all that trouble to move a stall a few inches? We need to ask him if there's a quieter, easier alternative."

Partial Sue held up a hand. "Wait. What if he's the murderer? I'm not sure how the moving stall fits into all this, but we'd be tipping him off that we know about it. He could do a runner or, worse, silence us like he silenced Clive."

Daisy shrank in her seat. "Oh, I don't like the sound of that. Sue's right — we need to be careful with this information."

This thought sobered Fiona up immediately. The moving stall played a huge part in all this somehow, but for now they needed to keep it close to their chests, which meant keeping Graham out of the loop.

CHAPTER 33

Fiona pulled out her phone, cleared her throat and prepared her best journalistic voice. This was the default character she adopted when she needed to extract information without revealing who she was — an amateur detective investigating a murder, which would have the recipient hanging up faster than Simon Le Bon pouncing on a dropped sausage.

She had remembered Graham stating that Christmas market stalls were much of a muchness, and from the various websites the ladies had perused, he wasn't wrong. A temporary yet ubiquitous feature of towns up and down the country at this time of year, the stalls were essentially the same glorified garden shed, some bigger, some smaller, with a few slight embellishments here and there. It was no wonder Graham was hoping to become the leading supplier with his unique Dickensian creation. However, for now, with the very limited choice of stalls on offer, the ladies were hoping that the same techniques would apply to moving them around, which would allow them to pick the brains of someone other than Graham. A supplier who would be far away enough to be insulated from the goings on in Southbourne.

After a cursory search, they settled on a supplier in Norwich, imaginatively called Norwich Timber Buildings. Fiona dialled the number and put it on speakerphone so Daisy and Partial Sue could earwig.

"Yeah?" a brusque voice answered. "I mean, Norwich Timber Buildings."

"Oh, hello. I'm from—"

"Whatever it is you're selling, I ain't buying."

"Oh, sorry. I'm not selling anything. I'm a journalist writing a feature on Christmas markets. I wondered if I could ask you a few questions."

"Long as it's not too many. Fire away."

Fiona's first forays were intended to be dummy questions. Trivial icebreakers to get the ball rolling — how many stalls do you supply each year? What are they made of? Why do you think people love Christmas markets?" Then she moved onto the real nitty gritty. "So how do you move all these market stalls into place? It must be a Herculean task."

"Nah, we have a flatbed truck. Load it up with as many stalls as we can, then crane them into place. Repeat the process till the job's done."

So far it was consistent with Graham's account. "Are there any other ways to move a stall?" Fiona asked.

"Not really."

"Okay, say a stall was already in place and the stall-holder wasn't happy with the position. How would you move it?"

The guy snorted. "Oh, yeah. That happens all the time. Stall-holders whingeing 'cos they think someone's got a better pitch than them. We just turn up with the flatbed again. Sling the harnesses underneath, shift it somewhere else."

"Is there any other way to move a market stall?"

"S'pose you could use a forklift. Not the little electric ones in B&Q. I mean the big fellas you get on building sites. Like a diesel Manitou."

The answers were not dovetailing with the idea of a stall being stealthily moved in the middle of the night. Fiona had one more avenue to explore. "Okay, now this is a bit of fun for our readers. We want to ask them a little quiz question. How many people would it take to move a stall? Not far, maybe just three inches."

An exhalation of air distorted the line. "You'd need a lot of strong backs. Maybe a rugby scrum could do it. Say, eight big fellas. That would be shunting it along the ground. Not lifting it. A stall's too unwieldy. Nothing to grab hold of. Anyway, I'd better go . . ."

"So, is there no other way you can move a stall?" Fiona asked desperately.

"Not that I can think of. Not without something big and mechanical."

"Thank you, that's been very helpful." Fiona hung up.

"Okay," said Partial Sue. "So our options are either a big diesel forklift or half a rugby team. Both of which would be very hard to come by in the middle of the night, especially for the Southbourne Stalker doing this alone, on the spur of the moment."

"And noisy too," Daisy added. "Half a rugby team trying to keep their voices down in the early hours? Impossible."

Fiona sighed. "And it's all far too over-engineered just to move a stall three inches. It doesn't make sense. We're missing something."

A discussion would have ensued, probably a heated one, like the last time. Ideas and theories being proposed and debated, mercilessly scrutinised and analysed to test their robustness. But the ladies had nothing. Not an idea, a thought or an utterance to offer up. The illogical nature of the situation had them stumped. The slightly shifting stall refused to budge any further. Silence reigned as minds cogitated, brain cells straining at the edge of reason, attempting to twist and grapple with the problem and bring it into submission. Trouble was, the problem itself had the ladies in a headlock without a hope of breaking free.

Half an hour later, Fiona's phone buzzed. She recognised the area code for Norwich.

"'Ello?" said a gruff voice. "Is that the journalist I was talking to earlier about the stalls?"

"Er, yes," Fiona replied.

"Right, I haven't been totally honest with you."

Fiona thought the supplier was about to confess to Clive's murder. "Oh, how so?"

"There is a way you can move a Christmas stall without a crane or a forklift."

"Yes, go on . . ." Fiona attempted to calm her excitement, while around her Partial Sue and Daisy did nothing to contain theirs, nearly falling off their chairs as they leaned closer, straining to hear.

CHAPTER 34

A tantalising pause hovered on the other end of the phone as the supplier of Norwich's Christmas stalls gathered his thoughts. "There are a few places where the streets are too narrow for our flatbed. We can't drive up to the site and offload the stalls with the crane."

"So, what do you do?" Fiona asked.

"Well, mostly I try to avoid supplying to places like that because it's too much hassle. Sometimes I whack more on the bill to cover the extra time, or hope it puts them off."

"And if it doesn't?"

"We deliver the stalls in kit form. The parts are loaded onto the flatbed — walls, floor, roof and doors stacked up on the back. We park as close as we can, then carry them the rest of the way, one by one. Reassemble them at the other end. It's a two-man job, mind. Each piece is too heavy for one person to carry."

"And how long does it take to reassemble a stall?"

"'Bout half an hour for each one. But that's not including lugging each bit. Sometimes takes us all day to put up seven stalls."

"That's so interesting," Fiona replied. "Our readers are going to love hearing about this."

The supplier didn't seem convinced. "Really? Sounds pretty dull to me. But then I've been doing it for donkey's years."

"Believe me, this is great stuff." Fiona thanked him again and hung up. The muscles of her face couldn't help contorting into the widest of grins. She glanced at her colleagues, but they didn't mirror her gleeful expression. Their initial excitement had swiftly subsided, replaced by crushing disappointment. "Why so glum? This answers a lot."

"Does it?" Partial Sue fired back. "Are you suggesting our killer grabbed a screwdriver from somewhere and started taking a market stall to bits in the middle of the night, just so he could move it three inches?"

"Clive was with him," Daisy said. "Maybe he helped him. After all, that chap said it was a two-man job."

Partial Sue glared at Daisy. "Why would Clive help him?"

Daisy shrugged. "People do silly things when they've had a bit to drink."

"Yep, I agree with that," Partial Sue said. "Except Clive had just witnessed him attack someone in an alleyway. I doubt he'd give him a hand moving his stall. And why move it just three inches?"

"Okay," Fiona agreed. "I don't know the whys and wherefores of what happened that night. But this answers one very big question."

Her two colleagues were stupefied, clearly not catching her drift.

"The locked-room mystery."

Their expressions didn't improve, still clueless as to how Fiona could have arrived at this conclusion.

"How does it solve the locked-room mystery?" Daisy asked.

Fiona was baffled that they couldn't see it. "The stalls can be disassembled. The killer removes a wall. Puts Clive inside — I don't know, maybe Clive's unconscious at this point or too woozy to put up a fight. He murders him, then slides the bolt across from the inside to make it look like Clive's locked himself in. He exits the stall where the wall's missing, then reattaches it. That's the only way it could've been done."

Partial Sue winced, not buying it. "That poses too many problems for our killer. Assuming he can get the wall off, he has to shift it to one side, all by himself. Remember, the supplier said those things are heavy, takes two people to lift them. If he accidentally loses his grip and it falls over, it's going to make such a racket. And he has to do all this while Clive's unconscious or semi-conscious, then hoist him up from a rafter. That's going to be a struggle. Then he has to lift the wall back in place and reattach it. This killer has to be one hell of a cool customer, not to mention strong as an ox, to do all that out in public. Okay, I know it's Southbourne in the dead of night but it's still a massive risk."

"Don't forget, he also has to break into Clive's phone and leave the suicide note," Daisy pointed out.

"Oh, yes," Partial Sue said. "Even if he uses facial recognition, that's still going to take time. Every second he's out on the pavement doing all that, he's exposed. Risks being discovered. It's too much of a stretch."

"And we still don't know why the stall has moved three inches," Daisy added.

The euphoria that had flooded Fiona's mind moments earlier suddenly evaporated. She'd convinced herself that she'd cracked the locked-room mystery and had become so overwhelmed by it that she hadn't stopped to consider all the very awkward implications. She bit the inside of her lip self-consciously, accepting the inevitable reality of the situation. "You're right. It is a bit of a stretch."

"I'm sorry," Partial Sue apologised. "It's a really good solution in theory but in practice it's just not feasible."

The atmosphere became drenched in negative energy as, once more, the case refused to give up any of its secrets, at least none that were credible. It had them beaten at every turn. The ladies descended into silence, one that threatened to stretch out indefinitely.

Daisy finally broke the quiet deadlock with an extraneous issue that had been troubling her. "What I can't understand is if Christmas stalls can be taken apart, what's to stop thieves removing a wall in the night, then stealing everything inside? Well, apart from it being very conspicuous."

"Hm," Partial Sue murmured. "We're not investigating a theft, but that is an interesting point."

For want of something better to do — Fiona couldn't stomach another defeated silence — she picked up the phone. "You know what? I'm going to ask our Norwich supplier."

Daisy became worried. "Oh, it was just a silly thought. I don't want to waste his time."

"Well, I'd like to know," Partial Sue said. "Plus, we haven't got much else on our plate. Apart from a case that makes no sense at all."

Fiona dialled the number. It was answered first ring. "'Ello."

"Oh, hi. It's Fiona again, the journalist. I just thought of another question to ask you, if you don't mind."

"Oh, er, sure. Go ahead."

"When you said the stalls can be assembled, what's to stop a couple of burglars unscrewing a wall, then taking everything inside."

"Why, you're not thinking of breaking into one, are you?" he chuckled.

"Good gracious, no," Fiona replied. "It's just, I didn't want to put that information out there and encourage a spate of Christmas market burglaries."

"Ah, yes. Well, you don't need to worry," he reassured her. "Firstly, they're not screwed together, they're bolted. We use an industrial impact wrench to do them up. Can't be undone by hand. And secondly, each bolt is secured with a lock nut."

"So what's an impact wrench and what's a lock nut?" Fiona had a vague idea but wanted to make sure she was on the same page.

"You'll have seen them before," he replied. "You've probably got lock nuts on your car wheels. They have a special shape to stop thieves stealing them, and an impact wrench is the gun that garages use to remove wheel nuts. Sounds like a dentist drill."

Daisy and Partial Sue's mouths became shaped like doughnut holes and their eyes equally wide. Fiona nearly dropped the phone. "Sorry, did you say a garage?"

"That's right, 'cept theirs are hooked up to compressed air hoses, whereas ours are rechargeable electric ones because they have to be portable."

Fiona hung up without saying goodbye. She didn't mean to, but the massive revelation caused her finger to jab the "end call" button quite spontaneously.

This time, the ladies all shared the same expression. One of alarmed disbelief. They all spoke one name at precisely the same moment. "Tony De Costa."

CHAPTER 35

Cold, debilitating shock ensnared Fiona's body — the realisation blindsiding her. It would've knocked her off her feet had she not been sitting down. The friendly mechanic with a penchant for bratwursts, and possibly Fiona, had to be the killer. He had access to everything he'd have needed to pull off Clive's murder. Specifically, an impact wrench. Indeed, they'd heard them, buzzing away every time they'd passed his garage. Removing lock nuts would be a doddle for him. He could've had them off in a jiffy.

"Are you okay, Fiona?" Daisy asked.

"Why wouldn't I be okay?" A wave of heat passed over Fiona's skin.

"Well, he seemed to take a shine to you," Partial Sue added.

Fiona waved away their concerns. "I told you, it's nothing." But it wasn't nothing. If Fiona truly examined her feelings, she'd taken a shine to him too, but she had to put those feelings to one side. Treat him like a suspect, cold and dispassionate.

Usually, with startling revelations such as this, Daisy's delicate sensibilities would be triggered and she'd have one or both hands clamped over her mouth to prevent any almighty gasps from escaping, but on this occasion, they remained firmly in her lap. "Er, I don't want to be a Daisy Downer, but don't we still have the same problems as before?"

Fiona and Partial Sue both studied her, unsure where she was going with this.

"Clive's stall is out on the pavement," Daisy explained. "Tony De Costa's tools are in his garage."

"Oh, don't worry," Partial Sue reassured her. "Those impact wrenches are connected to really stretchy hoses, like the curly cables on old telephones. They'd easily reach Clive's stall. It's only a few metres away."

Daisy frowned. "No, it's not that. Tony De Costa has to do all this out on the street, using noisy power tools, then removing a heavy wall all by himself."

Partial Sue became crestfallen. "Oh, I see what you mean."

"We shouldn't lose heart," Fiona said. "Tony De Costa is the best suspect yet. He's ticking a lot of very big boxes. We just have a few small ones left empty."

"I'll say," Partial Sue agreed. "Small but pivotal."

"Yes, small but pivotal." Fiona liked that phrase. Something about it had sparked a light at the very darkest recesses of her mind. Barely a flicker, it had illuminated briefly then snuffed out. "Small but pivotal." She repeated the three words like a mantra.

"Fiona, are you all right?" Daisy asked again, probably worried about her romantic entanglement with the mechanic.

Nothing could be further from Fiona's mind, for now. "Yes, I'm just thinking out loud. Tony De Costa definitely has the know-how and the tools to pull this off. We just haven't figured out his technique. Maybe something in his garage enabled him to do this without being seen or heard."

"Like what?" asked Partial Sue.

Fiona shrugged.

"Maybe we should go and have a gander at his tools, right this instant," Partial Sue suggested.

"But what would we say?" Fiona asked. "Hi, Tony, can we have a nose at your stuff? We think you used it to kill Clive and cover up his murder?"

"No, we make something up," Partial Sue huffed. "Pretend you're writing a piece on garages, just like you did with the chap in Norwich."

"Tony knows I'm not a journalist and I don't want to tip him off that we think he's guilty. If we suddenly go poking around his workshop, he's going to put two and two together . . ."

"And murder us," Daisy shuddered. "Just like he did Clive. I'm not setting foot in there."

"Plus, I think we need more evidence," Fiona said. "At the moment it's all too circumstantial. The only thing linking him with the murder are some lock nuts and an impact wrench. Other garages in Southbourne have them."

"Yes, but Clive's stall wasn't right outside theirs," Partial Sue pointed out.

"Again, circumstantial," Fiona replied.

Partial Sue sighed defeatedly. "Okay, but how are we going to get evidence if we're too frightened to go in his garage? Hey! Maybe you could . . ." Her voice trailed off.

"Maybe I could what?" Fiona asked, convinced she was going to suggest something along the lines of Fiona going in there to flirt with him while slyly extracting the information like a modern-day Mata Hari.

Knowing this wouldn't be a good idea, Partial Sue swiftly snuffed out her suggestion. "Nothing."

Daisy had been fiddling away on her phone. She held it up as if it were the Holy Grail. "We can use the power of the internet."

The other two ladies peered at the screen.

"Tony's garage has a social media account?" Fiona couldn't grasp why anyone would want to follow a garage online, much less gaze at something so banal as cars having their brake pads changed or oil topped up. Okay, food she could sort of understand, but everyday runabouts in various states of disrepair? It didn't track with her.

"Tony's son does all the posting." Daisy began swiping through image after image. It wasn't what you'd call visually appealing, unless you had a fetish for cars on ramps, cars with bonnets open, cars jacked up, missing their wheels or body panels. Daisy scrolled faster and faster as the images merged into one monotonous blur of a busy back street garage, cluttered with grease-smeared tools and parts strewn over the floor. Daisy's finger abruptly halted as one image stood out from the rest. Tony reclined on a beaten sofa by the reception desk, toasting the end of a busy week with a shot of whisky.

Fiona stabbed at Daisy's phone screen. "If he makes a habit of celebrating every Friday with a nip of whisky, he's bound to keep a bottle on site."

"That could be where the extra drink in Clive's system came from," Partial Sue said. "A couple of shots of whisky is about the equivalent of a pint. Tony probably lured him back to the garage with the offer of a drink, promising to explain his antics in the alleyway." Partial Sue held up her hands and attempted an impression of the mechanic. "'I wasn't attacking him. We were having a laugh. He's my son's friend,' or something like that."

"Yes, and Tony drinks at the Countess of Strathmore now and then," Fiona added. "He's probably seen Clive a few times getting dozy by the bar at last orders. He knows he just needs to get him back to that sofa, get another drink down him and he'll be out in no time, or at least very pliable. Let's keep scrolling."

Sure enough, a similar picture appeared of Tony celebrating a different end of the week, except in this one, he was cracking open a brand-new bottle of Scotch.

"Okay, so he definitely keeps a bottle in the garage," Partial Sue said. "He's got the booze to ply Clive with another drink, he's got the tools to get into the stall, and he's got the motive — silencing the one and only witness to his crimes. We just need to figure out how he did it — unless he was extremely foolhardy and did everything out on the pavement and just got lucky."

"No, I don't think so," Fiona replied. "He'd been discovered once already that night. He wouldn't risk it again."

"We've got two parts of the mystery that make sense," Partial Sue said. "The beginning and the end, we're just missing the middle."

"It's a mystery sandwich," Daisy muttered, still flicking through pictures of the garage. A self-confessed social media addict, she enjoyed a good swipe through anything, even if it was a sea of automotive repair work.

"Okay, let's try the Sherlock Holmes technique," Fiona proposed. "Eliminate the impossible and whatever remains, however improbable, must be the truth."

"Everything about this is impossible," Partial Sue grumbled.

"Okay, what's the most impossible way he could remove a wall, kill Clive and lock him in the stall without anyone noticing?"

Partial Sue thought for a moment. "He lifts up the stall all by himself and silently carries it into his garage, then shuts the metal sliding door behind him, so no one can see or hear what he's up to. Totally impossible. Unless he's Superman."

"But he lifts cars every day," Daisy said.

"Who, Superman?" Partial Sue scoffed.

"No, Tony." Daisy flipped her phone around and showed them an image of him working on a Toyota Corolla up on one side, supported by a red trolley jack. "That car must weigh the same or more than a stall."

"Aha!" Fiona exclaimed. "Small but pivotal."

Partial Sue didn't share their optimism. "While I would concede that the trolley jack in that picture is easily capable of lifting a stall, and has wheels to potentially move the thing, it is, as you said, Fiona — pivotal. It can only lift one side at a time. The other side's not going anywhere, so neither is the rest of it."

"What if he used two trolley jacks?" Fiona suggested. "I bet Tony's got more than one. What if he put one at the back and one at the front?"

"Too unstable," Partial Sue replied. "It's going to seesaw all over the place."

"But he doesn't need to lift it very high off the ground," Daisy said. "Just an inch or two."

"One side is still going to end up dragging along the ground," Partial Sue countered.

"What if he uses four jacks?" Fiona said. "One at each corner. Then it wouldn't tip over."

Partial Sue rolled her eyes. "A stall isn't meant to move. Even with wheels at each corner, that thing's going to be a nightmare to push, if he's able to get it going at all. Let's not forget, he's in a hurry. Has to get it inside before anyone sees him. Look, I know it only has to travel a few feet across flat pavement, but it's going to be at a snail's pace. Not to mention, trying to control the thing. Can you imagine trying to pull and steer a market stall at the same time? It'd be impossible for one person."

"What if he had help?" Fiona asked.

"Where's he going to get help from in the early hours of Saturday morning, and just who would be willing to be an accomplice to murder?"

In the grim light of reality, the promising theory began to fade, until Daisy came to its rescue. "Okay, there are problems with it, but I do think that's what's happened in some form or another."

"Come on," Partial Sue protested. "It's bunkum."

"But think about it," Daisy replied. "If he's wheeled the stall inside the garage somehow, removed a wall and done the horrible deed, he then has to wheel it back out again. No matter how cool and calm he is, Tony's going to be desperate to get it back out onto the pavement, quick as a flash. Except he's not quite managed to get it in the same position. The chewing gum proves that."

Fiona clicked her fingers. "Of course! That's it, Daisy. That's why the stall's moved only three inches. Either he hasn't realised it's slightly out of position because he's in a hurry, or he's hoping no one would notice."

Partial Sue shook her head. "Sorry, I can't see it myself."

"Okay, but we should at least test out the theory," Fiona said.

Partial Sue baulked in her seat. "I hope you're not suggesting we hire four trolley jacks, wheel them around the corner and start hand-cranking market stalls up in the air."

Daisy had her nose deep in her phone. "The trolley jack in the picture is called a Mighty XL. It's written on the side. I'm on their website now. Says it's capable of lifting five tonnes and has some interesting features." She flipped her phone around and showed them a promotional shot of the trolley jack in all its shiny red glory, with annotations littered around the edge, highlighting its many benefits. "Look at that round thing on the end of the arm that lifts up. It's the bit that the car rests on. Says it's called a saddle and those circular ridges around the outside are to stop the car from slipping off. Now, I don't know anything about trolley jacks, but I do know about wood. The stalls are spruce. Hardy, but it's still a softwood. If a trolley jack was to lift Clive's stall, those ridges will have dug into it."

"They'll have marked the bottom of the stall," Fiona agreed. "Where no one, not even the police, would've looked."

While still not fully on board with the idea, Partial Sue had to concede. "There'd be proof, one way or the other."

Like a single entity, the ladies rose from their seats. Partial Sue grabbed her car keys and Fiona clipped Simon Le Bon's lead to his collar. They shrugged on their coats and left the shop, pausing briefly to lock the door behind them. Without conferring, they all knew their next destination — New Forest Wooden Buildings.

CHAPTER 36

Fiona called ahead to inform Graham that they were about to pay him an impromptu visit, accompanied by the bizarre request to examine the underside of Clive's stall. He refused, of course, saying he was far too busy, not to mention how difficult it would be. Fiona pleaded a few more times and each time, Graham denied her request. This forced Fiona's hand. She had to do whatever it took to see what was under that stall. She decided to drop the M-bomb. "Let me give Malorie a ring. I'll probably leave it to her to organise a more convenient time with you."

Graham's tone became laced with fear. "Oh, I'm sure Malorie doesn't need to be involved in this."

"Well, she is the organiser of the Christmas market, so officially everything has to be run past her. I'm sure you understand."

Under the threat of Malorie's freckled fist, Graham immediately capitulated. "You know what, I'm just looking at my schedule. I do have a window if you can get down here now."

"We can certainly do that."

Twenty minutes later, they pulled into New Forest Wooden Buildings to find the car park dominated by Graham's flatbed truck. Clive's stall dangled in the air about six feet above the ground, suspended by two thick harnesses.

As they exited Partial Sue's car, Graham climbed out of the cab, a hesitant smile playing in his lips. "I thought I'd get it all ready for you."

"Thank you so much." Fiona thought she'd put the cooperative supplier at his ease. "No need to involve Malorie in this. In fact, when I see her next, I'll say how helpful you've been."

His shoulders relaxed and his smile turned into a proper one. "Oh, er, okay. Great."

Simon Le Bon regarded the stall, a disconcerted growl escaping from his sneering lips as it swayed very slightly in the December breeze.

"Can I just check something first?" Fiona asked. "Are your stalls bolted together?"

"And secured with lock nuts?" Partial Sue added.

"Yes, that's right," Graham replied.

Now that was out of the way, the ladies began crunching across the gravel to examine the stall, but Graham obstructed them. "Can I just ask what it is you're actually looking for?"

"Marks," Daisy replied.

"Marks?" Graham asked.

"We think someone moved Clive's stall using a trolley jack," Partial Sue explained.

"Why would they do that?" Graham asked innocently.

"We're not a hundred per cent sure," Fiona fibbed. "It's just a theory at the moment. Would it be possible to have a look?"

"Of course, be my guest." Graham gestured to the hanging stall.

The ladies assembled around it, but Daisy hesitated. "Is it safe to go under there? It's not going to drop on our heads like Dorothy's house on the Wicked Witch of the East?"

Graham chuckled. "No, I've delivered hundreds of stalls like this. I'll come under with you if you don't believe me." He ducked his large frame beneath the hanging structure as it creaked and groaned. The ladies edged warily behind him, although they had no need to lower their posture. Their fears, however, were quickly allayed, as they became distracted by the evidence they sought. The marks were immediately obvious in the otherwise unsullied wood. Three large, deep, circular bite marks, as if an animal had sunk its teeth into the pine. Two at the front and one at the rear.

"Well, I'll be," said Graham, fingering the splintered indentations.

"That's what you call conclusive proof," Partial Sue chirped.

"How did you know they'd be here?" Graham asked.

"Bit of deduction. Bit of luck," Daisy answered.

"Well," Graham said, "if these were made by a trolley jack, they've definitely been put in the right place."

"What makes you say that?" Fiona asked.

"Well, the front two are about a metre apart, wide enough to keep the thing stable but close enough so one person can pull both jacks at once. They can steer the thing too. The one at the back is dead centre and can be used to push."

"That implies it's a two-man job," Partial Sue said.

"Oh, yes. Even with industrial trolley jacks it would take more than one person to move a stall. But they also knew what they were doing. See how they've placed the jacks under the frame, where it can take the weight? If they'd placed them under the floor, they would've ripped straight through it."

Was this further evidence that a mechanic had done this? Possibly, but then again, most people who owned a car knew the importance of placing a jack in the right spot. However, not everyone would've thought of that when lifting up a stall. Fiona certainly wouldn't have.

Daisy began snapping pictures of the marks with her phone, taking close-ups and shots from all angles. When she'd slotted her phone away, Fiona said, "Well, thank you, Graham. You've been extremely helpful. We'd better be on our way."

"Oh, just one last thing," Daisy asked. "Do you have a tape measure I could borrow?"

CHAPTER 37

At last, everything was lining up and pointing to Tony as the killer. All they needed was one last piece of evidence for it to be indisputable. "Tony had to have had an accomplice," Fiona stated.

Partial Sue pointed the car towards Southbourne as they emerged from the forest. "But like we've already said, where's he going to get help in the middle of the night, and who's going to be silly enough to take part in a murder?"

Fiona remembered Tony's disparaging words about his son. "What about Joe?"

"Oh my gosh," Daisy gasped. "Do you really think Tony would be that cruel to involve his own son in a murder?"

"Why not?" Fiona replied. "If Tony is the stalker and cold-hearted enough to terrorise people late at night, I don't think he's going to think twice about involving Joe. And he's desperate. But Joe is the perfect choice. Loyal to his father and trusted to keep his secret. Blood's thicker than water."

"Okay, let's assume he did," Partial Sue said. "How's he going to convince Joe to leave his bedroom in the middle of the night? What's he going to say, 'Er . . . hi, son, I'm the

Southbourne Stalker and I need to kill someone whose just caught me in the act. Can you give me a hand?'"

"Do you really think Joe would fall for that?" Daisy asked.

"I'm not sure," Fiona replied. "I think Tony would probably spin it a bit better than that. But Joe always does whatever his dad tells him to do."

Partial Sue suddenly sat upright. "You've just given me an idea. If Tony needed help, regardless of who it was, he'd have needed to call them. We should check his records."

"That's a brilliant idea." Fiona pulled her phone from her pocket. When it came to advanced telecoms technology, the ladies had absolutely no idea how to acquire such not-strictly legal information, but they knew someone who did. Freya ran the local computer repair shop on Southbourne Grove, an innocent little outfit that sold dusty, refurbished PCs with unusual names, replaced cracked screens and uploaded new versions of Windows for the neighbourhood's not-so-computer-literate community. But what most people didn't know was that Freya, a towering female athlete with an addiction to cage fighting, had left a highly paid position in a London tech company to look after her father's shop when he retired. The capital's loss was the ladies' gain. Ever since she'd arrived, they'd had access to her alarmingly brilliant IT skills and, more importantly, she wasn't afraid to bend, twist and tickle the rules. She didn't do this for anyone. Only the ladies. One, because she liked them, and two, because she knew they only ever called on her when they wanted information that would put away bad guys.

Freya's breathy voice came on the phone. "Hi, Fiona. What can I do for you?"

"Are you okay to talk? You sound puffed out."

"No, I'm fine. Just done a minute on the speedball." Half of Freya's shop had been converted to a gym so she could work out during the quieter moments. "Please, fire away."

"Sorry to bother you with this, but we need the mobile phone records of someone called Tony De Costa — he runs the garage adjacent to Fisherman's Walk."

"Yeah, I know the one."

"Specifically, any calls he made in the early hours of Saturday the twentieth of November and who he made them to."

"Consider it done. I'll get back to you as soon as I have an answer."

"Thank you so much." Fiona gave her Tony's mobile number, then hung up.

"This should be interesting," Partial Sue remarked. "Final nail in the coffin, methinks."

"I hope so," Fiona replied. "We'll definitely have enough to go to the police, and we can update Daph. Make sure Scott gets the payout he's due."

"And we can get our fee," Partial Sue added. "I can get my new toaster."

"Then we should donate the rest of it to Dogs Need Nice Homes," Fiona added.

"Yes, of course," Partial Sue agreed. "Unless there's anything you want?"

"No, I've got everything I need. What about you, Daisy?"

Daisy gazed up from her phone. "Sorry, I wasn't listening. I've been looking at trolley jacks."

"I was just wondering if you needed anything from Daph's fee?"

"Oh, no," Daisy replied. "I'm fine. But there are a couple of other things I need."

"What's that?" Fiona asked.

"A very quick fact-checking mission around Southbourne. Won't take long."

"What's the other thing?"

"A cup of tea. I'm gasping after all the excitement."

Partial Sue licked her lips. "Now you're talking."

"Well, it's going to get a whole lot more exciting once we get those records from Freya," Fiona said.

The fact-checking mission didn't take very long, and as soon as they'd returned to the shop, the kettle went on and the tea came out. After the initial "ahhs" of heartfelt satisfaction and bursts of "Oh, that's better," subsequent sips were made in contemplative silence as they waited for Freya's call. Nothing could really move forward until they had the final necessary component that would make Tony's nocturnal stall-shifting possible. Without this accessory to murder, none of it could've happened. It wasn't physically possible and would therefore be very difficult to make the evidence stick — apart from the chewing gum, of course.

All eyes gravitated to Fiona's phone laying idle on the table as they collectively urged it to ring. They drained their cups and poured another but still the thing refused to light up with a call. A few customers entered the shop and browsed around, forcing the ladies to abandon their phone monitoring and return to their day jobs, offering advice and ringing purchases into the till. At least this was a pleasant if momentary distraction, even if it didn't bring the phone any closer to ringing.

Finally, at about four o'clock, it happened. Fiona snatched up her phone before it had a chance to ring a second time. She put it on speakerphone. "Hello, Freya!"

"Hi, Fiona. Okay, I've got the information you wanted. So, Tony De Costa never made any calls in the early hours of Saturday morning. Last one he made was Friday evening about 7.08 p.m. to a pizza restaurant, I'm guessing to order a delivery or make a reservation."

"He didn't make any calls later on?" Fiona asked.

"None whatsoever."

"Are you sure?" Partial Sue asked.

"Positive. The records don't lie. However, he did receive a call in the early hours of Saturday morning."

Fiona felt her brow rippling with confusion. "Wait, what?"

"Someone called him at about five past one," Freya replied.

"Who?" Partial Sue asked.

"Not sure, but it came from his garage's landline."

"His garage's landline?" Fiona's brain stalled, its cells and neural pathways going into lockdown.

"I'm guessing that doesn't fit with the narrative you've got for this guy," Freya remarked.

"No, it doesn't. Unless . . ." The phone slid through Fiona's fingers. She managed to grasp it before it hit the floor. She held it up once more, as her mind fizzed and raced. "Oh my. Thank you, Freya. We've got to go."

"My pleasure." Freya hung up.

Fiona tossed the phone on the table as if it were live with electricity. Both her friends shared the same stunned expressions — eyes wild and mouths mute with disbelief at the unexpected twist that now had their heads whirling. Only two people worked at that garage and, as far as Fiona knew, had access to it. If a call had been made from its landline in the early hours of Saturday morning to Tony De Costa's mobile, there was only one person who could've made it.

CHAPTER 38

The last vestiges of blue were chased from the winter sky, pursued by the oncoming night. Though still on the mild side, the air quickly turned damp, and Fiona's lungs tightened with each moistened breath. She coughed slightly as they rounded the corner and were confronted by the dazzling little carnival of festive joy. How she wished she could be part of it, indulging in the delightful frivolity of snacking on food that she knew wasn't good for her, while browsing the stalls for the perfect gift. Although, to be fair, on previous sorties, she hadn't spotted anything among the tat that she would deem present-worthy. However, that wasn't the point. It was all about the ambience, the magic and glitter, the warm hug of Christmas, which was strangely incongruous to what they were about to do.

Confronting suspects was always the hardest part of a case. Harder than the investigation itself, which on this occasion had been pretty taxing. Fiona didn't like confrontation, and this was probably the most confrontational situation you could find yourself in. You never knew how they would react. Anger, denial, confusion — whatever their reaction, she would always doubt herself and her methods, which of course were, by her very nature, amateurish. Had she got her deductions right? Thought through the logic and considered every counter-argument?

However, in this instance, Fiona had an extra complication to deal with. A possible romantic element that had ensnared her, try as she might to deny it. Maybe romantic was too strong a word — a gentle flirtation would be more apt. Nevertheless, the awkward situation had the potential to soften her resolve, which she simply could not allow to happen.

A stone-cold rock of dread weighed in her stomach as she contemplated the encounter ahead. She jutted out her chin and reminded herself that this had to be done. There was no way around it. They had questions that needed answering, but she took comfort in the fact that her two best friends were by her side.

They took a second turn and quickly found themselves at the entrance to the garage. Inside, past the opening with the heavy sliding door, Tony perched on the arm of the battered sofa, the garage's landline in the crook of his neck as he ran through a quote with a customer.

As they stepped inside, Fiona glanced down and noted that there was no change in level between the concrete forecourt outside and the smooth workshop floor inside. A strip of flush metal sat snugly between the two — a track for the well-greased wheels of the sliding door to run along. A comforting observation — nothing would have a problem crossing that threshold, no matter how big or small.

In the corner, they caught sight of Joe skiving off, leaning against the door pillar of a Toyota, gazing at his phone. Most importantly, Fiona spotted three scuffed-up red trolley jacks scattered against the wall like discarded shopping trolleys.

"Hi, ladies." Tony smiled at them.

"Hello, Tony," they chorused back.

"What can I do for you?" he asked. "Although, I must warn you we're shutting early tonight. Me and Joe are out on the town."

"What are you celebrating?" asked Partial Sue.

"Nothing," Tony replied defensively. "Just a bit of father-and-son bonding."

Fiona glanced at Joe. By his non-committal expression, she couldn't tell whether he loved or loathed the idea.

"So, what can I help you with?" Tony asked once more.

"We need a trolley jack," Daisy said.

"Do you need a wheel changed? Joe will do that, won't you, Joe?"

The teenager nodded slightly, although it was more of a reluctant quiver.

"Oh, I don't need a wheel changed," Daisy clarified. "I just need to take a measurement. Would you mind?" She pulled a tape measure from her pocket. Unlike the one she'd borrowed from Graham, which had been a hefty, battered device, this was her own pristine Cath Kidston floral number.

Tony's face became a mask of befuddlement.

Joe finally found his voice. "Why do you want to measure a trolley jack?"

"You can learn a lot from trolley jacks," Daisy replied. "And chewing gum."

Father and son exchanged confused glances.

"Trolley jacks and chewing gum?" Tony chuckled nervously. "Sounds like a messy drinking game."

"It's not a game," Partial Sue replied. "But it is messy. Although, I'm guessing you two might know more about that than we would."

Tony shrugged. "I have no idea what you're talking about."

"Start with the chewing gum," Partial Sue suggested.

Tony's eyes narrowed. "Chewing gum? What's chewing gum got to do with anything?"

"Well," Daisy said, "there's a blob of it out there on the pavement — you can't miss it, it's shaped like an appendix. It was right in front of Clive's stall, about four inches away. But after he died, it magically moved three inches closer.

We know chewing gum can't move. It's a swine to get off, especially if you get it on your clothes. I always put them in the freezer . . ."

"And why's that important?" Tony interrupted Daisy's life-hack digression.

"Oh, sorry," she apologised. "Chewing gum can't move, so Clive's stall must've moved."

Tony stared blankly. "O-kay."

"The only way to move a stall," Fiona said, "even three inches, is if you have a flatbed truck with a crane or a heavy-duty forklift handy. But we did discover another way, using trolley jacks. There was evidence on the underside of his stall."

"Three circular marks in the wood," Partial Sue added. "Pattern matched the saddle on a trolley jack — the bit that the car rests on."

"Yeah, I know what a saddle is," Tony smirked.

"Specifically, those ones." Fiona pointed to the jacks near the wall.

The smirk dropped from Tony's face. Without asking for permission, Daisy carefully chicaned around the scattered car parts and spanners towards the trolley jacks. Extending a length of tape, she bent over and measured the saddle on the top of each one, then straightened up. "Exactly five inches across. Same as the marks on the stall. I mean, we already knew it would be five inches because it says so on the Might XL website. But we had to check."

"Never assume anything in our line of work," Partial Sue said.

"What, volunteering in a charity shop?" Tony snorted derisively.

"No, investigating murders," Fiona replied.

Anger flashed across his face. "Do me a favour. I hope you're not insinuating what I think you are."

"Measurements don't lie," Partial Sue grunted.

"Doesn't mean anything," Tony replied. "All the garages around here use trolley jacks. Not just ours."

"Well, that's just it, they don't," Daisy explained. "The ones you use are made in the States, which is Serengeti puss for us."

"Serendipitous," Fiona corrected.

"Sorry," Daisy said. "I meant serendipitous. Mighty XL jacks are made to imperial measurements, which is why the saddle is exactly five inches across, which gives a bit of an odd size of 12.7 centimetres in metric."

"We did a quick recce earlier of the other garages around here," Partial Sue said. "Didn't take long. There aren't that many. Theirs are all European with saddles that are exactly ten, twelve or thirteen centimetres across."

Tony shook his head. "What about people with jacks at home? Did you check in their garages? Because there must be hundreds."

"That's true," Fiona said. "But why would any homeowner need more than one jack? Most people just use the one that comes with their car. Very few people have trolley jacks and of the ones that do, I doubt they'd need three of them lying around, all identical."

"It took three trolley jacks to move Clive's stall," Partial Sue explained. "We know that because of the three marks underneath. However, the stall was put back in the wrong position. Three inches out, as Daisy said."

"And the stall was tidy inside," Fiona added. "One thing we knew about Clive, he was a very messy person and so was his stall. Cups and sprinkles everywhere. But on that morning when you broke through the doors, everything had been put away. It didn't make sense until we discovered that the stall had moved. Whoever moved it must have thought they'd accidentally made a mess, dislodged everything while they were shifting it. So they had a quick tidy-up. Put things in cupboards so they wouldn't fall out when they moved it back. That was the first giveaway."

Anger flared in Tony's eyes. "Giveaway to what? What's a moving stall and flaming chewing gum got to do with us? Clive took his life, remember? Locked himself inside his stall."

"That's where the moving stall comes into it," Fiona explained. "Only way to make it look like suicide is to remove a wall and put him in the stall with the door bolted from the inside. Then, put the wall back, making it appear as if he'd locked himself in. Trouble is, it's too risky doing that out there on the pavement, not to mention noisy. The walls of the stall are secured with bolts and lock nuts. Can't be undone by hand. But you've got everything you need right here, including powerful impact wrenches." She nodded to the metallic guns hanging from their twisty compressed air hoses. "They're noisy, but once that thick sliding door is closed, no one's going to see or hear anything. Like changing a car wheel, but bigger. Oh, and I bet, as an experienced mechanic, you know how to get around a lock nut."

Fiona sneaked a glance at Joe, whose feet shifted uneasily, as if he wanted to make a run for it or burst into tears.

Tony laughed. "This is ridiculous. You three have lost the plot. Can you imagine shifting a stall? It's nonsense."

"Not really," Partial Sue explained. "It's only a few metres away. Once the jacks are underneath, it's no different to moving an oversized pallet. Your garage is plenty big enough to accommodate. You could slip it inside in seconds, shut the door, do what you have to do, then slip it back out before anyone notices."

Tony folded his arms and shook his head. "Apart from it being a load of rubbish. Why would I do any of this? I didn't have anything against Clive. Hardly knew him."

Fiona answered his question with one of her own. "Can I just ask how many people have a key to this garage?" She was already aware that just the two of them worked there.

Hesitating, his eyes flickered, as if his mind was performing calculations, running through scenarios, attempting to avoid being caught in a trap that was slowly closing in around him. Considering whether to tough it out, or cut his losses and do something drastic, he was the proverbial cornered animal.

CHAPTER 39

"It's a simple question," Partial Sue reminded him. "Who has access to this garage?"

Tony stalled. He couldn't exactly feign ignorance. No business owner would lose track of who had a spare key. And if he made up fictitious keyholders, they could be easily checked. He had no choice other than to tell the truth. "Just me and Joe."

"Interesting." Fiona had everything she needed. Time to bring out the big guns and start pounding the beach. "Something else that's interesting is we spoke to one of the last people to see Clive before he died. Told us someone jumped him in an alleyway in the early hours of Saturday the twentieth. Almost certainly a victim of the Southbourne Stalker. Poor lad was traumatised. Said he wouldn't have escaped if it hadn't been for Clive passing by when he did. Now here's the interesting part — he didn't see his attacker, was too busy running away, but Clive did, and he recognised him."

"Who was this lad?" Tony asked, his hands making fists by his side.

"He wouldn't say his name," Fiona replied. "But that's not the point. Clive knew the identity of the person terrorising our streets. Now put yourself in the shoes of the stalker. He has to get rid of Clive before he can tell anyone. Otherwise, he's done for. Next thing we know, Clive winds up dead in a stall with marks underneath it that only your trolley jacks can make."

Tony shook his head. "No, no, no, impossible. I was at home minding my own business."

"What about you, Joe?" Fiona asked. "Where were you?"

All attention turned on the young apprentice, whose eyes became as wide as saucers. "Er, I can't remember."

"Okay, fair enough," Fiona said. "But can I ask, did either of you make or receive a call in the early hours of Saturday morning?" She knew they had from the information Freya had given them. But she couldn't mention this, of course, because it was inadmissible evidence. Though she could hint at it innocently.

Tony shrugged. "No, I never made any calls."

"What about you, Joe? Did you make any calls?"

Joe rapidly shook his head. "You can check my phone if you want."

"What about from a landline?" Partial Sue asked.

Joe's face flushed with crimson, confirming that he had.

"Okay, that's enough," Tony bellowed. "Joe's not a murderer or a stalker."

"Why would making a call from a landline imply that he's either?" Partial Sue asked.

"Look at him. He's not even twenty," Tony snapped.

Fiona had to admit, behind the awkward teenager in ill-fitting clothes, it was hard to picture a prowler and even harder to imagine a killer. But that didn't mean he wasn't guilty. Never judge a book by its cover.

"See, I think he's capable of one but not the other," she said. "The stalker part, maybe. The thrill of the late-night chase. Sidling up to victims. The power over them, perhaps fuelled by low self-esteem."

Partial Sue threw Tony a filthy look. "I wonder where he got that from."

Fiona turned her attention on Joe's father. "But not the murder part. That requires a different set of skills. A second person for the practicalities of moving a stall. But also, more importantly, for diagnosing the problem and creating a workable solution. Sorry, Joe, but as an apprentice, I don't think you possess that experience yet. But your father does."

"Combined with a parent's automatic instinct to protect their child," Daisy said. "Even if he's just discovered his son's the Southbourne Stalker."

"That's enough!" Tony roared. "You three are out of order! You need to leave right now, before I do something I regret."

"What? Are you going to put us in a Christmas stall and make it look like suicide?" Partial Sue snorted.

Tony looked ready to grab a spare car part and throw it at them. But it wasn't the ladies he should have been worried about. Joe's gangly frame had been shrinking ever since they'd mentioned trolley jacks and moving stalls. His face swelled with a mixture of terror and guilt, as if it were ready to burst. Suddenly, in a bid for self-preservation he cried out, "Dad killed Clive!"

"Shut up, Joe!" Tony hissed. He would've no doubt throttled his son if the ladies weren't there to witness it.

Joe kept going, gabbling out a full confession. "Clive saw me in the alleyway. Accused me of being the Southbourne Stalker. I swear, it was just a prank. But he didn't believe me."

"You were playing a practical joke?" Fiona asked.

Joe nodded eagerly.

"So who were you playing a practical joke on?" Fiona asked.

"W-what?" Joe stuttered.

"Most practical jokes are played on people you know," Partial Sue pointed out. "So what's the name of your friend in the alleyway?"

"The eyewitness we spoke to," Fiona reminded him.

The ladies didn't know his name, but neither, it seemed, did Joe. His face contorted as he struggled to conjure a name. "It was John, er John Smith."

"John Smith?" Fiona raised a suspicious eyebrow. "And what's his number? So we can verify that you know each other."

"And have a history of jolly japery." Partial Sue smirked.

The awkward discomfort in his face was painful to observe, as he realised he was painted into a self-incriminating corner. "Well, he's not really a friend."

Fiona didn't bother dignifying his excuse with a response. "It's not looking good, Joe. The evidence is irrefutable. Stacked up high. Better to come clean."

"Don't listen to them!" Tony barked.

Joe shook. His conflicted gaze switched rapidly from his father to the ladies several times.

"Don't say another word," Tony warned.

"You're the Southbourne Stalker, aren't you, Joe?" Fiona said. "Clive caught you in the act, so you called your father in the early hours of Saturday morning because you didn't know what else to do. Remember, there'll be a record of any calls you made, so it's pointless denying it."

He weighed up his options and finally broke. "Okay, okay. But I didn't kill Clive. He did." Joe pointed to his father.

Tony swore at his son. "You ungrateful little swine. I was trying to protect you. Stop you going to jail. And this is the gratitude I get."

Joe ignored his father. "Clive was going to call the police. I told him to speak to my father. He'd back up my story."

"Hold on a minute." Partial Sue pointed at Tony. "Did you know your son was the Southbourne Stalker all along?"

For once, Tony remained quiet, his face drenched in shame, confirming Sue's assumption.

Joe continued. "I said Dad was working late at the garage. We could go and talk to him right now. Clive agreed and followed me here. Dad wasn't here, of course. I said he must have gone home but I could call him. So I did, using the landline. Dad said he'd sort it out, but I needed to keep Clive occupied until he arrived — told me to give him some whisky. Clive had a couple and dozed off on the sofa by the time he got here. Then everything happened just as you said. But it was all his idea."

Tony remained quiet, then he gazed towards Fiona, his eyes relaxing and his mouth softening. "Come on, Fiona. You don't believe all this, do you? It's me, Tony. You and I like going for bratwursts, having a natter. We get on well together, you know we do. I was hoping that it could be something more than that — maybe even romantic." He raised his eyebrows, throwing her a demure, puppy-dog look.

And there it was. The last-ditch attempt of a man on the ropes. Appealing to Fiona's tender side.

Fiona had to admit, the euphoria of thinking someone liked her had sweetened her days, like honey in her tea. But all along she'd been suppressing these delectable emotions for the simple reason that she didn't quite believe them. On the rare occasions she'd been in this situation before, it had never amounted to anything — so why should this have been any different? Sadly, Fiona was a perennial singleton, and it looked set to stay that way for the foreseeable future, which made her cynical and a tad angry. "You must think I was born yesterday. As if I believed your clumsy flirtations. Romance? More a case of keep your enemies close, I think."

If Tony was shocked that his little deception hadn't worked, he didn't show it. Silent and emotionless, he stood unmoving, possibly simmering beneath the surface and weighing up his options.

"Well, that is a shame." He slowly shook his head then reached down to pick up a hefty wrench. "I'd been turning a blind eye to Joe's antics. I mean, I'm not going to snitch on my own son. And this is how he repays me." Tony raised his gaze and glared at Joe. "So much for loyalty. Have you forgotten how desperate you were when you called? Begged me to make the Clive problem go away. Said you'd do anything. That makes you an accessory to murder, you idiot."

"Actually, he's an accomplice," Partial Sue pointed out. "Which is a lot worse. If you help out during a murder, it's a similar or the same charge as murder."

"What!" Joe blurted. "No, I just helped get the stall inside."

"And you helped me hang him. See, you've shafted both of us. Which means these three meddling do-gooders need to be dealt with. And you can help me." Tony stepped across the entrance, putting his back to it, blocking any means of escape. "Sorry, ladies. I can't let you leave knowing what you know. I have no choice — or should I say, my idiot son has left me no choice. After this, I might bury him too for all the trouble he's caused. Unless he helps me. Joe, you're fond of hitting people over the head — grab that mallet by your feet and shut the door."

Joe obeyed, snatched up the heavy tool and headed for the entrance, while his father moved towards the ladies, gripping the wrench, ready to strike.

Fiona held up a palm to halt him. "Er, how stupid do you think we are?"

Both father and son stopped in their tracks, caught off guard by Fiona's distinct lack of fear.

"What?" was the only response Tony could muster.

"I said, how stupid do you think we are? Do you really think we'd waltz in here, lay out a raft of damning evidence, the kind that will put both of you away for years, without first taking precautions?"

Tony held her gaze, unblinking, then his eyes crinkled and his mouth curved into a smile and then a laugh. "I see what you're doing. Don't worry, I've seen all the TV shows. This is the bluffing bit where you have to improvise, or distract us to get away."

"What, like saying 'look behind you'?" asked Partial Sue.

"Yeah, that kind of thing."

"Well, you really should look behind you," Daisy said.

Tony rolled his eyes. "Oh my god. Surely you can do better than that. I mean, how stupid do you think—"

His words were cut short by Joe's mallet clattering to the floor. He glanced over his shoulder to witness his son backing away, slowly raising his hands, an expression of abject terror clawing at his young face. The source of his dread was a horde of uniformed police officers trooping into his garage, several of them shouting at Tony to drop the wrench. He did without hesitation and raised his hands.

They were followed in by a pair of plainclothes officers that the ladies knew very well — DI Fincher and DS Thomas. For once, the young female DI was dressed casually, although still managed to look immaculate in wide-legged jeans, Ugg boots and a fur-lined flying jacket. DS Thomas was his usual scruffy self in an eclectic mix of sportswear, which paired perfectly with the unimpressed scowl permanently stuck on his face.

"We sent all the evidence to the police," Partial Sue informed him.

DI Fincher flashed the ladies a modest smile. "We'll take it from here."

Roughly translated this meant, "We appreciate the tip-off, but really want you to get lost now."

The ladies took the hint and shuffled out, while the uniformed officers whipped out their cuffs and DI Thomas's monotone voice read the mechanics their rights.

CHAPTER 40

The morning sun of the winter solstice shone mercilessly bright, slicing through the shop's front window at the acutest of angles. However, it signalled a new optimistic start to the ladies' lives, not to mention Christmas being tantalisingly close.

"Well, we got there in the end." Partial Sue squinted as she poured tea.

"All's well that ends well," Daisy added, plating mince pies and nudging them towards her friends. "Tony and Joe De Costa are going away for a long time."

DI Fincher had assured them of this, in the briefest of post-arrest phone conversations she'd had with Fiona. Although to define it as a conversation would be a tad generous. A hurried brush-off would be more precise. The DI had claimed she was too busy to talk, but did offer up a small but important sop — both father and son would be facing the harshest of sentences.

The police had also discovered that Tony had a record. Nothing serious, just a history of scuffles, one of which had resulted in a minor sentence of six months in prison. However, his time inside, mixing with other more serious offenders, would've given him a good idea of what his son would be facing if he ever got caught. Multiple assault with a mallet was classed as GBH with intent, carrying a sentence that would stretch well into double figures. The lad's life would be over before it had properly got started. Which is probably why Tony was so quick to try and make his problem go away, and embroil them both in Clive's murder.

The DI offered no words of thanks or a pat on the back for the ladies, despite them handing her the collar of the year, complete with a watertight body of evidence, most notably proving that the impossible locked-room mystery was eminently possible, if you had access to an impact wrench, a few trolley jacks and your garage was located on the other side of the pavement. What's more, to further strengthen the case, another piece of the puzzle was conveniently provided a few days later by an environmentally conscious customer. The woman didn't actually buy anything, and Fiona had quickly surmised that she'd come in to vent (the ladies had a notoriously sympathetic ear and were regularly inundated by serial grumblers). On this occasion, the woman had turned up at Tony De Costa's garage for her MOT, only to find it shut up tight. It had been this way ever since his arrest, and she was most put out by her wasted journey but even more vexed because she wanted to have words with him. "I saw him dumping a nearly full tin of paint in a public bin. Would've gone straight into landfill if I hadn't hoicked it out. Toxic, that stuff is. He must've known he was up to no good because he did it on the night of the carol service, when he thought no one was looking. But I saw him."

Either she hadn't heard that a stall had been graffitied with red paint or, more likely, hadn't put two and two together, being distracted by her own outrage. However, it was immediately clear that Tony had been the one stirring up trouble between shop owners and stall-holders with petty acts of vandalism, presumably as a bit of misdirection. Fiona had immediately texted DI Fincher this information but never received a response.

They were used to the DI's radio silence and could count on one finger the times she'd praised them for bringing murderers to justice. Most people would have considered this rude and ungrateful. But Fiona didn't blame the young detective. She was a dedicated professional and it must have smarted that yet another murder had flown under her sophisticated radar and had popped up on the ladies' rather basic and decrepit one. Not that they had had anything to do with this. If it hadn't been for Daph subcontracting their services, they too would have remained equally clueless.

On the subject of radio silence, this reminded Fiona that she needed to give the eccentric claims investigator another ring. Daph had been strangely quiet ever since Fiona had left a message on her voicemail informing her that Joe and Tony had been arrested. Fiona had called her several times since but with no response. Perhaps she'd been busy, compiling a comprehensive report on the matter. Which begged the question, why had she not contacted the ladies to fill her in on the details? Details were important in insurance investigations, Fiona imagined, and she'd only given her the barest of bones in her short voice message. Certainly not enough to compile a report with facts, evidence and dates and times, which her employers would certainly demand before they reluctantly agreed to pay Scott what he was owed.

Fiona pulled out her phone and dialled her number.

"Are you calling Daph again?" Partial Sue asked.

Fiona nodded.

"Good," Partial Sue grumbled. "She owes us a fee."

"Is that so you can buy your new toaster?" Daisy quickly got to the source of her griping.

"Well, okay, there is that. But it's also a hefty lump of cash she's denying the homeless dogs — once I've deducted the money for a toaster, of course." Partial Sue had plenty of money for a toaster, but, as was her nature, she would much prefer to use someone else's to buy such things. "You know, the one I've got my eye on has an app."

"Why do you need an app for a toaster?" Daisy asked.

"In case you're out and think, you know what, I really fancy some toast when I get home. Use the app and it'll have it ready by the time you get in."

"But wouldn't you have to put the bread in first before you went out?"

"Well, I suppose you just leave it in there at the ready."

"Wouldn't it go stale?"

Partial Sue became flustered. "Look, I don't know how it works exactly but it just has an app, okay?"

Fiona held the phone away from her ear as if it had suddenly become hot. "That's weird. Now it's saying that the number has not been recognised."

"She's avoiding us. Doesn't want to cough up."

"I'm not worried about the money," Fiona replied. "I just want to know why she's avoiding us."

"Try calling Tyndale," Daisy suggested. "They'll know how to get hold of her."

"I'll give it a go, but I doubt they'll tell us. One, because that information is confidential, and two, she said this was all hush-hush and there could be no mention of Tyndale in all this."

Nevertheless, Fiona called the life assurance company, only to receive the expected reply: "I'm sorry, we can't give out that sort of information."

Fiona hung up. "Okay, so what now?"

Daisy shrugged. "I don't know, but last time Daph was in here she was definitely acting odd."

"Odd in what way?" Partial Sue asked.

"Well, she's a bit intense, isn't she?" Daisy replied. "Eccentric but intense. Focused on her job. But last time she was here, halfway through the conversation, she became all laces fez."

"*Laissez-faire*," Fiona corrected, casting her mind back. "Yes, I noticed that, now you come to mention it. What were we talking about at the time?"

Partial Sue snapped her fingers. "We were bandying about the idea that Scott did it. Maybe that's why she relaxed. She was hired to find out if he murdered his dad, so Tyndale wouldn't have to pay out. Job done. Could take her foot off the pedal. Probably thought she was in for a nice big bonus too. Remember, she looked embarrassed when I mentioned bonuses — she must've had a guilty conscience."

"That makes sense," Fiona agreed.

However, Daisy appeared to think otherwise, squirming in her seat, but reluctant to utter anything that would upset the consensus.

"Something on your mind, Daisy?" Fiona asked.

"It's the wrong emotion," she replied.

Her colleagues were nonplussed.

Daisy explained. "Relaxed is the wrong emotion. It'd be excitement if she thought she'd got a result and was getting a bonus."

"But not at that point," Fiona pointed out. "She couldn't be either relaxed or excited. It was only a theory. We had no proof and, in the end, it turned out to be wrong."

"Maybe she'd convinced herself it was in the bag," Partial Sue said.

The ladies ummed and ahhed, then a mystifying silence enveloped the shop. There'd been plenty of these while they'd been investigating Clive's death and had thought they'd seen the back of them. But here they were. Back to considering events that didn't make sense.

Fiona tapped her phone in a bid to help her think. She cast her mind back to the conversation on that day, examining it in minute detail. Something had shifted in Daph, for sure. The pressure had been taken off her. Fiona replayed their verbal back-and-forth again, slowing down the tape in her head, pausing it now and again, slowly filling in the gaps and following the flow of their chat. On her third run-through, something occurred to her.

"You know, we weren't talking about Scott being the killer, not at first — that came later. We were actually talking about the victim in the alleyway. The lad who came in here. That's when she started acting differently. I thought Daph would be disappointed because we didn't know his name, but instead she looked relaxed, almost relieved."

"Relieved?" Daisy questioned. "Why would she be relieved?"

Fiona shrugged.

"What else did we say?" Daisy asked.

Partial Sue scratched her chin. "We told her that the lad didn't see his attacker, but that Clive saw him and recognised him. Oh, and that the lad didn't want to go to the police. Wanted to remain anonymous."

Fiona clapped her hands. Simon Le Bon's smushed furry head popped up, as he was woken from his snooze. "That's it! Daph became all laid-back when we told her the lad hadn't seen his attacker, and never wanted to come forward."

"Why would she act like that?"

"I can think of a reason," Fiona grinned. "The only reason anyone would act like that." She lifted her tea to her lips and downed it in one to celebrate. "Daph had a stake in all this, and it wasn't money. Daisy, can you have a look for someone on social media for me? Sue, can you remember which cup Daph drank from the last time she was in here?"

The pair didn't respond immediately, wondering what new cryptic conundrum had befallen them.

CHAPTER 41

The waiting area of the Canford Building Society was pleasant enough. Cheerfully lit but not so bright that you thought you were about to be strip-searched, it had a posh coffee machine and a Chesterfield sofa for waiting customers. While the ladies perched on its firm upholstery, Partial Sue informed them that a Chesterfield was without a doubt the best sofa in the world. A design classic — although, in recent years, it had been "mucked up" by pastel colours and weird-shaped arms. In her mind, there was only one Chesterfield and that was a traditional brown leather one — the scruffier the better.

When Partial Sue had finished her sermon on furniture, Fiona smiled at the cashier, mostly to signal that all was well. There were four cashiers' windows opposite their current position, but as with all banks and building societies, and sometimes supermarkets these days, only one was occupied.

The cashier smiled back. "She won't be long."

"Thank you," Fiona replied. They'd come to see Celia Trenton. According to the building society's website, she specialised in opening new accounts at this particular branch, and they had booked an appointment online using the name Mrs Tumnus — Daisy's affectionate suggestion, after the faun in

The Lion, the Witch and the Wardrobe. Daisy didn't want to be married to Mr Tumnus, or be a faun for that matter — she didn't fancy having goat's legs — but always wanted to live in his cosy cave of a house that had rugs on the floor and a big open fire. Until Partial Sue destroyed the illusion by reminding her that it got ransacked in the book by the Queen's secret police.

The ladies' attention was suddenly distracted by the security door with a keypad at the back of the building society. It clicked and swung open. A well-presented woman in a navy-blue trouser suit and name badge stepped through. Her high, glossy black ponytail swished merrily from side to side as she purposefully strode towards them, a well-rehearsed smile on her face. The epitome of professionalism, she clutched an iPad and a leather documents folder in her well-manicured hands. However, as she neared the ladies, her smile and strides faltered ever so slightly. "Oh, er, I didn't realise there would be three of you. Would you all like to open accounts?"

"No, just one of us," Fiona replied.

"I'm so sorry. Where are my manners? I'm Celia Trenton," she greeted them but didn't make eye contact. "Would you like to follow me?" She quickly ushered them into a glass meeting room with a round table and shut the door behind them. "Please take a seat."

They all sat down. Celia opened her documents folder and quickly extracted several forms but was still reluctant to make eye contact. She appeared to be in a hurry. "Right, let's get started. Here's a pen you can keep." She withdrew one from the inside of her suit jacket. It was a smart metal instrument with the society's logo on the side. She slid it across the table. "I can do most of this electronically. But there's still a little dreaded paperwork to sign." She punctuated the end of her sentence with a brittle laugh.

"Oh, that doesn't look like too much paperwork," Daisy said.

"No, not as much as the last time we saw you," Partial Sue added. "You had bags of the stuff."

"I'm sorry?" Celia gave a nervous smile.

"When you first visited our charity shop," Fiona explained. "It was the world cup of paperwork. All these bulging bags of the stuff. I can see why you went for the eccentric-expert look, with the mismatched clothes and the messed-up hair. Complete opposite of how you really are."

"It's a very good disguise." Daisy offered genuine praise. "I wouldn't have known it was you if I passed you in the street."

Celia's eyes flicked between them, desperately weighing up her options. She continued feigning ignorance. "I'm sorry. I don't know what you're talking about."

Fiona took a more direct approach. "You're Joe De Costa's mum, aren't you? Were married to Tony De Costa. Divorced three years ago. Reverted back to your maiden name of Trenton."

Celia hesitated, then offered a nervous smile. "Er, it's against corporate policy to discuss personal information with customers."

"Well, it says it on your name badge," Partial Sue remarked. "And we had a look back through Joe's social media. There are a few pictures of the two of you together, celebrating birthdays, et cetera. That's a fact. Here's another fact — Joe and your ex-husband have been arrested for the murder of Clive Preston."

Celia's gaze immediately dropped to her lap and her complexion lost all its colour.

"You and your husband may be divorced," Fiona continued. "Probably don't like each other. But you still care about your son. Like any parent, you want to protect Joe, keep him from harm, stop him from getting into trouble. He seems extremely prone to that last one. How long have you known he was the Southbourne Stalker?"

Celia's head jerked upright. "How dare you!"

Partial Sue ignored her protest. "Did you know all along or did you only just find out when his father bumped off Clive? I can imagine Tony tried to keep it a secret from you."

Celia didn't answer.

Partial Sue waved it away, as if it were trivial. "Doesn't matter. Maybe Joe told you. Has a habit of blurting things out, but the conversation you had with Tony afterwards must've been difficult. A blistering argument. I bet he reassured you that everything was fine and nobody would find out. To be fair, he did a pretty good job. The locked room had everyone fooled. Even the police. No other verdict possible except suicide. However, you couldn't shake the fact that he'd left a loose end — the lad in the alleyway. You needed to know if Joe was still at risk. Could he still be identified? I'm sure Joe reassured you that he hadn't been seen. But you couldn't rest with that sword of Damocles over him. Had to find out who the lad was. What were you planning for him? Get Tony to make him disappear? Another suicide, perhaps? But you had a problem. How could you find out who he was without raising suspicions?"

"That's when Daph was born," Fiona said. "Your alter ego who could ask the questions you couldn't. But you needed an excuse for her to poke her nose into things without any repercussions. I'm sure working in a building society, you might know someone who knows someone who could check to see if Clive had life assurance. You mocked up a few forms to sell the deception, which, conveniently we only glimpsed briefly because they were confidential documents. Your husband sometimes drank in the same pub, so you had a fairly good idea of how much alcohol he'd had. I'm guessing you didn't see the autopsy report, but then you didn't need to because you made your husband tell you everything. You had to be accurate on the off chance we found out what was in that report. Most importantly, that there were no signs of a struggle because Clive had passed out or was extremely pliable. Then you hired us, under the guise of investigating Scott, but of course, making us promise to keep it all hush-hush. It was a little risky. However, no one else had figured out that Clive's suicide was a murder, so what hope would three amateurs have?"

"You nearly gave yourself away at one point, but we all missed it," Partial Sue said. "I asked you about bonuses for every claim you discredit. You never answered. At the time we thought it was because you felt too embarrassed to admit it. But you didn't answer because you didn't know. You'd swotted up on everything else, and working in a building society, you probably had a good knowledge of life assurance products, but that's something only a genuine claims investigator would know."

"So, off we went," Fiona continued. "During our investigation you hoped we'd uncover the lad's identity. It was a long shot, but even if it didn't work there was still the possibility that Clive's death could be pinned on Scott. Another layer of protection for Joe. Then as good fortune had it, we were paid a visit by the lad in the alleyway himself. Poor thing was terrified. Traumatised. Okay, we didn't discover his identity, but we gave you the next best thing. He swore he'd never go to the police. Wanted to stay anonymous. Good enough for you, so much so that you took your foot off the accelerator. Stopped returning our calls. You could relax in the knowledge that Joe's identity was safe. Is that about right?"

Celia put on her best poker face. Not a hint of emotion or fear. "I'm really sorry, ladies, but I have no idea what you're talking about. I've never been to your shop. Did you say it was a charity shop? I don't use them, if I'm honest." There was a hint of arrogance in that last remark.

Fiona sighed. From inside her coat she produced a clear ziplock bag containing a dirty mug, the largest one they had in the shop. She placed it on the table. "Trouble is, you have been to our shop. This is the mug you drunk out of. Covered in your DNA and fingerprints."

"You are partial to a cup of tea," Partial Sue remarked. "Or should I say Daph is."

Celia glared at the mug. Her face remained as still as a portrait, but her brain was either racing out of control or had stalled like an old British Leyland car on a frosty day in the seventies. She reached for the bag. Fiona snatched it away. "Oh, no you don't. This is evidence that you've been in our shop, drank our tea."

In reality, the mug had been scrubbed within an inch of its life, several times, by Daisy's fastidious hands. However, Celia didn't know that, and they'd made tea in it again, which Partial Sue had drunk, never one to let good tea go to waste, but they'd left the remaining dregs to dry and stain. To all intents and purposes, it looked as if Daph's cup had not been touched since the last time she had visited, DNA and fingerprints intact.

Celia's composure faltered. She swallowed hard.

"So," Fiona said, "you've dealt with one sword of Damocles only to find another one above your head, hanging by the barest of threads."

"Definitely conspiracy to pervert the course of justice," Partial Sue said. "Maybe even conspiracy to commit murder, depending on how much the police think you were involved."

"Turn yourself in, or we will." Fiona held up the ziplock bag and jiggled the contents.

The ladies got to their feet and left the meeting room, but at the last second Partial Sue darted back to the table and snatched up the free pen.

CHAPTER 42

The ladies officially had no idea about the fate of Celia Trenton aka Daph Richardson. They dared not ask DI Fincher. One, because she probably wouldn't tell them, and two, they didn't want to explain that they'd coerced Celia into turning herself in with a dirty teacup, of all things. They could just deny it, of course, and after they'd returned from the building society, Daisy had immediately gone to work on the mug with great gusto, a bowl of soapy water and a scouring pad. She had eradicated all evidence of their very trivial deception while alleviating her disdain for leaving anything unwashed for longer than was absolutely necessary.

However, unofficially, there was more than a good chance that Celia was now in police custody. Fiona had called up the building society, innocently asking to speak to her with a query. The chap on the other end of the phone had become tongue-tied at the mention of his colleague's name. He'd stuttered and fumbled an embarrassed excuse that she was taking some unexpected time off to deal with a family matter. Fiona had asked when she would be back in. He couldn't furnish her with an exact date but assured her that he could help with whatever enquiry she had. Fiona made some excuse then hung up, satisfied that Celia was probably sitting in a police cell.

The carols were cranked up and every cup of tea poured was accompanied by a mince pie. Not that this was any different to previous days, but they could now enjoy their festive indulgences, knowing that the three miscreants involved in Clive's murder were safely behind bars. Thankfully, neither Partial Sue nor Daisy ever mentioned anything regarding Fiona's doomed flirtation with the murderous mechanic, and that suited her just fine.

Although the arrests weren't yet public knowledge, Fiona had felt a shift in mood, not just in the shop but in Southbourne as a whole. She might have been imagining it, but she had sensed an unconscious relaxing of the community's collective shoulders. Slowly but surely, customers began returning to Southbourne Grove. Just a trickle, but that would soon turn into a stream and then, before long, the place would be back to its happy, bumbling old self again, and that made her spirits soar.

As if confirming her thoughts, the doorbell jangled. Another customer. The fifth this morning.

The ladies' heads whirled around to observe the towering frame of Scott Preston making his way through the door, his head narrowly missing the top of the frame.

His face was pale, and his eyes told Fiona that he needed more sleep, of the peaceful, uninterrupted variety. In his right hand, he carried three small, rectangular Christmas presents.

Cautiously and with a great deal of sensitivity, the ladies greeted him with warm, gentle hellos.

"Scott, welcome," Fiona said, but stopped short of asking how he was. It would be better to give him space to volunteer that information, if he so wished, rather than pressure him into giving an answer. She couldn't imagine what he was going through, and he might not feel like sharing or opening wounds that hadn't even begun to heal.

"Would you like a cup of tea?" Daisy asked. "Pot's still warm."

"Or a mince pie?" Partial Sue added.

"I won't, if you don't mind. I've just come in to say thank you."

"Oh," Fiona replied awkwardly.

"You've done me a great service. If it wasn't for the three of you, I'd still believe that my dad had killed himself. Felt guilty for the rest of my life."

"It's the least we could do," Daisy offered.

His face darkened. "Instead, I'm left with grief and anger. Anger at that vicious toerag of a mechanic who murdered him, all to save his vile son. Which isn't much better. But you brought them to justice. Made them pay for what they did to my dad. And for that I'm grateful."

Fiona wasn't sure whether the police had informed him that Joe's mother had also been involved. She thought it best to leave it for now and let them tell him when they were good and ready. "They'll be behind bars for a long time," she reassured him.

"I hope they throw away the key. They've taken my father away from me and—" He paused momentarily. Fiona thought he was about to become tearful, but a rare, small smile broke across his face. "A grandfather to be."

"Grandfather?" they all exclaimed.

"Angie's pregnant."

Abandoning all restraint, the ladies crowded around the sub-postmaster, smothering him in congratulatory hugs.

"Oh, that's wonderful news," Fiona gushed.

"Yes, it couldn't have come at a better time. It's brought some much-needed happiness into our lives."

"Do you have any names lined up?" Partial Sue asked. "I've heard Susan is making a big comeback."

Scott gave a brief snort. "I'll bear that in mind. But we're thinking of Sadie for a girl, or Tom if it's a boy."

"Both wonderful names." Daisy dabbed a happy tear from her eye.

"Dad would've loved being a grandfather."

"I bet he'd have been fantastic," Partial Sue remarked. "Good fun, I imagine."

"Yes, fun but not particularly responsible," Scott replied. "Anyway, I have something of his for you. Just a little thank you." He handed each of them a Christmas present with their name on. "As you know, my dad was a hoarder. Flat full of stuff for flogging on eBay. But he was also a collector, and knew a good piece when he saw one, especially when it came to antiques."

Partial Sue was first to relinquish her present from its wrapping, ripping off the paper with wild abandon to reveal a plain, white cardboard box about the size of a DVD case. She flipped open the lid. "Oh my gosh." Her slender fingers plucked out an exquisite antique magnifying glass with a thick carved oak handle and a hefty circular brass frame. "It's beautiful."

Daisy opened hers, carefully picking at Scott's expert wrapping. Inside was a smaller, more delicate magnifying glass, entirely made of brass with an intricate swirling filigree where the hooped frame met the handle. She clutched it to her chest. "I love it! Thank you so much."

Everyone turned to Fiona expectantly. Her present was also a magnifying glass. Made of solid brass with a plain handle, it had a thick, sturdy frame resembling the porthole of an ocean liner.

"They're all Victorian. Very rare," Scott informed them. "I thought they were apt, seeing as you're all expert sleuths."

Partial Sue held hers up to her eye, turning it huge. "They're amazing."

"We'll cherish them for ever," Daisy added.

"This is so kind of you," Fiona said. "But we can't keep them."

"We can't?" Partial Sue baulked.

"They're your father's heirlooms," Fiona explained. "They should stay in your family. Be passed down to your children."

"Not to diminish their worth," Scott said. "But we have boxes and boxes of his antiques. Too many to keep. And I want you to have these. It's my way of saying thank you. Please accept them with my sincerest gratitude."

Fiona paused, thinking it through. The other two ladies patiently awaited her answer. They'd defer to whatever Fiona decided was morally right.

She smiled. "Okay then, we'd love to accept these wonderful gifts — but on one condition. You stay and have tea and a mince pie with us."

"I think I can manage that." Scott smiled back.

CHAPTER 43

"Oh, would you look at that?" Partial Sue blustered. Her Marigolded hands heaved a tyre from out of the cold murky water. "That'll fit my Fiat Uno. There's good tread on that. Honestly, the things people throw away." She waded over to the side and flung it on the bank.

They were around the back of Matalan, up to their wellingtoned ankles, cleaning out the stream of litter and other detritus. This was at the behest of Malorie, who, failing to think of a suitable recompense or, more accurately, penance for her favour, had resorted to the old favourite of hers — Christchurch's equivalent of painting the Forth Bridge, i.e. cleaning out the shallow waterway behind the giant superstore that served as a local dumping ground.

Daisy had endured this unenviable task once before, made a little more palatable this time with her two friends by her side. However, Malorie had thrown in an extra twist (of the knife) by insisting that they do it on Boxing Day morning. They had all protested, apart from Partial Sue, who maintained that nothing ever happened on Boxing Day, and it was therefore pointless giving it a name when all the good stuff happened the day before.

"I thought we'd have seen a shopping trolley by now," Partial Sue remarked. "There's usually always one in the stream, what with all the big retailers around here."

"Yes, it's mostly crisp packets and empty vapes," Fiona added, clutching the aforementioned items in her fist and stuffing them in a binbag.

"How much longer do we have to do this?" Daisy took a moment to straighten up and stretch her back.

"Two more flaming hours." Partial Sue tutted but it didn't sound genuine.

Fiona suspected she was secretly enjoying this. She'd already snagged a free tyre and was, no doubt, hoping to score more unexpected booty from the shallow depths.

Daisy's head suddenly pricked up, like Simon Le Bon's when he'd heard a cat or a food cupboard door opening. "I can hear footsteps. Someone's coming."

"Who'd be around here on Boxing Day?" Partial Sue asked. "Unless it's to dump rubbish."

"I do hope its Malorie," Daisy replied. "Saying we can go home."

A distinctively sinister figure sashayed around the corner. Dressed in a long black puffa coat that reached down to her ankles and a matching fur ushanka hat, she looked as if she were about to hit the slopes, or assassinate James Bond in some bizarre, convoluted way. It was the last person they expected.

"Sophie?" the ladies chorused.

"Yes, your eyes do not deceive," she uttered, as if it were some rare treat like unexpectedly spotting a film star. Gail scuttled along behind, engulfed by a pair of vast fisherman's waders. The dutiful assistant was carrying a folding chair in one hand and large brown paper bag in the other.

"What are you two doing here?" Fiona asked.

"Not come to gloat, have you?" Partial Sue added.

"Not at all. I, like you, owe Malorie a favour."

"Why, what did you do?" Fiona thought it must have been something serious if she was making Sophie, her best friend, muck in with her rivals from across the road. Perhaps it was for ordering the surplus Christmas market stall, which had caused the tragic chain reaction.

Sophie tapped the side of her nose. "I'd rather not say. However, I intend to honour her request and repay the debt." Even the self-appointed Queen of Southbourne had to pay fealty to Malorie — the real power behind the throne.

Partial Sue screwed up her nose. "What, you're going to jump in here with us and clear up rubbish?"

Sophie guffawed. "Oh, god, no. Gail's going to do that on my behalf, aren't you, Gail?"

"'S'right," Gail nodded, as she unfolded the chair beside the stream, which Sophie immediately plonked herself down on. Gail then pulled a takeaway coffee from the paper bag and handed it to her lord and master. The ladies looked on enviously.

Sophie rolled her eyes. "Oh, please. Will you three stop staring like lost kittens and come and join me? I've bought one for everyone, even Gail."

The ladies looked at one another, wondering if this was some sort of trap or prank designed to humiliate them.

"'S'right," Gail reassured them.

"I'm not a monster," Sophie barked. "It's Christmas, for heaven's sake. Come on, take a break and have some refreshment."

The ladies didn't need telling twice. They climbed out of the stream and stripped off their rubber gloves as Gail handed them each a steaming latte.

"This is lovely coffee," Daisy said. Everyone agreed, thanking Sophie for her generosity.

However, Fiona still felt uncomfortable, wondering if there was a catch to all this. Perhaps she'd laced their drinks with sleeping pills so they'd pass out by the time Malorie arrived to inspect their progress. However, Fiona's politeness was stronger than her scepticism, and she carried on sipping. "Well, this isn't how I thought I'd be spending my Boxing Day."

"How do people spend Boxing Day?" Partial Sue asked. "I keep saying, nothing ever happens on Boxing Day."

"Well, in my heyday as a PR guru," Sophie replied, "I suggested to a rather large greeting cards client that if they wanted to sell more products we should rebrand Boxing Day as second Christmas Day — that's what they do in some countries on the continent."

Daisy's eyes lit up. "Oh, I love that idea!"

Partial Sue winced. "I can't think of anything worse. Can you imagine? Twice the postage. Twice the presents. Twice the food. Twice the expense."

"Exactly!" Sophie barked. "My client would've sold twice as many products, so would everyone else. It was a genius idea."

"So what happened?" Fiona asked.

"Idiots didn't go for it. Pearls and swine, honestly."

"What a shame," Daisy frowned. "Two Christmases. It's a brilliant idea."

Sophie immediately warmed to Daisy's fawning. "Thank you. It was a brilliant idea, wasn't it?"

Although she was loath to admit it, Fiona had to confess her fondness for the idea but with one small tweak. "What if you had a gap between first and second Christmas? Stick it on the last day of January. Give everyone something to look forward to."

"That makes good sense," Sophie agreed. "You'd have a chance to restock. I can see the headline now—" she moved her hand from left to right in a flourish — "*Christmas. Once is not enough.*"

"*Second Christmas. Twice the fun,*" Daisy suggested.

"Yes!" Sophie got to her feet, pontificating. "We should start planning a campaign, right this instant. Make it happen."

The ladies all agreed, even Partial Sue, who reluctantly accepted that another Christmas would break up the New Year's blues. Although she grumbled that it still didn't answer what to do about Boxing Day, the spare part of the festive season.

The stream clearance was put on hold as the five ladies excitedly brain-stormed ideas like a group of small children, eyes full of wonder. Fiona knew it wouldn't come to anything, and the concept would probably be swallowed up and forgotten once the decorations had been stuffed away for another year. However, right at this moment, it was nice to sip good coffee and indulge. Let imaginations run riot. Share a joyous moment with friends and bury the hatchet with enemies. Surely that's what Christmas was all about.

THE END

ACKNOWLEDGEMENTS

I must admit, I'm a complete sucker for Christmas and jumped at the chance to write a book centred around my favourite time of the year. I'm sure the reason for this is that I associate the festive period with my two children. They're both December babies, so I'm always reminded of the time they were born whenever Christmas comes around. The nervous drive to the hospital in the middle of the night was accompanied by the surreal sight of inflatable Santas and fairy lights, almost guiding our way. It's a joyful but extremely hectic time in our house. Try arranging two consecutive kids' birthdays before you've even got on to the business of Christmas presents and organising the big day. However, I wouldn't swap it for anything. So huge, huge thanks, as always, goes to my wonderful, funny and supportive family, to Sha, Billie and Dan, and to my mum and my sister Jane.

Any book always involves a bit of research and for this I never take chances. Yes, you can use the internet, but I find that nothing compares with talking to a real expert. For the police procedural parts I always call on the help of the amazing Sammy H.K. Smith, a real-life detective whose knowledge and ideas are indispensable. On this occasion, I also dabbled in the world of life assurance and for this I relied on the wonderful talents of financial wizard and all-round nice guy Michael Duff.

It takes a lot of people to get a book off the ground, and I am so grateful for the amazing people I have behind me. They are my brilliant publisher Laura Coulman-Rich, superb structural editor Cat Phipps, highly skilled line editor Matthew Grundy Haigh and sharp-eyed proofreader Julia Williams. Plus, the whole team at Joffe Books who are constantly working hard to ensure my books are a success. Massive thanks must also go to agent Lorella Belli and her team, securing deals in far-flung places and taking my books to some truly dizzying heights.

Finally, biggest thanks must go to the people who read my books and say such lovely things about them. One in particular, Sally Smith, has been a fan since day one and tirelessly recommends the series to everyone she meets.

THE JOFFE BOOKS STORY

We began in 2014 when Jasper agreed to publish his mum's much-rejected romance novel and it became a bestseller.

Since then we've grown into the largest independent publisher in the UK. We're extremely proud to publish some of the very best writers in the world, including Joy Ellis, Faith Martin, Caro Ramsay, Helen Forrester, Simon Brett and Robert Goddard. Everyone at Joffe Books loves reading and we never forget that it all begins with the magic of an author telling a story.

We are proud to publish talented first-time authors, as well as established writers whose books we love introducing to a new generation of readers.

We won Trade Publisher of the Year at the Independent Publishing Awards in 2023 and Best Publisher Award in 2024 at the People's Book Prize. We have been shortlisted for Independent Publisher of the Year at the British Book Awards for the last five years, and were shortlisted for the Diversity and Inclusivity Award at the 2022 Independent Publishing Awards. In 2023 we were shortlisted for Publisher of the Year at the RNA Industry Awards, and in 2024 we were shortlisted at the CWA Daggers for the Best Crime and Mystery Publisher.

We built this company with your help, and we love to hear from you, so please email us about absolutely anything bookish at feedback@joffebooks.com.

If you want to receive free books every Friday and hear about all our new releases, join our mailing list here: www.joffebooks.com/freebooks.

And when you tell your friends about us, just remember: it's pronounced Joffe as in coffee or toffee!

www.ingramcontent.com/pod-product-compliance
Ingram Content Group UK Ltd.
Pitfield, Milton Keynes, MK11 3LW, UK
UKHW041718101025
8343UKWH00023B/258